Olivia's Gift

Nancy Carabio Belanger

AUTHOR OF THE AWARD-WINNING **Olivia and the Little Way**

ILLUSTRATED BY

Sandra Casali LewAllen

Selected quotes excerpted from:

Broome, CSP, Francis. *The Little Way for Every Day: Thoughts from Thérèse of Lisieux.* Paulist Press. 2006. Mahwah, NJ.

Dr. Seuss, *Horton Hears a Who!* Random House Books for Young Readers. 1954. New York, NY.

Edmondson, Robert J. *The Complete Thérèse of Lisieux.* Paraclete Press. 2009. Brewster, MA.

The New American Bible, St. Joseph Edition. Catholic Book Publishing Co. 1991. New York, NY.

Saint Thérèse of Lisieux, *The Story of a Soul.* TAN Books and Publishers, Inc. 1997. Rockford, IL.

Society of the Little Flower. Darien, IL. www.littleflower.org

Descouvemont, Pierre. *Thérèse and Lisieux.* Wm. B. Eerdmans Publishing Co. 1996. Grand Rapids, MI.

"Our mission is to provide books that celebrate our Catholic faith, modesty, and a wholesome childhood."

www.harveyhousepublishing.com
P.O. Box 81841
Rochester, MI 48308

Printed in the United States of America

*Praise for **Olivia and the Little Way**:*

"This book offers a unique and fresh way to celebrate the life of St. Thérèse of Lisieux. It is a wonderful and engaging novel suitable for all but especially for tweens. They can share Olivia's life lessons as she deals with different relationships and real challenges."
—*The Catholic Press Association announcing* **Olivia and the Little Way** *as an award winner,* *Catholic Press Association 2009 Book Awards*

"This is a really lovely book, beautifully crafted with gorgeous illustrations. It's a book that children and adults will enjoy, maybe even together." —*Donna-Marie Cooper O'Boyle, author of* **Mother Teresa and Me** *and EWTN TV host*

"...most definitely a gem worth owning is **Olivia and the Little Way**, by Nancy Carabio Belanger. Belanger makes the message of St. Thérèse of Lisieux relevant to children today through the plight of Olivia Thomas…Olivia is a wonderful character, sinful, yet repentant.... Truly, this is one of the best saint stories for children that I have ever read. My daughters loved this book, and I even caught my 13-year-old son reading it. Highly recommended!"
— *catholicbookreview.blogspot.com*

"**Olivia and the Little Way**, by award-winning author Nancy Carabio Belanger, is an engaging book for children and families that celebrates the great dignity of each individual within the context of a very entertaining story. This book is a winner, and my children and I can't wait to read the sequel."
—*Michele Elena Bondi, award-winning publisher* *and author, www.Godisatworkinyou.com*

"Nancy Carabio Belanger's debut book, *Olivia and the Little Way*, is a successful melding of St. Thérèse's life story and a modern-day story about a fifth grader named Olivia."

— *Faith and Family* magazine *(July/August 2009)*

"It's not hard to find a book that deals with problems like moving to a new place, trying to fit in, or fear of being shunned by popular kids. But few pop books get straight to the heart of the matter: It's spiritual warfare....It is with the added prayers of Thérèse before the throne of God that Olivia overcomes her own weaknesses and learns to exercise true charity. In the end, there is no good guys vs. bad guys, but instead a growth in understanding and grace for all. Of course, no saint would pray for less."

— *Treasure Chest for Teens book review blog: www. booksnblather.blogspot.com*

"Nancy Belanger captures the struggles children deal with when their peers are unkind and untruthful. She has good insight into the motives which often lead children to do what they shouldn't, and she understands the need children have to feel accepted....This is a book that nourishes the soul and teaches while it entertains."

— *Fran Rutherford, book reviewer—Tiber River, Catholic product reviews*

"Acclaimed author Nancy Carabio Belanger's *Olivia and the Little Way* is an excellent book that allows children to enjoy reading as they learn about their Catholic faith."

— *Andre Bottesi, co-author of the award-winning* **Your Teen Apostolate**

"The life lessons shared in this book are wonderful for a middle-school-aged audience, but the story will capture the hearts of a much more broad audience (including the moms of those middle schoolers!). I'm hoping that this will be the first of many books to come from author Nancy Carabio Belanger and that you will enjoy this book as much as I did!"

—*Lisa Hendey, webmaster of Catholicmom.com and author of **The Handbook for Catholic Moms: Nurturing Your Heart, Mind, Body, and Soul***

"Nancy has written a new novel that explores how St. Thérèse can be a guiding force in the lives of kids and teens...I'm an adult and I read it and I loved it." —*Monsignor Jim Lisante, host of "Personally Speaking," SIRIUS Radio*

"In this well-written and engaging novel, author Nancy Carabio Belanger illustrates St. Thérèse's Little Way in a delightful and unique approach without being preachy or dogmatic. I highly recommend this wonderful book not only for children, but for anyone interested in following the Little Way." —*Ellen Gable Hrkach, author of the award-winning **In Name Only***

"Not only is this book helpful for young people that WILL eventually be faced with the same situations Olivia is faced with but it will also help adults remember how difficult it was for them when they had to make decisions of right and wrong at such a young age. Reading **Olivia and the Little Way** just might slow us all down enough to think about the outcome of anything that we do, good or bad. I recommend this book for ALL ages."

—*Martha A. Cheves, American Author's Association, author of **Stir, Laugh, Repeat***

I dedicate this book to my beloved friend Saint Thérèse, who holds my hand and never lets go. *Ma chère Sainte-Thérèse, vous êtes une amie de mon coeur. Comment beaucoup je vous aime.*

Hugs and kisses to Lauren and Anna.

To John-Paul, Vincent, and Paul: How very much I love you!

"Before I formed you in the womb I knew you. Before you were born I dedicated you, a prophet to the nations I appointed you. 'Ah, Lord God!' I said, 'I know not how to speak; I am too young.' But the Lord answered me, Say not, 'I am too young.' To whomever I send you, you shall go; whatever I command you, you shall speak. Have no fear before them, because I am with you to deliver you, says the Lord."
—*Jeremiah 1:5-8*

"Holiness consists simply in doing God's will, and being just what God wants us to be."
—*St. Thérèse of Lisieux*

ONE

"Do not fear. If you are faithful in pleasing Jesus in little things, He will be obliged to help you in the greater things." —St. Thérèse

Olivia sat cross-legged on her bed, furrowing her brow in concentration as she counted.

"One hundred twenty-six, one hundred twenty-seven, one hundred twenty-eight..."

She set the paper money down and picked up the plastic box, shaking it and listening to the jingling of the coins inside. How much was in there...maybe a few dollars?

She opened the box and emptied its contents. Onto her bedspread she divided up quarters, nickels, dimes, and a few pennies in change: four dollars and thirty-six cents' worth, to be exact. She frowned. A total of $132.36. A lot of money for a twelve-year-old girl, certainly. But not enough, not by a long shot. Even the $45 she had received for her birthday recently from relatives was not helping much.

"Olivia, all of that dirty money on your fresh clean bedspread?"

her mother tsk-tsked from the doorway, balancing a basket of clean laundry on her hip. Mrs. Thomas had a thing about money, said it was germy and had been all over who-knows-where. She always made Olivia wash her hands after counting her money, which Olivia seemed to be doing every day now.

She looked at Olivia's fallen face and her voice softened. "What's the count at today, honey?"

Olivia looked over at her mom, a wad of dollar bills in her hand. "I'm $200 short, Mom," she moaned. "I'll never make the difference up in time."

Her mom came over and sat on the edge of her bed. "The change didn't help much?"

Olivia shook her head.

"Don't worry, honey. You'll find a way. There's still plenty of time."

Mrs. Thomas set the laundry basket down and picked up a few stray hangers off the floor. She looked around the cluttered bedroom and saw art supplies, bottles of hand cream, little religious statues and pins on her dresser, a handful of mini notebooks, a colorful necklace tree, and plastic trinkets from vending machines. Her mom did not say anything, but Olivia knew her mom was thinking she should straighten up the mess.

To Olivia, however, her room was no mess. She liked to think of it as a room full of collections, just like the bedroom once was of her favorite saint and heavenly friend, St. Thérèse of Lisieux. Olivia's grandmother had given her a couple of books about Thérèse, and Olivia had read them over and over, enjoying learning new facts and details of the life of the Little Flower in her native France in the late 1800s. The more she read, the more Olivia felt they had in common, and a room filled with little treasures was something that seemed to connect the two, in Olivia's mind. One of the books mentioned that young Thérèse had a variety of things in her room: "It was a real bazaar," Thérèse had written, "a collection of pious articles and curios, a garden and an aviary."

Olivia felt relieved that her mom knew it wasn't the time to mention the mess, seeing as she was feeling so down in the dumps at the moment. She was grateful. A lecture from her mom right about now wouldn't help matters.

Mrs. Thomas looked at Olivia with a small smile. "Grandma's coming for dinner," she said, hoping to cheer her up. "Why don't you put the money away and help me set the table? Dad's going to grill hamburgers."

"In a few minutes, Mom. I just want to finish up here," Olivia said. Her mom nodded and left the room.

Olivia collected the dollar bills and the change and put them back into the purple pencil box she had kept from the last school year. It had an old sticker with "Olivia Thomas, Grade 6" on it. Hayley had seen the pencil box a week earlier and frowned.

"It's summer vacation, Olivia! You still have that pencil box?"

"It's where I'm keeping the money for The Project," Olivia whispered, although she wasn't quite sure why she was whispering. It wasn't a secret cause. That's just what she and Hayley had agreed to call her project: The Project.

Why did money have to be such a problem? Not much she could do about it, not now anyway. She would just have to find a way to earn more, that was all.

She placed the pencil box in her nightstand drawer and closed it a little louder than she should have. It just wasn't fair. After all, the money wasn't for herself. Sure, there were things she wanted, like a new bike and some new books and things. For her twelfth birthday a few weeks ago, people had gotten her clothes, pajamas, and a purse: nice presents, to be sure, but she just wasn't that interested in those things. She secretly still liked games that other girls her age thought were too babyish.

One of her favorite gifts was a glow-in-the-dark basketball from her friend Hayley. It was fun to play basketball at night with her dad. She loved spending time with him, be it in the kitchen making homemade pizza or cookies, or out on the driveway shooting hoops and playing a game of H-O-R-S-E. Funny how she hadn't really been into the sport before, but when her dad had come home one day in late spring and announced that their driveway needed a basketball hoop, she had to agree. She had always enjoyed basketball when Mrs. McCune had them play in gym class.

The day the new net was installed, Olivia and her dad had played until well after dark, when her mother had turned on the floodlights. Hayley had given her the perfect present with that glow-in-the-dark ball. Although she had to laugh when she heard her dad's steady thump of the ball hitting the pavement one night when she was trying to fall asleep. Her mom had to open the front door and tell him to come in at last, since he was waking up Olivia and anyone else in the neighborhood who wanted to sleep!

Hayley had tried her best to be helpful, giving Olivia tips on how to make some extra money. "The story of my life," said Hayley, who had learned a lot about pinching pennies from her mom since her dad died. One of her ideas was to have a lemonade stand. Hayley even came over one day to help out and brought chocolate-chip cookies to sell. They sold pink lemonade and cookies but only ended up making about five dollars the whole day. They both ended up with stomachaches from eating too much of the "merchandise." Olivia thought it was generous of Hayley to offer Olivia her share of the day's take for The Project.

It was just so hard to make money when you were smack-dab in the in-between stage: not a little kid, but not a grownup either. She was too young to get a real job at the mall, and even too young to babysit, at least for another year. Sabrina had a job lined up as a mother's helper for the summer, mostly, as Sabrina's mom had said, to "keep her from getting bored." Sabrina certainly did not need the money, coming from a wealthy family. It sounded fun, but there weren't any young children that lived near Olivia. She thought about how that would have been a perfect job, considering she had plenty of experience with her little sister Lucy.

Olivia lay back on her bed, her hands outstretched beneath her head. She felt guilty thinking about money so much. It certainly wasn't a nice thing to do, to be obsessed with making money. She knew God wouldn't approve of that, but consoled herself with the fact that she wanted the money for a godly purpose. That was okay, right?

"Dear God," she prayed. "Please help me raise the money I need."

Two

*"I am the smallest of creatures and I recognize my
worthlessness, but I also know how hearts that are
generous and noble love to do good."*
—*St. Thérèse*

It had all started with an advertisement she had seen in the
Catholic newspaper. Olivia couldn't get the picture out of her
mind. An underweight, impoverished child with missing teeth
stared back as Olivia munched on a toaster waffle. Olivia looked
at the disheveled clothes that hung loosely on the child's thin
frame, her brown, stringy hair, and her sad eyes, pools of tears
welling up in them. Suddenly, she felt extremely guilty, eating
while this child obviously had nothing. It actually made her feel
a little sick, and she found that her hunger subsided immediately.
She set the half-eaten waffle on the table and peered at the ad for
a closer look.

"This is Maria," the ad read. "She lives in Guatemala. She
walks nearly a mile every day to get water for her family from a
well near a creek. Her father and mother have no money to feed
her and her brothers."

This startled Olivia. To think of having to walk a mile every day to get fresh water, when all she had to do was walk a few steps to the nearest faucet.

The ad continued, "Her father has tried for years to find work, but there is none. She and her brother live in a shack with a mud floor. They do not go to school and do not know how to read and write."

Olivia thought of her house, which they had moved into a couple of years ago. At the time, she had been sad that because of her dad's job, they had moved to Michigan from Texas, the only home she had ever known. Her house wasn't anything fancy, and would be considered modest by some, but when compared to a shack? It was a palace.

Olivia thought of not being able to read and to write. Her wonderful school, St. Michael's, popped into her mind, with all of the kind and nurturing middle-school teachers from last year, and its beloved principal, Sister Anne Marie, who gave out butterscotch candy when kids stopped by her office.

She turned the page quickly. She couldn't look at Maria anymore. She tried to brush the picture out of her mind and picked up her waffle. Maybe it was a fake picture. Maybe Maria didn't really exist. But Olivia knew better. Somewhere out there was a Maria, and a girl or boy just like Maria. Millions of them.

For days, little Maria's picture haunted her thoughts. She found she couldn't let the tap water run anymore while she brushed her teeth. The thought of wasting fresh water when children like Maria had none was shameful. She found herself picking up her toys more often and taking care of her bedroom. And she quit saying, "I'm sooo glad school is out for the summer!" to her friends. She was glad for the break, of course, but thinking of

Maria and her brother having no school to attend made her feel strange every time she said it, so she stopped.

What would Maria say if she could see the excess in which Olivia lived? Her mostly uneaten ham sandwich she so casually tossed into the trash? The half-finished bottle of spring water she carelessly left on the driveway last night after playing basketball? The games she left lying around in the basement, pieces strewn all about?

She thought of the books she had read about her special friend St. Thérèse, the little French nun from the 19th century who yearned to be a missionary and spread the word of God to those who did not know Him. To this day, missionaries adore her, the patron saint of the missions, the little sister who never went anywhere beyond her cloistered convent. She prayed for missionaries from her tiny cell. Little did Thérèse know that she would become a missionary, even in her death, for teachings of her Little Way of serving God through sacrifice had traveled the globe.

In a small way, I can be a missionary, too, Olivia thought. *Just because I can't go to a foreign country, I can spread the word of God to a child like Maria, who may not know about Jesus.*

When Hayley had come over that afternoon, Olivia showed her the newspaper.

"Wow," Hayley had said quietly when she was finished reading. "I don't think I'll ever complain about my mom's pork chops again."

Olivia managed a small grin. "I know. Or my mom's spaghetti."

Hayley winced. "You got me on that one, Olivia." Olivia gave her a playful shove and Hayley responded, "I know, I know. But sorry, it's true."

Olivia laughed. Her mother's spaghetti sauce was…well, it

9

needed a little work. The couple of times Hayley had come over for dinner on spaghetti night, she had filled up on garlic bread and salad instead and Mrs. Thomas had been none the wiser.

"That's why my dad's the cook in our family," Olivia said. "And me!"

Hayley put the newspaper back on the table. "You know, I think Jenna's family does this."

"What?"

"Sponsors a child in a foreign country. She mentioned something one time about some boy in the Philippines."

Olivia looked back at the ad. "Yeah, it says something about sending money to help out. What does Jenna's family do for the boy?"

Hayley squished up her face, trying to remember. "I don't know. It was, you know…a long time ago that I remember her saying that." Hayley's voice faded off.

Olivia looked down. They both knew what Hayley was referring to. Even though it seemed like long ago now, their fifth-grade school year had been full of ups and downs. There was a time when Hayley and Sabrina were not very nice, and had gotten pleasure from making fun of Jenna, calling her and Chad geeks and other mean names. Olivia, the new kid in school, had been caught in the middle, trying to stay afloat between the two groups of kids. But Hayley had undergone a lot of changes, especially this past school year. Olivia had prayed very hard for that to happen. And certainly St. Thérèse, Olivia's great friend in Heaven, had played a large role in Hayley's transformation. Lots of prayers were sent up to the Little Flower that year, and sweet St. Thérèse had heard them all, interceding before God on Olivia's behalf.

She knew that being reminded of that time was painful for Hayley, who still felt ashamed of her behavior, two years later. But all was forgiven, even if Hayley didn't forgive herself. She had gone to confession, and Father Hansen had told her that God had forgiven her, but Hayley still carried the immense feelings of guilt. She knew it was wrong to feel that way, because her slate had been wiped clean with the sacrament. It was something she was still working through.

Olivia tried to cheer her up. "That's okay. A lot of my first year here seems to have slipped my mind. I don't remember a whole lot about it, really. Especially fractions!"

Hayley laughed, then groaned. "Speaking of math, my mom said something about math workbooks this summer. I hope she forgets!"

"Next time we see Jenna, let's ask her about it," Olivia said, looking at Maria's picture. "Gosh, I feel so terrible. Like I should do something."

That evening, Olivia got out her St. Thérèse chaplet and offered her prayers for children who were in need, all throughout the world. Then Olivia called Jenna and learned all about Rolando, a seven-year-old boy from Manila who sent letters throughout the year, thanking her family for sponsoring him. The money Jenna's mom and dad sent helped Rolando and his family with schooling, religious formation, and health needs.

Jenna said that her family had gotten a letter from Rolando around Christmastime thanking them for providing him with new shoes. Another letter said that the money they sent had bought him a new backpack he used for school. Jenna said that Rolando always sounded so happy and grateful for even the smallest things, items many American kids take for granted. After all, who that they knew didn't have a simple pair of *shoes*? Or pencils and scissors for school supplies?

"Every time we get a letter from Rolando, it makes me appreciate everything I have," Jenna said solemnly. "Then a day or so later, my brother and I forget and we start to fight with each other or whine about stuff we want." Jenna said that during those times, her mother took Rolando's latest letter and displayed it on the refrigerator as a silent reminder of what is important in life. It worked every time.

Jenna said she would give Olivia the name of the foundation for more information.

After she brushed her teeth before bed, Olivia sat down with her parents and told them she wanted their family to sponsor a child.

She showed them the newspaper clipping and told them about Rolando.

"I want to do this with my own money," she said.

"You certainly have a kind heart," her dad said. "And I know God must be very proud of you."

"Livvy, are you sure?" her mom asked. "The suggested donation is over $300 a year. That's a lot of money for a little girl like you to raise every year. I don't think it can be done, to be honest."

"I know I can do it, Mom!" Olivia cried. "Remember the baby blanket drive for the Peabody Center in fifth grade? And last year with the charity book auction? I did that on my own."

"I know, honey," her mom said gently as she tried to reason with Olivia. "But buying baby blankets and books was a lot less money than what is needed in this case to support a child."

"Well, maybe we can work something out," her dad said. "I'll look into this foundation and see what it's all about. Mom and I can help you out a little, but..." his voice trailed off and he looked down. Her mom shifted in her seat.

Olivia sensed something, but she didn't know what. Her parents looked a little sad at that moment, and she didn't know why.

"Thanks, Dad, but this is something I want to do all on my own. At least for the first year. Maybe next year you can help out. Please?"

"We'll think about it," her dad said.

Olivia smiled. That was certainly better than an outright "no."

"We'll see" and "We'll think about it" usually meant yes... eventually.

"And Mom?" she asked very carefully, not wanting to press her luck. "Um...well...I'm not a little girl, you know?"

Her mom smiled and kissed the top of her head, and gave her a side hug. "I am beginning to realize that, Livvy. Is it still okay to call you Livvy?"

Olivia managed a grin. "Sure, Mom. Just not in public, okay?"

"Agreed...*Livvy*!"

And she kissed Olivia again.

THREE

"He set before me the book of nature; I understood how all the flowers He has created are beautiful, how the splendor of the rose and the whiteness of the lily do not take away from the perfume of the little violet or the delightful simplicity of the daisy. I understood that if all flowers wanted to be roses, nature would lose her springtime beauty, and the fields would no longer be decked out with little wildflowers. And so it is in this world of souls, Jesus' garden. He willed to create great souls comparable to lilies and roses, but He has created smaller ones and these must be content to be daisies or violets destined to give joy to God's glances when He looks down at His feet. Perfection consists in doing His will, in being what He wills us to be."
—St. Thérèse

After the hamburgers were eaten and Grandma had left, Olivia began to worry. She realized that it was going to be a long, slow process to earn enough money to support a foreign child. She decided to brainstorm ideas for earning money. There had to be some way a girl—no, make that an almost-teenager—could earn some money. Grandma would know, she decided, then chided herself for not asking her earlier.

After Mass that Sunday, she went to Grandma's house for a

visit. The two sat on Grandma's patio, eating butter pecan ice cream and enjoying the warm sunshine.

"Grandma, your flowers are so pretty this year," Olivia said between bites of her ice cream cone.

"Oh, thank you, sweetie," Grandma said as she dabbed at her mouth with a napkin. "Those orange tiger lilies over by the fence are new this year. I wanted to spice up the back yard!" she said, happily waving her hand toward the vast yard, filled with every perennial imaginable.

Olivia giggled. As if Grandma's yard needed any more spicing up! Grandma was not a fussy gardener, nor was she a prim and proper one. No matchy-poo rows of balanced flowers, all alike and color coordinated, separated by species. No, Grandma's back yard was filled with the plain and the exotic, all mixed together in a beautiful symphony of color and shape. Peach roses intermingled with lavender lilac bushes, hostas with ferns, red geraniums with purple garden phlox.

Some serious gardeners might say Grandma's color palette clashed, or didn't "flow" properly. Grandma wouldn't care if they did. Her only concern was that each variety was planted in the proper spot: sun-loving plants were planted in the sunny areas of the house, and shade-loving plants stayed in the cool, northernmost part of the house. Other than that, it was come as you were, do as you please in Grandma's yard.

The orange tiger lilies were planted next to purple coneflower and a butterfly bush, with separate pots of basil, rosemary, and geraniums intermixed among them. Grandma saw no need to separate herbs from flowers. "They all keep each other company," she liked to say. Grandma's garden was a mishmash of statuary, flowers, and plants, and to Olivia it was simply beautiful.

Grandma liked to pick up perennials on sale at the end of the season at the local garden center, when their blooms were spent and turning brown. "Just think what a pretty surprise we'll get next year when it's their time," Grandma would remark to Olivia as she placed a pot with a clearance sticker into her cart. "You just wait and see, Livvy," she would say as she perused the sale tables. "We'll see what this little fella can do."

One time, Grandma mentioned that a few years ago, an uppity couple named Mr. and Mrs. Farnsworth who lived next door used to make snide remarks about her patchwork garden under their breath. "They said it was tacky!" Grandma had said at the time, incensed at such a word. "Can you imagine?"

But eventually Grandma was able to laugh at the stuffy couple, who would stare at her yard from their fence and shake their heads. When Grandma saw them, she would call, "It IS beautiful, isn't it? Why don't you come over for a glass of iced tea and a closer look?" To which the staid Farnsworths would look away, embarrassed, and suddenly become extremely interested in a section of their shrubbery.

"This year I planted pink wax begonias for Our Lady," Grandma announced proudly, gesturing toward the concrete statue of Mary. "I think Our Lady deserves the prettiest pink possible."

Olivia had to agree. She also thought that yellow daylilies were a perfect fit for the St. Francis statue, although why she felt that way she couldn't say. They just seemed to go together naturally.

A little green ceramic frog frolicked among the blue creeping phlox groundcover, while a garden gnome Grandma and Olivia lovingly named "Mr. Heffenpfeffer" kept the purple clematis company by the trellis. Olivia joked that Mr. Heffenpfeffer was the boss of the yard, and kept the squirrels, birds, and chipmunks in line. Grandma agreed: No backyard creature was to mess with Mr. Heffenpfeffer. She noted that in all the years Mr. Heffenpfeffer stood guard, no bird ever decided to leave its messy mark on him, and wouldn't if it knew what was good for it!

"Yes, Mr. Heffenpfeffer is keeping everyone in line this year," Grandma said as she admired her yard and all its trimmings. "Although I daresay he needs a new paint job. His little red hat is peeling, and so is his coat."

"I'll do it for you, Grandma," Olivia offered.

"Of course you will, because you're so sweet," Grandma said and winked. "But tell you what: I'll give you a little something to scrape and repaint Mr. Heffenpfeffer. It's a bigger job than it looks. I already bought the paint; it's in the garage."

Olivia refused, even though she could have used the money. "No, Grandma, really. You're my grandma; I don't mind doing it for nothing. But I do want to ask if you know of any of your neighbors who have little children that I could babysit? I'm trying to raise some money."

Grandma thought for a minute. "Mrs. Blakely across the street just had a baby a few months ago. But you're awfully young for such a big responsibility, honey."

"Oh, I don't mean babysitting on my own. But I could be a mother's helper, and watch the baby while she did some things around the house during the day," Olivia offered. "Sabrina's doing that. She watches a little boy so the mom can catch up on bills and make phone calls, that sort of thing. She even helps fold laundry."

"Sabrina?" Grandma was surprised that Olivia's wealthy friend had a job, and at her age.

"Grandma," Olivia pointed out politely, "we're both twelve years old now."

Grandma smiled. "Oh, yes, that is evident, honey. You're getting to be quite a young lady. And you'd make a fine mother's helper, but the Blakelys are pinching pennies nowadays, I think. Her husband just got laid off from the car company."

"Oh."

Olivia finished her ice cream cone and wiped her sticky fingers off as best she could. It seemed like a lot of people were pinching pennies nowadays, and trying to make do with less. She knew of a couple of kids who were not able to return to St. Michael's in the fall and were either moving out of state or enrolling in the public school in town because their parents could not afford to pay the tuition any longer.

Grandma seemed like she wanted to say something more, but chose not to. "What are you saving up for?" Grandma asked instead.

"It's a surprise," she told Grandma. She wanted to surprise Grandma with her sponsored child's picture and biography. "But Mom and Dad said it was okay and they approve."

"Hmmm…" Grandma was intrigued. "I can't wait to find out, whatever it is. I'm sorry I don't have any ideas for you right now."

"That's okay." Olivia stood up. "Well, if you want, I could get started on Mr. Heffenpfeffer today. I'll go put on one of Grandpa's old painting shirts," Olivia said.

Grandma smiled. "I'm sure Grandpa is smiling down at us from Heaven, and laughing at your old pack-rat grandma who saves everything, even his old work shirts!"

"You have to admit, Grandma, that they are coming in handy!" Olivia stepped away from the patio table and stretched.

"Why don't we just play a game of Crazy Eights instead? You look a little tired. Mr. Heffenpfeffer can wait."

Olivia laughed. "Grandma, you know Mr. Heffenpfeffer is a crabby little gnome, and he's probably angry that he looks so bad!"

Grandma laughed, too, at their over-the-top silliness. "Yes, you're probably right. Don't want to upset him any more than he is already! Follow me to the garage."

On the way there, they passed Olivia's favorite spot, where the St. Thérèse statue was. Dressed in her Carmelite habit with her long, black veil, Thérèse smiled lovingly at her savior Jesus on the crucifix. Red rosebushes of various hues bloomed all around her in a beautiful and delightful pattern. Sometimes when Grandma took a short afternoon nap and Olivia was all alone in the yard with her thoughts, she would wander over to the St. Thérèse statue to have a word with her favorite saint.

"Thérèse," she would say, sometimes desperately when she felt particularly sad about something, "Please don't ever leave me. Please always stay with me."

Olivia would lovingly stroke the statue and smile. "I like Hayley and Jenna and Chad and Sabrina a lot, but Thérèse, you're my best friend," she would whisper.

These words would come to Olivia in the silence of her heart: **"One phase of Heaven causes my heart to beat faster—the love that I shall receive and that I shall be able to give."**

Thérèse would keep smiling her lovely smile, the one that told Olivia that she would never leave her, that she would be her friend forever.

Grandma nodded at the statue as they passed. "There's your special friend, Olivia. Let's give her a little *bonjour* from us. *Bonjour, ma petite Thérèse. Vous êtes si belle!* My, aren't you lovely today? But then again, you always are," said Grandma as she patted the statue on the head and kept on walking.

Olivia smiled to herself. Grandma could be a little eccentric sometimes, but there was no better grandma around—she knew that for certain! She loved how Grandma always said the same thing to the Thérèse statue: *Vous êtes si belle.* You are so beautiful.

She turned to Olivia. "You ask your dear friend for advice, ask her to pray for you to God. She'll let you know what you should do."

The rest of the afternoon passed quickly, as it always did when Olivia went to visit Grandma. Later, Olivia's dad came to pick her up and they drove home. She was pleasantly tired and had bits of red and blue paint on her hands.

Seated in the back seat of the car, she rummaged through her little purse for some lip balm for her chapped lips. Tucked inside, to her surprise, she found a newly folded ten-dollar bill.

⁹FOUR

"To live by love is to go through life sowing peace and joy in hearts!"—St. Thérèse

"**O**livia, can you come downstairs for a minute?" her mother called from the staircase.

Olivia sighed. She was just getting to the good part in her library book. "Can it wait a few minutes, Mom? I just started a new chapter."

"Sure," said her mom brightly. "But I think you're going to want to hear this."

Now Olivia was intrigued. Whatever it was, it sounded good, so she closed her book with a snap and scurried downstairs. Her mom and dad and two-year-old Lucy were in the kitchen. Lucy was gnawing on some animal crackers at the table, quite pleased with the mess of crumbs she was creating for herself.

Mrs. Thomas was holding a couple of photographs and a letter in her hand and had a big smile on her face.

Mr. Thomas had his calendar laid out on the kitchen table.

Olivia had the feeling it was something big and exciting. And she was right.

"Olivia, we got a letter from Aunt Peggy and Uncle Jack that I'd like to share with you."

Olivia's aunt and uncle were legendary on her mother's side of the family. They were always going somewhere exotic: a year in Provence, a summer in Italy, a cruise to Alaska. They were world travelers and very wealthy. Aunt Peggy loved to tell stories about their travels and the people they met. And Uncle Jack had a crazy sense of humor, always making good-natured practical jokes and laughing. They were nice people, and Olivia missed living near them in Texas.

Olivia perked up. Once in a while, her family would receive a funny letter from them from a faraway country. She assumed that this would be another letter relating tales of their life abroad.

Mrs. Thomas held up a photo of Aunt Peggy and Uncle Jack in southern Italy next to a grove of lemon trees. They looked happy and tanned.

Her mother unfolded the letter and read:

> Dear Steve, Claudia, Olivia, and Lucy:
>
> Greetings! Well, I guess you can tell from the post-mark on the envelope that we're stateside, at our home sweet home in Texas. After all of this traveling, it sure is good to be home for a bit. How are you all doing? Are you getting used to those Michigan winters? We hope Olivia is still enjoying her school and her friends. We love hearing all about the girls and what they are up to.
>
> Uncle Jack and I are doing well, but we think we need to take a respite from all of this traveling and stay put for the summer here in Texas. Uncle Jack has to have an operation on his knee and the doctor feels that it would

be best for us to clip our wings for a while, at least until the fall. This means that we will not be spending the summer at our beach house in Keane Harbor. We are a bit disappointed, especially since we have had so many beautiful renovations done to the place while we were away in Italy this year.

We would like to extend an invitation for you to use the house this summer for a month or so, however long you would like. We would hate for it to sit empty all summer; it is such a lovely home right on the Atlantic Ocean. We would be more than happy to have you stay there and enjoy yourselves. No sense having it go to waste, right? I'm not sure about Steve's work schedule, but perhaps you could work something out. There are plenty of bedrooms, so please feel free to bring Grandma Rosemary, a friend of Olivia's, or one of the cousins. It would be a comfort to us to know the house was being looked after in our absence.

Please let me know what you think. We'll be awaiting your reply.

Love to all of you,
Aunt Peggy

Olivia's eyes were as big as saucers. Spend part of the summer at the beach in North Carolina? Could life get any better? Would Mom and Dad say yes?

"We said yes!" her mom and dad said in unison. "For one month—all of July," her mom clarified.

Olivia jumped up and down and clapped her hands in glee. Yipeee! A whole month at the beach!

She ran over and gave them a big hug. "I can't believe it! This is going to be so fun!"

"And the best part," her dad said, "is that you can invite one of your friends, if you like. This way you won't be lonely."

"Really? Really and truly?"

Her dad laughed. "Really and truly."

"What about Grandma?" Olivia asked.

"We asked her, but you know Grandma. She's more of a homebody. She really prefers to stay put. Besides, she's not big on the ocean," her dad said.

Olivia frowned. "Well, I can understand that. But Dad, what about your job? You can't skip work for a whole month, can you?"

Mr. Thomas cleared his throat. "Well, honey, the thing is, I found out last week that I've been laid off until August. Nothing I can do about it; it's the company's decision."

"Oh," said Olivia, thinking of the Blakelys, who were pinching pennies for some reason. Would that mean they'd have to as well? And what did it mean exactly, exactly, to "pinch pennies"? Olivia had an image in her mind about people holding coins and squeezing them, and wondered whoever came up with that term.

"It's nothing for you to worry about, but it does mean that we won't be able to have any money for extras. We'll be eating in a lot, and won't be able to do a lot of expensive things. But since Aunt Peggy and Uncle Jack were so kind to let us stay in their house, we figured we shouldn't pass up the opportunity to have a free summer vacation." Her mom smiled. "What do you think?"

"I think I have to pick someone to come with us!" Olivia laughed. "But who? I don't want anyone to feel bad. And when do we leave?"

"We'll leave at the end of this month—June 30. My last day of work is two days before. It will take us over a day to drive there. It'll be a long car ride," he warned.

"I don't care!" shouted Olivia excitedly. "I can't wait!"

"You think about who you want to invite, and we'll call her parents to talk it over," her mom said.

Olivia went outside to mull it over. She thought about Jenna, but remembered her saying that they were going back to her native Massachusetts to visit family for a couple of weeks in July. A quick phone call to Jenna confirmed her suspicions.

"Oh, you are so lucky," Jenna had said when Olivia called. "Your trip sounds so much more fun than mine. I have to stay with my cousin Ellie and her family," she moaned.

"That doesn't sound so bad," said Olivia, thinking about the stories Jenna had been telling her of her fun, wacky cousins who lived in an old farmhouse.

"I think they're going to put me to work on the farm," Jenna moaned. "They get up at the crack of dawn to feed the chickens and clean out the coop."

Olivia stifled a laugh, thinking of Jenna getting up with the crow of a rooster on her summer vacation and milking cows. "Well, at least you'll have your cool cousin Ellie to hang out with."

"Not really," Jenna said, sighing. "Ellie turned sixteen last month."

"What's so bad about that?"

"She can drive now. She'll be hanging out with her teenage friends and going out all the time. I'll be left doing all the chores!"

"Well," said Olivia, trying to improve Jenna's mood, "maybe she'll take you with her to the mall and stuff."

Olivia's suggestion made Jenna feel a little better. The prospect of hanging out with her cool older cousin and her friends seemed to cheer up Jenna enough to suggest other travel companions for Olivia, like Hayley, Sabrina, or Chad.

Unfortunately, Chad was most definitely out. Not only because he was a boy, but his grandparents needed him to stay with them and help with their many needs. Hayley and Sabrina were kind of a matched set, but lately, since Hayley lived closer and seemed to have more free time, she seemed to be getting closer to Olivia. Sabrina also had lots of friends in her neighborhood that she hung out with at her swim club. And with Sabrina's job as a mother's helper, Olivia knew she wouldn't be able to come.

Olivia would love to ask Hayley. What a treat that would be for her, to go on a fun vacation. Hayley had never really been on a vacation like this; her father had died when she was younger, leaving her mom to work full time and take care of her and her older brother Ryan. There had never been any extra money for fun vacations or extras in Hayley's family.

Olivia wondered if Hayley's mom would let her go away with her family. It seemed like such an extravagant thing to ask. She doubted her mom would give permission. A month was a long time to be away from your mother. Olivia had to admit that she herself wouldn't want to be away from her family for a whole month. Would Hayley even want to go?

"Are you kidding?" shrieked Hayley when Olivia called her up. "I'm going!"

"Wait, Hayley," cautioned Olivia. "Your mom might say no."

"She's just *got* to let me go!" moaned Hayley. "If she doesn't, I'll just *die*." Hayley had a way of dramatizing things.

"Wait, why don't you let one of my parents talk to her and give her the information? Maybe coming from them first, it might go over better. It might sound more *parental* or something."

Olivia silently congratulated herself on such a mature idea. It was bound to work.

Mrs. Thomas and Mrs. Stewart talked for over thirty minutes, going over the fine details. By the time they had hung up, Hayley not only had permission to go, but she had dragged a suitcase out of the attic and began to pack, even as the two mothers still chatted.

"Yay!" Hayley shouted into the phone when the girls retrieved the phones from their mothers.

"You've saved me from an entire month of visiting colleges with Ryan!" breathed Hayley. "I can't thank you enough. I would've died of boredom!"

"I think that's one of the reasons your mom said yes," said Olivia. "She knew you'd hate being dragged from campus to campus this summer with your brother. BO-ring!"

"Really! Hey Olivia, let's get together tomorrow and make a list of the stuff we should bring. You have to bring your Tyler Twins CDs."

"Of course! And you have to bring your UNO cards and your MP3 player."

"And movies!"

"And you bring your inline skates!"

"OK, if you bring yours and your glow-in-the-dark basketball!"

"Sure! And flashlights for flashlight tag on the beach!"

"So cool! Olivia?"

"Yeah, Hayley?"

"We are going to have the most awesome summer *ever*!"

⸮FIVE

"How can my confidence have any limits?"
—St. Thérèse

ather Hansen set his Styrofoam coffee cup down on the table and took a seat next to the Thomas family.

"One of my favorite things about Sunday: the coffee and doughnuts after Mass!" he said to Olivia and winked as he took a big bite of his chocolate-frosted doughnut.

Olivia smiled. Father Hansen was the nicest priest she'd ever met. She remembered the first time she went to confession with him at St. Michael's; she was so nervous that she thought she was going to throw up while waiting in line. She didn't have anything especially bad to confess, she thought, but still she worried.

She had still been nervous entering the confessional, but something made her think of the story of St. Thérèse's first confession, and she couldn't help but smile. Grandma, who in Olivia's mind was an expert on St. Thérèse since she had read all about her, had told her that Thérèse was only seven years old at her first confession, and too little to even see over the armrest in the confessional. The priest even had to ask her to stand up.

Olivia could just imagine cute little Thérèse with her long, light brown hair, nervously making her first confession, and the priest not even being able to see her!

As it turned out, Father Hansen was a very friendly priest who was very understanding. He had given her a few Hail Marys to say and had her work on her temper as penance.

Mrs. Thomas subtly motioned to Olivia that she had some powdered sugar on her face, and she quickly wiped it off, embarrassed to be looking like such a mess in front of the handsome young priest.

"Father, we won't be at too many of these this summer; we're going to Keane Harbor for the whole month of July!" Olivia said.

"Yes, so I've heard," he said, taking a sip of coffee. "You are one lucky girl. I remember going there when I was a boy…when the dinosaurs roamed!"

"Oh, Father, you're not that old," laughed Mr. Thomas. "I know you're younger than I am!" he said to the priest.

"Well, let's just say the gray hairs are starting to come in, and leave it at that," he said. "I hope you all have a great time and get to relax and swim and have fun at the beach."

Little Lucy banged her hands on the table. "I go in the water!" she cried happily, and everyone at the table laughed. Now that Lucy was beginning to talk up a storm, she said the funniest things when you least expected it.

They chatted for a bit, and then Father Hansen got up to leave so he could visit with some of the other parishioners. He leaned over to Olivia and whispered, "Don't forget to take St. Thérèse with you this summer."

Olivia smiled. As if she would ever forget! "I know, Father. She's always with me."

"Of course she is. Remember how determined she was to enter

the convent when she was only fifteen? She doesn't let go easily! Hello, Chad, young man. How is your summer going so far?"

"Pretty good, Father, thanks." With one hand, Chad O'Toole waved to Olivia and her family while he balanced a paper plate in the other. "My grandpa wants another doughnut. He's had two already. Plus hot chocolate."

"Well, never question your elders. Your grandpa is a wise man. Maybe I'll have another doughnut also," Father said as he walked away with a grin.

Chad sat down in Father's chair. "Hi Mr. and Mrs. Thomas. Just wanted to wish you all a fun time," he said. "When do you leave?"

"In two days," Olivia said, beaming. "I can't wait!" Then her face softened. "I sure wish you could go, too."

Chad shrugged his shoulders. "Nah, not for me."

"You don't like the beach?" her mother asked Chad.

"Are you kidding? I get seasick!"

Olivia groaned. "Chad, you are one crazy kid." That was just like Chad.

"I'll be looking for postcards in my mailbox. And put some interesting news in there, not just boring stuff like 'The weather is great, wish you were here.'"

"What kind of stuff do you want to hear?"

"Good stuff. Like, you and Hayley went fishing and caught a 30-pound sailfish, or went parasailing or something. Something really cool."

"A 30-pound sailfish?" Mr. Thomas cried. "You don't really think Miss Olivia is going to go deep-sea fishing in the Atlantic Ocean?"

Olivia pretended to pout. "What do you mean? I like fish…I think." But she knew she wouldn't be believed. That was one thing she certainly didn't have in common with St. Thérèse, who loved going fishing with her father in the river near her home.

Chad shook his head, trying to imagine Olivia out on the ocean, struggling with a big, slippery fish.

"Come on! You didn't even like Jumper," he reminded her.

Hmm. He had her there. She had even been afraid of Chad's pet tree frog a couple of years ago.

"Well, if you do go in the ocean, don't get eaten up by a shark. I'm going to need your help with social studies next year and you can't help me if you're dead."

Olivia laughed.

"So what are you and Hayley going to do on the beach all month besides study ocean wildlife? Meet boys?"

Olivia turned bright red. "Yeah, right."

Boys were the furthest thing from Olivia's mind. Well, except for the lead singer of the Tyler Twins. She'd begged and pleaded with her parents to let her hang a poster of the popular teen band on her wall. After much talk about making holes in the freshly painted wall, her parents had finally relented, remembering, no doubt, their own infatuations with the bands of their day.

While some of the girls in her class were starting to get what her mom called "boy crazy," Olivia had not and was glad of it. *Besides*, she told herself often, *with these ugly freckles, who would think I'm pretty anyway?*

Anyway, she liked hanging around both boys and girls and was not interested in the least in acting silly around boys, calling them and asking fake questions about homework, and trying to impress them like Beth and Riley, girls in her grade, were doing.

It especially irritated her how Beth, the smartest student in the class, would call boys she liked to ask them about homework assignments. Bright Beth could practically teach the lesson and here she was, calling up Tim DeMayo to ask him about math homework. As if Beth, a straight-A student, needed Tim's help— a kid who got straight Cs!

She was glad Hayley, Sabrina, and Jenna were sensible about boys and weren't boy crazy. Although lately it seemed as if Hayley was more interested in her hair and clothes than usual. Olivia also noticed that Hayley had been mentioning Mike Ashworth's name more often: Mike liked to play baseball; Mike's mom and her mom worked together; Mike had a golden retriever named Casey. Things like that. Hmm. Olivia decided she'd have to keep a closer eye on Hayley to see what was going on there.

Chad grinned. "We'll see."

"I don't think so, Chad. Definitely not boys."

Chad made a face. "Okaaaay…"

"I think what Olivia means," her mom said, smiling to ease the tension, "is that she hopes to meet some nice friends at the beach."

"Well, just bring me back some salt water taffy and all will be forgiven," Chad said as he stood up to leave. "And one of those oval white stickers with a KH on it. Have a great trip!"

"Bye Chad!" She was going to miss Chad and his goofy sense of humor. She tried to picture what his summer was going to be like, helping to take care of his grandma, who was ailing and in a wheelchair, while his grandpa worked to make ends meet. Then she remembered Chad telling her that his uncle was coming to visit them and would be taking him to a Detroit Tigers game and to go camping at the lake for a couple of days.

She felt better knowing that he would be having some fun things to do. She also was glad he had such a positive attitude toward life, especially after having lost his parents in a car accident when he was very young. Having a friend like Chad, who could look at the bright side of things, was really cool, not to mention a reminder of what was really important in life. She promised herself that she was going to send him the funniest postcards she could find.

When the Thomas family pulled up in front of their house, they were surprised to see Grandma's car in the driveway.

"What's your mom doing here?" Olivia's mom asked her dad. "Is everything okay?"

"I'm sure if something was wrong she would've called me. She knows my cell phone number." Mr. Thomas sounded a bit concerned, though, as he remembered, "Although I turned it off before Mass."

He pulled the car into the driveway and parked behind Grandma's car, a large, old Buick that was rarely driven and had only 40,000 miles on it. Olivia's dad liked to joke that whoever bought Grandma's car when it was time to sell it would be getting quite a vehicle: For ten years, Grandma had only driven it to the market, church, her doctor's office, and the card shop, which all together took up a two-mile radius.

When Grandma saw them drive up, she got out of her car, looked at her watch, and shook her head.

"Did that young priest go over again?" Grandma went to Our Lady of Good Counsel, the church on her side of town, whose pastor was Father Decina, an older man who could do no wrong in Grandma's eyes. He'd been the pastor of her church for as long as anyone could remember, and anyone who said a negative word about Father Decina, even to criticize one of his homilies, never heard the end of it from Grandma.

"No, Mom, coffee and doughnuts," said Olivia's dad as he bent down to give Grandma a kiss. "St. Michael's has it every Sunday, remember?"

Grandma's face turned sour as she remembered. "Hmm. Very extravagant. We only have it once a month. Well, how was I supposed to remember?"

Olivia went over and hugged Grandma. As she held Grandma close, she caught her parents giving each other a concerned look.

But nothing got by Grandma.

"Oh you two, don't look so worried. I'm an old lady, and old ladies sometimes forget things. Just you wait 'til you're my age."

"Is everything okay, Grandma?" asked Mrs. Thomas gently.

Grandma's face brightened. "Of course everything's okay, Claudia! In fact," and she turned toward Olivia, "better than okay. I've decided to hit the big, open road with you after all. I'm going to Keane Harbor!"

The family was silent and in shock. Only the birds made noise. Even Lucy remained quiet on her mother's hip. No one could believe it. They all thought back to the week before, when Grandma had adamantly refused their offer to go.

"No, no, no," she'd said at the time. "I thank you for the offer, but I need to stay put right here and keep an eye on things."

No one had been too surprised, since Grandma wasn't much of a traveler. Besides, they all knew Grandma wouldn't trust just anyone to watch her house and take care of her garden.

Mrs. Thomas smiled now, obviously happy with the news. "What changed your mind, Grandma?"

Grandma had a faraway gleam in her eye. "Last night I had a dream about Grandpa," she said. "We were sitting on the porch swing, just like we used to all the time after dinner and drinking that chamomile tea he used to like to settle his stomach, and he looked at me and said, 'Now Rosemary, you have got to go and keep the family company at the ocean this summer.'

"I looked at Grandpa like he'd lost his mind. I'm sure you've heard all the stories from your folks about how I almost drowned in the sea on our honeymoon a million years ago," she said to Olivia. "It was quite traumatic. He raced me to the hospital and was sure I was dead. Of course I wasn't, but he didn't know that at the time! I spent three days of my honeymoon in the hospital. I couldn't believe that Grandpa was telling me to go back after all of these years."

Olivia nodded, having heard the frightening story before.

"'Frank, have you lost your mind?' I asked him. 'There is no way on God's creation that I'm stepping these old toes onto sand again. It's been 55 years since I've breathed the sea air and it'll be another 55 before I do again!'"

Grandma's face got very serious then. "And then he told me that it was time I go back, to face my fear. He told me he'd be watching me every step of the way, that I wouldn't be alone."

She put her hand on her hip. "And then I woke up. Grandpa told me to go and go I will. If," she asked tentatively, "the offer's still good?"

The four of them enveloped Grandma in a big embrace.

"Grandma, we thought you'd never ask!"

"Good, then it's settled. I promise I won't be in anyone's way."

"Oh, Grandma, you could never be in anyone's way," Olivia said with a chuckle.

"Well, we'll see. But don't count on me going down to the water. I'll just admire it from afar," she said firmly.

Everyone went into the house to draw up a list of the things Grandma should pack.

SIX

"I do everything for God, and in this way I lose nothing,
and I'm always well repaid for the trouble I go to for other
people."—St. Thérèse

The Blue Ridge Mountains seemed to go on forever, like bumpy waves of different shapes and sizes, filling the horizon with their towering pines. Everywhere Olivia looked, she saw blue hills dipping up and down. They looked so serene, and once in a while she'd spot a simple cabin or house tucked away on the edge of the mountain. She wondered who lived there, and what the little houses looked like inside. What would it be like to live in a cute hilltop house in the middle of the Blue Ridge Mountains, instead of her town in the suburbs of Detroit? She decided that living on a rural mountaintop, even though it probably got lonely sometimes, sounded quite peaceful. Just think: Only nature to keep you company. Birds and squirrels and the wildlife that lived there would probably be a welcome change from the noisy lawnmowers that populated her neighborhood.

Olivia leaned up against the minivan window, imagining living in one of the little cabins when she grew up. She knew just what she would do: She would can her own produce from her garden, she decided. Tomatoes and corn and peaches. She would have a little larder where she would keep her jars, along with the large bags of flour and sugar she would likely need for baking bread each day. She would hang her laundry out on a line in the back, and it would flap in the breeze as it dried. She'd have a phone for emergencies, she mused, but no TV or computer. She would spend her time reading, baking, and writing novels on an old-fashioned typewriter, like the one Grandma had in her spare bed-room that didn't even have a plug for electricity. She would sew her own clothes and curtains, and would have a cast-iron skillet for making cornbread, and a big black pot for making beef stew. The deer and rabbits would come to her door and she would give them bits of food to nibble on. Once a week she would venture into the nearest town to pick up her mail and supplies from the store, and to go to Mass. Maybe she would meet a nice man and they would get married and live in the little house and have chil-dren who she could teach to help her in the garden. It all sounded so romantic.

"Whatcha thinking about?" asked Hayley as she took her ear-buds out of her ears. She had been listening to the Tyler Twins. Olivia and Hayley were crazy about them, and had played their new CD over and over again all spring. Her parents could not see what all the fuss was about, this pair of blond-haired broth-ers who made preteen girls from all over the globe scream and faint.

"Your favorite song is on: 'You're So Random,'" Hayley said with a big grin, and she began to sing the song off key.

Grandma winced. "You call that noise music? You should let

me introduce you to the music of *my* day. Now *that* was music."

"Right, Grandma," answered Olivia dreamily as she watched the beautiful scenery go by.

"I was just thinking about when I grow up." She turned toward Hayley, who was sitting next to her on the rear bench seat of the van. In front of them, Lucy dozed off in her car seat. "Do you ever think about it?"

"Oh yeah," Hayley said, as she stuffed her MP3 player back into her tote bag. "All of the time. I'm going to live in New York City and be a famous news anchor. I'll have one of those gorgeous high-rise apartments on Fifth Avenue and take taxicabs all over Manhattan to cool restaurants and stores."

Olivia bit her lip. Their dreams of adulthood could not have been more opposite.

"Promise me you'll come and visit, Olivia. I'll take you to see the Statue of Liberty and Broadway plays." She kicked off her flip-flops and sat cross-legged on the seat. "What about you?"

"Well, my idea is a little different."

"How so?"

"Think a little less Big Apple and a little more apple pie," she laughed, and motioned to the mountains they were passing.

"What, here?" Hayley laughed. "Out here in the wilderness? Like Laura Ingalls Wilder?"

"Well, technically Laura didn't live in the mountains," Olivia corrected her.

"Olivia, I've seen the show a thousand times. There were always mountains in the background."

Olivia laughed. "I know, but Laura lived in Minnesota. No mountains there. The TV show was filmed in California. A little-known fact."

Hayley rolled her eyes. "Okay, okay, so Laura didn't live in the mountains. But you will?"

"Maybe. It seems like it would be fun. I don't think I am a big-city girl like you."

"Well, it has its pros and cons," Grandma interjected knowingly from the second row of the van.

"How so, Mrs. Thomas?"

"No, I'll have none of that 'Mrs. Thomas' on this trip, Hayley. You call me 'Grandma,' okay?"

Hayley seemed to ponder that for a bit. Olivia knew that Hayley already had two grandmas who had passed away, and she missed them a lot. She probably thought it might feel strange to call someone else 'Grandma,' as nice as Olivia's grandma was. "Is it okay if I call you 'Grandma Rosemary?'"

"I'd like that, Hayley," Grandma smiled. "Anyway, I've lived in both the city and the country, so I think I know a little about both. I grew up in a little town in Ohio called Bexley, in a big Italian family with four sisters and four brothers."

"Wow!" cried Hayley. "Such a big family!"

"That's right," said Grandma. "And we all got along, the nine of us, most of the time. We were too busy working the family farm to have much time to argue. My father—Olivia's great-grandpa—owned a small produce company, so even though it was the Great Depression, we always had enough to eat. We grew all of our own produce right there on our farm. We were one of the lucky families back then. Once a week, I remember Mama taking huge baskets of our vegetables like tomatoes and carrots, food we had canned, and our homemade bread and cookies to our neighbors, the MacFarlanes, who were going through a hard time and needed food. I used to tag along with her. We'd leave the food on their front porch and leave as quietly as we could."

"Why?" asked Olivia, curious.

"I asked my mama the same question at first. The first time we went there with food, I was ready to knock on the door and stay to play with the MacFarlane children, who I was best pals with."

"Why didn't you stay?"

Grandma closed her eyes, remembering. "Your great-grandma said something I'll never forget. She said: 'We give in secret.' And we'd go home and return a few hours later instead to visit, just as if we had never been there earlier that day." She opened her eyes. "I never forgot that, and from then on I never asked her why again."

Hayley and Olivia exchanged confused looks. Why would they return a few hours later instead?

Grandma smiled kindly. "Girls, think of it this way. If you were one of the MacFarlane children, how would you feel if you knew it was your best friend who was putting your food on your table?"

Olivia stared out the window. She thought she got it now: It was a matter of helping the MacFarlanes keep their pride. When they returned later for a visit, Mrs. MacFarlane was able to welcome them as guests and serve tea with the cookies they'd brought earlier. Grandma's family had never let on that they knew they were eating their very own food.

"I see what you mean, Grandma Rosemary," Hayley said. "That way none of the family would be embarrassed."

"Yes, because every human being deserves dignity," she said with a nod of her head to emphasize her point.

"Mom, did they ever know it was you and Grandma who were

delivering the food?" Mr. Thomas asked from the driver's seat. "I always wondered that."

Grandma shook her head. "If they did, they never let on. We did it for quite a while and it was never mentioned, ever."

"That's nice, Grandma," Olivia said. "You were able to help out your neighbors."

"Well, God calls us all to help our neighbors," Grandma said. "And to do it without thinking about it. You know, so the left hand does not know what the right hand is doing. Otherwise, you could start to feel pretty important about yourself."

"That kind of sounds like the Little Way, Grandma," Olivia said. "Like St. Thérèse always said, doing little things with great love."

"That's right, Livvy. Saint Thérèse is a good person to teach us to renounce selfishness and do little things with great love. Little things that anyone, rich or poor, can do. We weren't rich by any means, but compared to some of our neighbors, we were."

"What does that mean, Grandma Rosemary?" Hayley wanted to know.

Grandma smiled at Hayley's use of the affectionate term, and she was pleased to continue talking about her favorite saint.

"It means being a servant to other people, denying yourself and your wants and needs, and following Jesus. Thérèse spent much of her life doing for others, and not complaining about it. She did it for God, to show Him how much she loved Him."

Olivia beamed, proud that Grandma knew so much about the saint she herself had introduced to Hayley two years ago.

"I'll tell you something else, though: A few years later, the MacFarlanes did something for us that we were always grateful for. When my oldest sister Connie got married, a terrible

thing happened! All spring and summer, my mother had carefully grown gorgeous flowers for the Mass and the reception at
our house. They were really something to see! So beautiful. The
night before, we had gone outside to check on the flowers in our
yard one last time. We wanted them to stay as fresh as possible,
so we agreed to cut them early the next morning before the Mass.
When we woke up and went outside to cut them, they were all
gone, every last one of them! The deer had come by in the early
morning and eaten them all: lilies, roses, and daisies; every last
one but a few stragglers."

Olivia's jaw dropped. Imagine that! "Oh no! No bouquet for
Great-Aunt Connie!"

"Not only that, but no flowers for the altar, for the Blessed
Virgin statue, for the party. It was terrible. It was the only time
I ever saw Mama cry," Grandma remembered. "In all of those
years, through all of the hardships and sicknesses our family en-
dured, that was the only time. She was heartbroken for Connie
that we had no flowers on her wedding day."

"What happened next?" asked Hayley with bated breath.

"We gathered up the best ones we could, which were trampled
on but still usable, and brought them to the church. We made
makeshift bouquets: one for Connie and one for Our Lady. They
were pretty but small. The Nuptial Mass was still beautiful, but
there was a bit of sadness in the air that all of my mother's hard
work that spring and summer had been destroyed."

Olivia thought that was terrible. *Why had the deer chosen that
time, that very day, to eat the flowers?* she wondered.

"After the wedding Mass, we all went to our house for the reception. Mama had made a big pot of spaghetti sauce, which was
on the stove, and we even had *spiedini*, rolled beef, simmering in

the sauce. It was a treat to have meat in those Depression days. We girls went straight to the kitchen to put the water on to boil for the pasta, when out of the blue we heard a lot of commotion coming from the back yard. We raced outside, worried that something had happened. When we got to the back yard, we couldn't believe what we saw. It was filled with flowers, the most gorgeous ones you've ever seen! They were on the tables, draped over the arbor my papa had built, all over the lawn, even!

"Geraniums, pansies, daisies, wildflowers of all different colors; it was stunning, girls! I wish I had a color photograph of it, but we have so few pictures from back then. Connie and my mother just stood there, without saying a word, and hugged each other. That moment is etched in my memory. I knew the significance of what had happened. It was absolutely beautiful."

"Grandma, do you think it was the MacFarlanes who did it?"

"Well, for years afterward, we wondered. They never mentioned it and we never asked them, but deep down we knew it had to have been them. No one remembers seeing them at the Mass, but we dismissed it because they weren't Catholic."

"I can't believe it! Where did they get all of the flowers from?" Olivia asked.

"Heaven knows," Grandma answered. "But I did notice their yard was quite barren that fall. They blamed it on the deer too, but I don't think so. Mama told me to never ask them."

"We give in secret," Hayley repeated. "Sounds like the MacFarlanes were doing the same thing. Maybe they didn't want you to feel like you had to repay them."

"Maybe," said Grandma. "I think they must have felt so happy to do something for us in return. But that's just how it was out in the country. We always helped each other and were there for people, in good times and in bad. In my opinion, it seems a little different in the city."

Olivia's dad asked, "When did you move with Uncle John and Aunt Stella to Detroit, Mom?"

"I was in my late twenties. That's when I got a job in the dress shop and met Grandpa. His last name was really Tommasino, but when he was a boy coming from Italy, the immigration people in New York changed it to Thomas."

"I never knew that, Grandma!" cried Olivia.

"Hmm. There are lots of things I could tell you about the old days," Grandma said. "Boy, what a change it was living in Detroit. We lived in a little flat on the east side, and it was so noisy, unlike our little town in Ohio!"

"Did you like it much?" asked Olivia. She loved hearing stories from Grandma's past; it was so fascinating—much more interesting than any history book!

"At first I hated it. But I got to know some of Uncle John and Aunt Stella's neighbors, and they were wonderful people. The whole neighborhood was Italian, so we had lots in common there. But it took some getting used to: no open spaces, no apple trees, no big gardens. I planted tomato plants in pots on our tiny porch; not enough for more than a couple pots of spaghetti sauce. For the first time in my life, I had to buy produce from the market. And let me tell you girls, it is not as good as home-grown. But you make do," she said.

"Reminds me of the saying, 'Bloom where God plants you,'" said Olivia's mom from the front seat. "I just love hearing your stories, Grandma," she said.

Olivia smiled. *Bloom where God plants you.* The saying reminded her of something St. Thérèse would have said. The Little

Flower was always trying to be content where she was, and made the best of any circumstance she was given.

"So I guess wherever I end up, in the city or in the country, I should just try my best to be happy, right, Grandma?" asked Olivia with a knowing smile.

"Bingo!" cried Grandma, who then put her wrinkled hands to her face in surprise. "Oh dear, that reminds me: I plum forgot to tell Madge Richardson that I'd be missing Bingo this month! Old Madge will *never* let me live this down!"

Everyone in the van laughed as the Thomas minivan passed over the curvy West Virginia terrain and through the sweeping hills of the Blue Ridge, heading east.

SEVEN

"Now I see that true charity consists in bearing with all the faults of our neighbors, in not being surprised at their weaknesses, in being edified at their least virtues."
—*St. Thérèse*

It was dinnertime when they pulled into the parking lot of a motel near the freeway.

"End of the line for today, y'all," Mr. Thomas said with a Texas flair, which never seemed to escape Hayley's attention.

"Y'all, I'm beat…and hungry," she said casually, trying out the term. Olivia rolled her eyes good-naturedly. Sometimes Hayley was a little eccentric.

Mrs. Thomas got out of the car and stretched. "What a long drive. It'll be good to take a breather and then start fresh tomorrow. I'll drive tomorrow, Steve," she said. "Let's go check in and get to our rooms."

Mr. Thomas had booked two adjoining rooms: one for himself, Mrs. Thomas, and Lucy, and the other for Hayley, Olivia, and Grandma to share. Everyone took in a few necessities that they'd need for the night.

Hayley flopped on one of the double beds in the room and

yawned. "It feels so good to stretch out," she moaned. "I never want to sit again!"

"Well, we're going to the restaurant next door for dinner," Olivia said as she flopped down beside her. "Unless you want to eat standing up?"

"Girls, Grandma? Ready to get some dinner?" Mr. Thomas asked.

"Come on girls, up and at 'em," Grandma said. "I'm starved!"

After a tasty meal of fried chicken, corn on the cob, and mashed potatoes ("Our specialty," the waitress had proudly said, so who could refuse?), everyone walked back to the motel. Hayley took out her cell phone and called her mother to let her know they had arrived for the night. Olivia thought Hayley was lucky to have her own cell phone. So many kids already had their own in the sixth grade and she knew some who were talking about getting one over the summer. In Hayley's case, her mother felt better knowing Hayley could be reached at any time. Her mother worked full time and sometimes childcare was an issue if Ryan couldn't watch her. But Hayley's mom had strict rules about using the phone; it was only for calling home and for emergencies. She wasn't allowed to text friends. When Olivia broached the topic of her own phone with her parents, they had said no before she even finished her sentence. Olivia took that to mean it was out of the question. She figured she would wait a year and try again. It couldn't hurt, right?

After Hayley was finished talking to her mom, she kicked off her shoes and yawned. "Think I'll take a shower," she said as she grabbed some pajamas and a robe and disappeared into the bathroom. Fifteen minutes later she emerged from the steamy room with a towel wrapped on her head like a turban.

Grandma excused herself to go the other part of the suite to chat with Olivia's parents and help Lucy get into her pajamas. "Should we see what's on TV?" Hayley glanced at the bedside clock. "It's nearly 8:00. *The New Clique* will be coming on."

Olivia, who was lying on the bed doing a crossword puzzle, frowned slightly. She wasn't allowed to watch *The New Clique,* a teenaged show about a high school's popular group. The characters kissed a lot, skipped school, and were disrespectful to adults. She had begged her parents to let her watch it a few months ago, since so many people at her school watched it and talked about it at school. Not knowing much about the show, her parents agreed to preview the show first, without her there. After a few minutes of watching immodestly dressed teens making fun of their teachers and using bad language on *The New Clique,* her mom and dad had turned off the TV, looked at each other, and said, "Not gonna happen."

Olivia had to admit that she wasn't surprised when they told her no and discussed with her their reasons why not. Deep down, she wasn't interested in watching teenagers kiss and be sassy, but watching *The New Clique* was the "in" thing to do. Every Friday morning, some of the kids would gather together and discuss the show from the night before: who went out with who, who was the cutest character, etc. She, Jenna, and Chad usually felt left out during that time. It was something she just had to deal with, she figured, since her parents had been absolutely firm on their decision.

"Um, how about the cooking channel? There's that show where they take you on tours of potato-chip factories and stuff like that. That's always fun to watch."

"Instead of *The New Clique?* No way," said Hayley, towel-drying her long hair. Then, in a lower voice, she said, "Olivia, if we close the door and keep the volume low, your parents won't even hear us watching it."

Olivia was tempted. She'd always been curious about the show. She'd heard so much about the characters that she wondered what they looked like. Surely it wouldn't hurt to watch the show just once. Just one episode, just so she could say she'd seen it. How much harm could that do, just once?

Hayley took Olivia's silence as the go-ahead she was seeking. She walked over to the adjoining door, closing it quietly. Olivia reached over to the nightstand where the TV listing card was and picked it up, checking the channels. She grabbed the remote, glancing around the room. Just then she caught sight of her pajamas sticking out of her suitcase on the floor, the pajamas with red roses all over them, reminding her of St. Thérèse. *Oh St. Thérèse*, she said inside her head, *you always know when I need your help. You always seem to know when it's time to step in to keep me from doing something stupid, something I'll regret.*

Olivia shook her head and clicked on the TV. She turned to the cooking channel, where an overzealous young man excitedly held up a chocolate candy bar. He had a thick southern accent.

"Hi, y'all! I'm Phil McGill! Ever wonder where Fudge Chewies are made? Come with me to a fudgy dreamland where your chocolate dreams will come true!"

"Uh-uh," said Hayley, shaking her head. "Turn on *The New Clique*, just for a minute. I want to show you Will, the cute guy I have a crush on."

"Sorry, Hayley," said Olivia as she got her rose pajamas out of her suitcase. "It's Fudge Chewies tonight. I've even got one in my purse we could split while we watch."

Hayley groaned as she combed out her wet hair in the mirror. She looked at Olivia for a long time, then sighed. "Fine. I don't want you to get in trouble on the first night of our trip."

"Or any night of our trip, right?" Olivia teased. She went into the bathroom to change into her rose pajamas.

That was a close one, St. Thérèse, she thought. She looked at herself in the mirror. She had almost made a huge mistake. Imagine how disappointed her parents would be in her if she had snuck around and watched a show they'd forbidden her to watch. She shuddered at the memory of the time she had gotten her ears pierced in defiance of their rules and she had gotten grounded for a whole month. She couldn't see any of her friends and felt generally horrible and guilty for four weeks. She didn't want to repeat that mistake again! She certainly was glad to have St. Thérèse keeping her on track to do the right thing. She felt lucky that God had sent the Little Flower to her as a special friend.

Glancing at herself in the mirror, she frowned at her reflection. A fresh pimple had seemed to pop up overnight. Lately she was getting more and more of these. It was getting embarrassing.

She looked around the bathroom, which was an utter mess of wet towels and washcloths on the floor. For Heaven's sake, how many towels did one girl need for a shower? She reached for a hand towel and washed her face. *Grandma and I won't have any towels for tomorrow morning*, she thought irritably. It was then that Olivia realized that this month-long vacation with Hayley would not be a walk in the park. They were going to have their ups and downs.

She said a quick prayer for patience and help in following the Little Way as she tried to straighten up the towels as best she could. Then she had to giggle. Olivia herself wasn't much better at home in her own bathroom. She thought of the globs of tooth-paste she absentmindedly let solidify on the bathroom counter, no matter how many times her mother told her to wipe it up as soon as it fell off her toothbrush. And the wet washcloths she left on the edge of the bathtub, which dribbled onto the floor and left puddles. Funny how she could sit there and judge Hayley for her mess when she herself wasn't much better most of the time.

Olivia left the bathroom and reached for her purse on the desk. She pulled out a Fudge Chewie bar, unwrapped it, and broke it in half.

"Here's to Keane Harbor," Olivia said with a smile as she gave Hayley her half of the candy bar.

"And here's to the 'fudgy dreamland' on Channel 37," said Hayley wryly as she bit into hers. She raised her eyebrows. "Mmm…not bad, actually. What's in here?"

They examined the candy bar. "Caramel, chocolate, and some chewy stuff." Olivia frowned. "Hayley, what's nougat, exactly?"

Haley pondered that for a moment. "You know, I don't exactly know."

Olivia laughed. "I don't think anyone really knows!"

They chewed in silence.

"Jenna introduced me to these," said Olivia as she bit into the candy bar again. "I'm addicted!"

Hayley considered this. "Not as much as I'm addicted to *The New Clique*." She got in bed beside Olivia and fluffed up her pillow so she could sit up.

"I think it started summer reruns anyway," Hayley said, biting into her candy bar again.

"Good," said Olivia, savoring her chocolate and putting on her southern accent extra thick. "Now y'all hush up so I can hear Phil McGill!"

EIGHT

*"I was six or seven years old when Papa took us to
Trouville. I'll never forget the impression that the sea
made on me. I couldn't keep myself from looking at it
without stopping. Its majesty, the roaring of its waves,
everything spoke to my soul about the Greatness and
the Power of God." —St. Thérèse*

veryone in the minivan was silent as they pulled up the
long driveway to Aunt Peggy and Uncle Jack's beach house. Little Lucy broke the silence with an excited yell.

"We here, Mama?"

Mr. Thomas sucked in his breath. "It's beautiful," was all he said.

"I had no idea," Mrs. Thomas slowly said, amazed.

Grandma Rosemary mumbled something in Italian that no one could identify.

Mrs. Thomas examined a piece of paper. "Steve, are you sure this is the right house?"

"Twenty-seven Ocean View Drive. This is the place," he confirmed as he read the numbers on the mailbox, but still unbelieving.

Ahead of them, the beach house stood majestically, towering over the lawn like a giant. The windows were numerous. Stately pillared columns stood at attention on the front porch, which housed gorgeous glass French doors with a beautiful scroll design. At the top of the house, a wooden cupola with a lighthouse-themed weathervane pointed due north. A white wooden fence divided the property and ran down to the beach.

"Look, it's even got an upstairs balcony!" cried Olivia.

Olivia rolled her window down, as if the house could talk and she wanted to hear. She was instantly struck by the sounds of the surf, and her excitement grew.

"If this is it, Dad, let's go in!"

Hayley was silent and looked a little unsure. She had never seen such a large home, except maybe in movies. But in person? And to actually stay in? This house was even bigger than Sabrina's.

Olivia turned her head to look around, instantly impressed by the grandeur around her. Most of the houses in this neighborhood were just as stately and large. Aunt Peggy and Uncle Jack sure had been very vague when describing their "summer home" at the beach.

The family got out of the van and began to walk toward the house, Mr. Thomas fumbling for the key that was in an envelope, and Mrs. Thomas balancing Lucy on her hip. Olivia stopped walking and noticed Hayley wasn't there.

"Hayley?"

Hayley remained seated in the van, staring at the house through the window. She looked a little disoriented. Olivia knew why: This was a far cry from Hayley's tiny, modest apartment back in Michigan.

"Aren't you coming? Let's go explore it," said Olivia, her eyes wild with excitement, trying to interest Hayley.

Hayley shrugged her shoulders. "It's gigantic." She tried to make light of it. "I'll probably get lost in there and you'll never find me."

Olivia patted her on the back. "It's okay. Come on. It'll be fun—a new adventure."

The inside of the house was decorated in a seaside theme, with gorgeous shells and beautiful ocean paintings. But the real thing stared out at them when Mrs. Thomas opened the drapes to reveal a wall of windows that presented the deep blue of the Atlantic Ocean. It was a breathtaking view.

"It's so beautiful!" Olivia cried as she ran toward the door-wall, which opened onto a three-tiered deck. She did a twirl right there in the living room. "I love it! And to think we get to stay here for four whole weeks!"

Grandma mumbled something in Italian again, which made her father laugh. When Olivia asked him what Grandma had said, her father wouldn't say, but just kept on laughing. Olivia figured it was grownup talk.

Hayley and Olivia ran upstairs to explore the second floor, taking steps two at a time on the large staircase until they reached a hallway containing six generous-sized bedrooms, three full baths, and a walk-in linen closet.

"Which room do you want?" Olivia asked. "I think I'll take the peach room if you don't care." She wandered into her chosen room, admiring the lovely shades of peach and the shell bedspread. She looked out the window at the ocean. "I don't think I'll ever get tired of looking at this view."

Hayley hesitated, then offered hopefully, "We could share the room if you want to. It has a big bed."

"Don't be silly, Hayley," said Olivia, motioning toward the room right down the hall that was done in all white, with a white eyelet comforter and matching shams. "With all of these rooms to pick from? Take that one. It has an ocean view, too!"

Then Olivia sighed contentedly. "I overheard Grandma in the kitchen. She said it's a gourmet kitchen, with real marble floors, stainless steel appliances, and a huge breakfast bar!"

Hayley smiled politely, not knowing what to say. Were those things supposed to be good?

Olivia exclaimed, "Wow, is this really how rich people live? I can't wait to cook something in that kitchen!" Then her face fell. "Oh, I forgot to bring my favorite recipe book, the one with the Mexican chicken recipe you like."

"That's okay, Olivia. Your mom or dad might remember the ingredients."

"Choosing a room, girls?" said Mrs. Thomas as she entered the hallway. She peeked in on Olivia's room, admiring it. "My, they are all lovely, aren't they? The master bedroom is on the first floor, but we'll let Grandma have it since it's hard for her to manage the stairs. Dad and I will take the one down the hall. Lucy can have the aqua one next to ours."

"Oh, let me see!" cried Olivia, skipping down the hall to inspect and leaving Hayley alone in the peach room. Then, wanting to see what Hayley's room looked like, she turned around.

Hayley slowly wandered down the hall to the white room and stood there, staring. She sat down on a white wicker chair with an eyelet cushion and studied the room: wicker desk with matching chair, wicker headboard and nightstand, and an antique whitewashed dresser with matching mirror completed the room.

"I've never seen so much wicker in my life," Hayley said with a nervous laugh.

"Really," Olivia agreed from the doorway, sensing that Hayley was feeling a little strange in these fancy surroundings. This room was way bigger than Hayley's tiny bedroom at home. Olivia wondered if Hayley would be a little uncomfortable, knowing she'd be sleeping in it alone every night.

"Want to share a room?" Olivia asked.

"'Course not," Hayley said quickly, not wanting to seem like a baby. Besides, with six rooms to choose from, sharing a room would be silly.

"So...you like it?" asked Olivia as she rolled Hayley's suitcase inside the room and lifted it on the bed for her.

"Sure. I mean, who wouldn't, right?" Hayley said with a laugh.

"This sure is heavy. Whatcha got in here, Hayley, a bunch of rocks?"

"Oh, just all of the stuff I thought I'd need. Maybe I did over-pack a little," Hayley said sheepishly as she unzipped it and revealed piles of clothing, toiletries, and a few books and magazines.

"Don't forget, there's a washer and dryer," said Olivia as she winked. "We aren't exactly going to rough it here at the beach."

Hayley peered out the window at the ocean. "Yeah, I can't think of anything this house *doesn't* have."

Mrs. Thomas peeked her head inside. "Oh, what a lovely room. Make yourself at home with us this month, Hayley. Help yourself to snacks and drinks in the kitchen—after we go grocery shopping, that is," she added with a chuckle. "Aunt Peggy made a list of some of the local stores, restaurants, and the nearest Catholic church for us and directions to each. That should be helpful. Well, I'll let you get settled in. I'm sure you and Livvy will want to explore the beach."

She left the room to help Grandma settle into her room downstairs.

"I'm going to get my suit on!" Olivia said happily as she left the room. "Put yours on too!"

Hayley opened the empty closet and found a bunch of hangers waiting for her. She carefully hung up each of her shirts, which were wrinkled from the trip, but she figured the wrinkles would fall out eventually. Besides, life was supposed to be casual at the beach.

Olivia appeared in the doorway a few minutes later, dressed in a one-piece floral bathing suit and flip-flops. She wriggled into a matching coverup as she talked.

"Almost done, Hayley?" she asked, her head inside the coverup as she struggled with the armholes. "There's still time to see the beach before it gets too late and it's time for dinner," she said.

"My dad said he'd go pick up a pizza in a little bit." She glanced around Hayley's room and found a bottle of sun lotion on her dresser. "Let's go!"

A few moments later, the pair was headed downstairs.

"Don't go too far, girls," said Mrs. Thomas. "Dad and I are going into town to pick up a few groceries and things. Grandma is here but she's resting for a bit from the long drive."

"Don't worry, Mrs. Thomas," said Hayley, who was beginning to cheer up at the thought of hanging out on the beach. "We'll stay right by the house."

Olivia went to Grandma's room and found the door ajar. Grandma was lying on the bed, her eyes closed. She opened them when she heard Olivia in the doorway. "Oh," she said sleepily. "I'm just resting a spell. You girls have fun at the beach."

"Want to come, Grandma?" Olivia ventured, hoping Grandma would. But she knew it was unrealistic for Grandma to get over her fear of the water the day they arrived.

"No, no," Grandma said hurriedly. "Too tired today. Another time."

Olivia was doubtful. "Okay," she said. "Well, maybe tomorrow you can—"

"Have a good time," Grandma said, ending the discussion.

It was Olivia's first time at the ocean. When she was living in Houston, Olivia had been to the Gulf of Mexico more times than she could count, but she was amazed at the strength and power of the waves of the Atlantic Ocean.

"The Gulf of Mexico is much calmer," she observed. "Look, Hayley! There's a ship way out there...see?"

"Wonder where it's going?" Hayley mused.

Olivia squinted out at the sea. "In that direction somewhere," she said vaguely, watching it slowly disappear. The two decided to look around for a good spot to lay their towels down on the sand so they could sit.

As they laid on their backs, their faces toward the westward sun high up in the sky, Hayley told Olivia, "You know what? This is the life!"

Olivia laughed and sat up so she could look out at the water again. She couldn't agree more. It sure was going to be fun to live in a rich house and spend their days on the ocean. The blue sea looked like it could go on forever, touching the horizon for miles. She loved listening to the surf as it came forth and splashed in rhythmic, foamy crashes. The two were silent for a bit as they enjoyed its beauty. Out in the distance, a red and white lighthouse stood as a beacon for boats.

Olivia wondered at the many different creatures God had made that lived beneath the waters. Olivia got to thinking about how God could create something so beautiful and huge at the same time. To Olivia, it was a mystery how God is so powerful, yet so gentle and loving, too.

"Hey."

A girl's voice interrupted the silence. Startled, Olivia looked behind her and stared up into the faces of two girls and a boy who looked to be about her age.

Hayley looked up, too, and was the first to respond.

"Hi," she said in a friendly manner. "Who are you guys?"

"We could ask *you* the same question," the boy said.

Hayley studied him closely. He was on the taller side with blond curly hair, sunglasses, and long swim trunks with orange and black Hawaiian flowers on it. He had on a faded Boston Red Sox T-shirt. Hayley blushed, looking instantly smitten.

"You're on our part of the beach," he said, as if to clarify. "Mine and my sister's."

Olivia was a little annoyed. "What do you mean?" she asked irritably. "This is our property." What she meant to say was that it was Aunt Peggy and Uncle Jack's property, but it didn't quite come out that way.

"Technically, it's nobody's property," the girl with the straight blonde hair interjected, and elbowed the boy. She wore a two-piece bathing suit that showed her navel, something Olivia's parents—and even Hayley's mom, who normally was a bit more liberal with rules—had disallowed.

Since they resembled each other, Olivia guessed that the two were siblings. "The beach belongs to everyone. It's just an unwritten rule here that owners usually stay right in line with their houses," the girl said nicely.

Olivia glanced back to Aunt Peggy's house, noticing that they had, in fact, strayed a bit to the right.

"Oh, sorry," she said. "We'll move over, then."

Gee, these kids sure are picky to make such a big deal out of a few yards, Olivia thought. She began to get up and shake off her towel. "Come on, Hayley."

Hayley began to get up too, when the other girl, who had long brown hair, said, "Wait, it's okay. We'll sit with you. My name's Abigail, but everyone calls me Abby." Abby smiled, showing a silver retainer covering the top row of her teeth. She wore a purple floral coverup over her bathing suit.

Olivia relaxed a bit and stood there, still holding her towel. "I'm Olivia, and this is my friend Hayley."

"I'm Brandon Dansbury," he said. "And this is my sister Brooke. We live right here," he said, gesturing to the huge house next to Aunt Peggy's. "Abby's our friend from home. We're from Massachusetts."

"Oh, we're from Michigan, but our friend Jenna is originally from Massachusetts," Olivia said brightly. She mentioned the name of the city Jenna had said she was from, and Brandon laughed. "We're definitely not from *there*," he said. "Are you the new owners of the Pemberley place? I thought I heard it was for sale."

Olivia took a closer look at the confident boy who stood before them, and she made up her mind that, although he was handsome, she didn't like him, not one bit. What a snob to make fun of Jenna's hometown. She didn't like the easy way he carried himself, standing there with his designer sunglasses, so confident, like he owned the beach.

She also had to smirk at Brandon's choice of words, calling her aunt and uncle's enormous house simply a 'place.'" *These kids must be super rich*, she thought with a pang of jealousy. *They probably don't have to worry about counting pennies and quarters like I do.*

She then thought back to a conversation she had heard last year when her mom received a letter from her aunt and uncle saying they were thinking of listing the house, which obviously they never ended up doing.

"As a matter of fact, um…we are the new owners." Olivia could not believe those words came out of her mouth. Did she really just say that? Hayley looked over at Olivia, eyes wide and questioning. Nearby, a couple of seagulls, squawking wildly, started to come toward them. Olivia waved her arm to shoo them away.

"Funny, I never saw a sign on the lawn," said Brandon suspiciously, then added, "But then again, we've only been here since mid-June." He seemed to get bored with the conversation then, and pulled out his cell phone to answer a sudden text message.

"How do you like the house so far?" Brooke wanted to know, directing the question at Hayley. "I've been inside a few times and it is really cool. Even nicer than ours," she said wistfully. "Yours has more bedrooms."

"It's not my house; we're just friends," said Hayley, uncomfortable with the way this conversation was going, and thinking *And it's not Olivia's house, either!* Olivia's lie had shocked her. It just wasn't like Olivia to tell an outright lie.

"It's, um, really great," Olivia piped up. "We're staying for all of July and just got here this afternoon." Olivia was feeling guilty but knew that it was too late now to take back her words.

"What grade are you guys in?" Brandon wanted to know, looking up from his cell phone.

"We're going into seventh," Olivia said. "How about you?"

"Seventh," said Brooke. "But Brandon's going into eighth. We go to The Crabtree School. It's a private boarding school outside of Boston. We live there during the school year and spend the summers here on the coast. Or sometimes we just go to Europe. We spent Christmas in Paris last year." She beamed.

"Oh sure, Paris," said Olivia, as if she knew all about Paris. She had a dreamy look on her face just thinking of it. She had always wanted to go to Paris. In reality, she had only been on an airplane a handful of times in her life, and had never left the United States.

Brandon, Brooke, and Abby took that to mean Olivia had been there. "When's the last time you were in France?" Brooke asked.

"Oh…it's been a while," Olivia answered, dodging the question.

"Oh, then you wouldn't know that Chez René closed. My mom cried for weeks," she said, shaking her head. "She said no one prepared *foie gras* like Chef René."

Olivia wasn't sure what that was, but it sounded French and, therefore, extremely fancy.

Hayley rolled her eyes. "Yeah, we were pretty upset when the Dairy-O closed," she said. "The owner couldn't make the rent and the soft-serve machines kept breaking down."

Olivia shot Hayley a dirty look. Why did she have to be so sarcastic? She was ruining any chances of making a good impression on these new kids.

Stop it, Olivia, she told herself fiercely. *What do you care, anyway?* She hugged her knees to her chest and stared down at her chipped toenails. They needed to be repainted. She glanced over at Abby's and Brooke's toenails, which were expertly painted, like a professional had done them.

"Oh…that's too bad. I liked it there," said Olivia, not knowing what Chez René was, but figuring it was some sort of fancy restaurant.

"Where do you guys go to school?" Brooke asked.

"St. Michael's," said Olivia, then adding rather proudly, "It's a private school too."

"Sounds religious."

"It's a Catholic school."

"Oh. We're not Catholic," Brandon said, turning up his nose. Abby frowned at Brandon.

Hayley, very irritated now, stood up and grabbed her towel. "Olivia, we should get going," she said abruptly. "Your dad will be back with dinner."

Olivia squished up her face and glowered, offended by Brandon's comment.

Brooke, sensing trouble, tried to smooth things over by changing the subject. "Wait, don't go. Hang out with us. It's so boring around here and we wouldn't mind making some new friends. Don't listen to Brandon; he's just crabby because our dad won't take him golfing tomorrow. So what do you like to do? Hey, do you guys watch *The New Clique*?" she asked excitedly.

Hayley stopped and dropped her towel back onto the sand. After all, they had been looking forward to spending the rest of the afternoon at the beach and it was still early. And they watched her favorite TV show; they couldn't be all that bad.

"Of course," Hayley said with a scoff. "I mean, who doesn't?" She glanced sideways at Olivia.

Olivia fumed inside and stared evenly at the pier in the distance, where people were fishing. This just wasn't going well.

Brooke, not knowing what to say, swept her foot from side to side in the sand and flicked an old cigarette away with her big toe.

"So, um, tell us about yourselves. Like, what do your dads do? Our dad is a cardiologist at Mass General."

Olivia faltered. She had always been proud of her dad and the fact that he worked hard for a living, always putting his family first. But she felt a little embarrassed to admit to these new kids her dad was laid off from his job at an automotive company.

"My dad's a doctor too," Olivia said firmly. The trio nodded their approval. *We seem to passing most of their tests*, Olivia thought. *But why do I care?*

Hayley narrowed her eyes at Olivia and said, "My dad died

when I was little. He wasn't a *doctor*," she said pointedly, for Olivia's benefit, "but he was a great mailman." Olivia could read Hayley's mind: *I'm* not embarrassed to tell the truth, unlike *you*!

Olivia herself had wondered what had gotten into her, and why she was so impressed with these new kids' lavish stories. After all, who were they?

"Well, welcome to the neighborhood," piped up Brooke, running a hand through her long blonde hair. "It's nice to meet you guys. We've been on the beach all day and we're just about to go in. Think you'll be around tomorrow?"

"Definitely," Olivia answered, without checking with Hayley.

They all waved their goodbyes and Brandon, Brooke, and Abby retreated down the sand in the direction of their house.

Hayley let Olivia have it. "I totally can't believe you."

"What?"

"Don't *what* me; you know what. Pretending to be a rich snob. Telling them you own that house! That your dad's a fancy doctor. What's gotten into you, Olivia?"

Disgusted, Hayley got up and grabbed her towel. "I'm thirsty. Let's go back to your house. It is *your* house, isn't it, Olivia?"

"Well, what was that crack about watching *The New Clique*? 'Who doesn't watch it?'" she mimicked sharply.

Hayley kept on walking, saying nothing.

Olivia sighed. "I honestly don't know why I did that, Hayley," she said as she gathered her things and watched their new acquaintances disappear down the beach. "I just really wanted to impress them, I guess."

"Why would you want to impress *them*? Who are *they*? Just some rich kids with no manners. Even the cute guy was rude."

"You think he's cute, Hayley?" Olivia teased.

Hayley turned bright red and chose to ignore her. "And a doctor? Why did you say that? Your dad is not a doctor!"

"Well, they were going on and on about their dads' jobs, and Paris, and a crabapple school—"

"Crabtree."

"Okay, Crabtree. Silly name anyway." The two trudged through the sand, carrying their flip-flops as they walked.

"I do *not* want to see them tomorrow, even the cute guy, Brandon," said Hayley. "Besides, he has nothing on Mike."

"Or the Tyler Twins," Olivia said, trying to be funny and get back into Hayley's good graces. "Hey, that's the second time you've mentioned that Brandon is cute. Relax; we won't see them tomorrow. I told them we would, but we can avoid them. If we see them out there, we just won't go, that's all," Olivia said.

"I don't want to sneak around and avoid them all summer," moaned Hayley. "If you had just told them the truth, they wouldn't want to hang around us in the first place; we wouldn't have met their high standards. We're too poor!" Hayley scoffed. "Imagine that!"

They reached the deck of the house and began to walk up the stairs.

Olivia stopped and looked at Hayley. "Okay, I'll tell them the truth. I'm sorry. It was totally stupid of me to pretend to be one of them."

Hayley stared at Olivia ever so slowly. Her frown turned into a smile and she started to laugh. "Good. But I just thought of something funny. Usually I'm the one messing up and being a bad influence. The tables are turned!"

Olivia exploded into laughter. "Too funny, Hayley! I hope you are still allowed to hang around with me!"

Hayley, her hand on the doorwall, turned to Olivia and said, "Hmmm. Maybe not, but I don't think I have much of a choice, Olivia my dear. I'm living with you for a whole month!"

The two shook off the sand from their feet as best they could and went inside, hoping Grandma wouldn't notice the sand they were trekking into the living room. For Olivia, getting scolded by Hayley was enough for one day.

ᑎINE

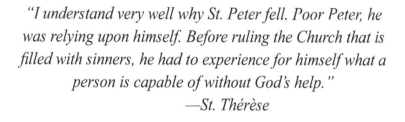

"I understand very well why St. Peter fell. Poor Peter, he was relying upon himself. Before ruling the Church that is filled with sinners, he had to experience for himself what a person is capable of without God's help."
—St. Thérèse

ayley walked into Olivia's room the next morning and found her dumping the contents of her purse onto her bed. Pens, a notepad, a wallet, lip balm, little notes, old gum wrappers, hair bands, and a green marker fell out, littering the bed.

"Sheesh, Olivia, what a pack rat you are." Hayley picked up a gum wrapper and held it up with mock interest. "Charming."

Olivia was not known for her neatness, and she knew it. Ah! There was her St. Thérèse chaplet, hidden in a zippered pocket in her purse. She had been looking for that.

"Good morning to you, too," Olivia said evenly. "Just cleaning out my purse."

"It's about time," Hayley said, eyebrows raised and reaching for the green marker. "And the purpose of this is…?"

Olivia snatched it back and opened up her wallet. She began counting out bills in an orderly fashion.

"Why did you bring all of that money?" asked Hayley incredulously. "Isn't that the money you are saving up for The Project? You're going to lose it."

"Well, I didn't want to leave it at home," Olivia said matter-of-factly as she counted.

Hayley smiled knowingly. "You just want to be able to count it every day. Trust me, it's not going to increase magically."

"One hundred forty-two dollars and 76 cents," Olivia said dejectedly. "It's just not going to be enough." She buried her head in her hands.

"Well, I'm sure you'll think of something," Hayley said as she patted her friend on the back to cheer her up.

Olivia hated that phrase. It always sounded so useless. "Gee, thanks."

"Well, I can't solve all of the world's problems. I'm too hungry. Come on downstairs. Your grandma's making eggs for breakfast. I told her we'd set the table."

Olivia stuffed the money back into her purse and hung it on the doorknob. She could hear her mom in the other room, getting Lucy ready for the day.

Breakfast was Grandma's special framed eggs—bread with a circle cut out of the middle and an egg fried in the middle. Ever since she could remember, Grandma had made framed eggs for her when she spent the night. Sometimes Grandma even made a spicy little tomato sauce to go with it as a garnish, but only when she used crusty Italian bread. Mr. Thomas couldn't find an Italian bakery nearby when he went shopping the night before, so Grandma just used sandwich bread.

"Grandma Rosemary, these are so good," Hayley said, impressed. "I've never had these before."

"My grandma makes them for me when I spend the night at her house," Olivia said proudly, and Grandma winked at her.

"Growing up, my mama made these for us boys and girls for breakfast, with day-old bread. The eggs were from our very own chickens, too," she reminisced. "And Grandpa asked for these all of the time. He liked extra pepper and a little garlic salt on his." Grandma's voice got very far away then. "So long ago," said softly to herself.

When Grandma got to thinking about the past, somctimes she would get very sad. Olivia knew she was remembering her youth, and all of the years she had spent with Grandpa before he had died of a heart attack. Grandma had her good days and bad since then, mostly good.

In an effort to distract her, Olivia asked, "Think you can teach me, Grandma?" Olivia had never done any stovetop cooking before.

"I think you're old enough to have a go at the stove, Livvy," Grandma said.

Olivia sat up a little straighter in her seat. She was secretly glad that her family was starting to notice that she wasn't a baby anymore, that she was getting older. She felt that sometimes they didn't notice, like when they balked at letting her ride her bike too far in the neighborhood, or not allowing her to wander the grocery aisles by herself to help out her mom at the store. She had to admit that there were times when she still wanted to be a little girl, though. Thunderstorms with lightning came to mind. She still liked to crawl into bed with Mom and Dad when the big booms came and woke her up from her sleep. That, and when she found spiders in the basement. Olivia and St. Thérèse had that fear in common, which made Olivia feel all the more close to her favorite saint.

But there were many times when Olivia wanted privacy and time to herself. And yes, sometimes her parents even embarrassed her on occasion, like when they used silly family nicknames like "Olive" and "Livvy" in public when other kids her age were near-by. When that happened, she felt like she wanted to run and hide.

The girls finished their framed eggs and brought their dishes to the sink.

"Just leave them there, girls. Your mom and dad haven't had breakfast, so no use cleaning up just yet." Grandma waved her hand. "You can go make your beds and get dressed."

Olivia groaned inwardly. There was never a vacation from making your bed, was there?

Beds made and swimsuits on, Hayley and Olivia peered tenta-tively out the doorwall, looking for any sign of Brandon, Brooke, and Abby. The beach was mostly deserted, except for a lady and her young child.

"The coast is clear," Olivia said, then laughed at her pun. "Oh, I crack myself up!"

Hayley rolled her eyes. "You're starting to sound like Chad," she said with a playful shove.

"What do you think Chad's doing now?" Olivia asked as she grabbed two bottles of water from the fridge.

"We should call him," Hayley said, taking one from her. "I want to tell him about the trip so far."

"And I want to tell him about this awesome house!" Olivia said excitedly, looking around the room. "He'd never believe how fancy it is."

"No, he wouldn't," Hayley said quietly. Chad lived in an old-er, small duplex with his grandparents. "But I don't think he'd be all that interested."

Olivia considered this. Maybe Chad would think they were rubbing it in. "Well, we can still call him. We'll tell him about the beach."

Olivia stopped by the bathroom to put her long, brown hair into a ponytail, and the two ventured out to the shore.

"Hello there girls," said the lady they'd seen from the door-wall, who wore a large sunhat. "It's a beautiful morning to relax on the beach," she said with a smile. Olivia noticed that the lady was due to have a baby soon, and she smiled back.

"Hello."

"Are you going to have a baby?" asked Hayley point-blank, and Olivia shot Hayley a look.

"Hayley!" she hissed.

The lady with the sun hat just laughed. "It's okay. Kind of hard not to notice, eh?" She rubbed her round belly. "Just four more months to go. I can hardly wait." She smiled at her young son, who was carefully digging into the sand with a yellow plastic shovel.

"I'm Hayley, and this is Olivia," Hayley offered, feeling guilty for being so forward. "We're staying at Olivia's aunt and uncle's house this month."

"Well, it's nice to meet you, Hayley and Olivia," said the lady. "I'm Mrs. Duggan, and this is my son Danny."

"Hi Danny," said Olivia to the little boy, who was filling a plastic bucket with sand. He looked up and smiled shyly.

"Where are you from, Mrs. Duggan?" asked Hayley.

"We're from London, Ontario," she said. "Up in Canada. We're renting this house until September. My husband thought it would be a nice place to relax before the baby comes. It's been wonderful so far, great weather." Then she asked the girls, "Where are you from?"

Olivia started to get a little nervous, talking and sharing personal information with a stranger. She had always been taught to keep her distance from strangers when her parents weren't around. Even if she was with Hayley, she still felt the need to keep her guard up. After all, they didn't know this lady; she was a stranger, even thought she seemed really nice and had a toddler with her.

"Michigan," Olivia said vaguely. She didn't want to appear rude, but her mom, dad, and teachers had always taught her that safety came first.

"Oh, what a coincidence! I grew up in Detroit," Mrs. Duggan said, but sensing Olivia's discomfort, she did not prod any further. "Well, have a nice time, girls. Don't burn up; the sun is going to be hot today."

Hayley and Olivia nodded and said goodbye, then moved a bit further down the sand until they found a spot they liked. They spent the next half hour talking and reading books they had brought. The sun kept getting higher in the sky, and it was starting to get hot.

"Let's cool off," Hayley suggested, and Olivia agreed. The cold ocean water would feel so good on her hot skin! For a long time they splashed and played and watched the tide wash over their feet into the wet sand at the water's edge. When they returned to their towels, they noticed Olivia's parents were there chatting with Mrs. Duggan. Lucy and Danny were sitting next to each other, putting sand into a sand pail together on a towel.

Olivia's mom waved. "Hi girls! Having fun?"

The girls went over to them, dripping wet but allowing the sun to dry them off.

"We just met Mrs. Duggan here, and Danny," her dad said. "She tells me y'all met."

"Yeah, Dad," Olivia said, squeezing water out of her hair. "Isn't Danny cute?" Danny looked up at the mention of his name.

"Turns out I know someone your dad went to high school with a long time ago," Mrs. Duggan said. "My brother, Bill."

"Small world," said Mr. Thomas, smiling. "I remember you as a little girl when you and Bill lived in Detroit," he said. "Your brother was a character, always getting into trouble with the teachers," he said. "Didn't he almost blow up the science lab our sophomore year?"

Mrs. Duggan laughed. "He's settled down some," she said. "He lives in California now with his wife and four daughters. But he does work for a chemical company, if you can believe that."

"Donna, would you like to have dinner at our house tonight?" Mrs. Thomas said suddenly. "It would be so great to talk and you two could catch up on old times. And your husband and Danny, of course. What do you say?"

Mrs. Duggan gleamed. "Oh, I wouldn't want to impose on your first day here…"

"Not at all," Mrs. Thomas said. "Grandma and the rest of us would love to have you! Please say yes."

"Well, I'm sure my husband Rich wouldn't mind," said Mrs. Duggan. "He's working here in Keane Harbor for the summer in his company's local sales office. He usually works until 5:30 or so, but anytime after that is fine."

"Then it's settled," Mr. Thomas said.

Olivia was happy to hear it; it would be fun to have company for dinner and entertain at her aunt and uncle's fancy house.

The group broke up and Hayley and Olivia went into the surf for one last dip in the waves, which were calm and inviting.

When they started back to their towels, Mrs. Duggan and

Danny had gone inside for lunch, and Olivia's parents were taking Lucy for a quick stroll along the shoreline. But there were others waiting for them, their towels laid out and a big sun umbrella perched into the sand. It was Brandon, Brooke, and Abby, each lying out on their towels. The first thing Olivia noticed was Brooke's bright-pink two-piece bathing suit. Olivia looked down at her own one-piece suit and frowned, feeling frumpy.

"Hey! Olivia and Hayley, over here!" Abby was waving them over. "We're invading your spot; hope you don't mind!"

Brandon smiled at the girls and gave Hayley a little wave, which did not go unnoticed by Hayley, who, in spite of herself, blushed a little, but continued to frown at the thought of running into them.

"How's the water? Yesterday it was freezing cold," he said to Hayley.

Olivia looked down at her feet before answering, "It's better today; I think it's warming up." *Ugh. How stupid was that to say? What am I, a weather forecaster, for crying out loud? Besides, the question was directed at Hayley, not me.* She guessed she was feeling a bit nervous because she knew it was time to own up for yesterday's batch of lies. *Ugh.* She didn't think she could do this. Why was it so hard to admit it when you made mistakes, especially big ones?

Then she realized that she wasn't alone. She didn't have to rely on herself: She had help. She had St. Thérèse, and most importantly, she had God.

Lord, please help me get the words out, she prayed. *I am so embarrassed. What will these new kids think of me? They'll think I'm a liar, a fake.*

"We were just about to go in for lunch," Hayley said, her voice clipped. "Ready, Olivia?"

Olivia glanced sideways at Hayley. "Not yet," she said, and took a deep breath. "I want to dry off a little." Her heart started to beat faster, in anticipation of owning up.

"I brought drinks," said Abby, gesturing to a cooler. She opened the lid to reveal lemonade in tall glass bottles on ice. "Want one?"

"Sure," Olivia said, and helped herself. She was relieved for the brief distraction. "Thanks."

She lay back on her towel, unscrewed her lemonade, and took a long sip. Olivia read the label on the bottle: It was sparkling lemonade from Italy. It fizzed and tickled her throat. She didn't like this fancy lemonade; it didn't taste like anything she was used to. She took another sip to be polite.

Hayley, resigned to the fact that they were going to stay put for a while, sat down as well.

"Listen, guys," Brandon began in his thick Massachusetts accent, "Sorry I was kind of a jerk yesterday. I gave you both a hard time when we first met. Start over again?" He held out his hand to Hayley first, waiting to shake.

Olivia softened. Maybe these kids weren't so bad after all. Brandon's apology seemed heartfelt, and he did have a nice smile, which wasn't really relevant, but...

"That's okay," Olivia said, taking another sip of lemonade to stall time. Then she said, "I...uh...sort of have an apology to make, too. You see, yesterday I told you a couple of things that aren't true."

Abby's eyes widened. "Like what?"

Olivia glanced nervously at Hayley, who nodded, urging her on.

"Well, my dad's not exactly a doctor," she said.

"What 'exactly' does that mean?" asked Brandon, a little irritated.

"It means he's not really—"

"Hey! Look at that lighthouse way out there!" Abby cried suddenly, interrupting the conversation and pointing toward a tower off in the distance. "Did you guys notice that before?"

Brooke looked over at Abby, very annoyed at this. "Abby, we've been here over a month and it's been here. It's a stupid lighthouse; big deal!"

"It IS a big deal," said Abby excitedly. "How could I not notice that before?" She squinted her eyes, looking at the faraway lighthouse. She turned to Hayley and Olivia. "I'm a big fan of lighthouses. I know, it's weird."

Brooke nodded in agreement. "How many girls our age are into lighthouses?" she scoffed.

"I am, and my dad is too," said Abby, hurt. "You know that," she added softly.

Suddenly, Brooke looked down and bit her lip. "Yeah, I know that. Sorry, Abs."

Hayley and Olivia looked at each other, confused. Olivia wanted to know more, but kept silent.

The group fell into an awkward silence and it seemed like everyone forgot what they had been talking about earlier—except Brandon.

"Hmmm…okay, then I guess we're even," said Brandon, lips pursed together. "But if we're going to be friends, then no more lies."

"And no more attitude," Hayley put in, sticking up for her friend. "You know, to be 'even.'" She raised her eyebrows in expectation.

"Deal," he said with a faint smile.

"Good," Hayley said.

Then Brandon asked her, "Do you like riding the waves? I've got some extra boogie boards."

Hayley's face lit up. She'd been talking to Olivia that very morning about how she wanted to try boogie boarding on their trip. Olivia could see Hayley's excitement growing as Brandon and Hayley talked about taking his boogie boards out into the surf.

Olivia felt bad that they did not have any boogie boards to use. From what she could see, lots of the kids on the beach had their own to use. She highly doubted that Aunt Peggy and Uncle Jack had some back at the house. She stifled a little laugh to herself, thinking about them riding the waves.

"Girls, come on in for lunch! I made sandwiches!" called Mrs. Thomas from the balcony. Olivia was mortified to see her mother waving to them, all worked up about sandwiches, in front of the new kids.

"Okay!" Olivia answered back, and she had to admit that her stomach was rumbling from hunger. She turned to the kids. "Um, maybe we'll see y'all out here later?"

"Yeah, maybe," said Brooke with a grin, trying not to laugh. "Better go have those sandwiches. See ya later."

As Olivia and Haylcy started to walk away, Brandon called out, "Hey, in a couple of days there's going to be a party with some fireworks on the beach. It's a tradition in Keane Harbor on the Fourth. You guys are welcome to come with us."

Olivia and Hayley were silent, considering this, when Hayley shocked Olivia and said, "We might, thanks." The two girls waved and turned around, trudging through the sand back to the house.

Without warning, Hayley turned on Olivia with a scowl. "You're such a liar. How can you lie to them like that?"

Olivia turned bright red, humiliated at her admonishment. "Hayley, I tried to tell them the truth, honest. Just...let me try again tomorrow."

"Yeah, right."

"Really, give me another chance. I wanted to, but then Abby and Brooke started to get into something about that lighthouse. Weird. What was that all about? Hey, why are you so mad?"

"Because, Olivia, you had the chance and you blew it. You act like you are ashamed in front of that group. Well, I don't care what they think. I am who I am." Hayley shook sand off of her legs as they climbed the steps to the patio. "Well, you'll have another chance tomorrow when we see them. And you'd better come clean."

Olivia glanced back at the group, still sitting on the beach. Brandon was still watching them as they walked away.

"That Brandon. I can't stand him. I thought you felt the same way. Now you want to see fireworks with them?"

Hayley stopped then and stared at Olivia, squinting in the midday sun. "Come on, Olivia, doesn't everyone deserve a second chance? You should know that better than anybody." She left Olivia standing in the sand, confused and staring after her. Hayley turned around and waved faintly at Brandon, then kept walking toward the house.

TEN

*"Let us not grow tired of prayer: confidence
works miracles."—St. Thérèse*

Olivia wiped her hands on the kitchen towel. Making lasagna sure was messy, but very fun. Her dad stood over her, watching her every move.

"You're doing great, Livvy. Save some of the cheese for the other layers, though."

Olivia noticed that her cheese supply was dwindling; she was going to run out if she kept up this pace.

Finally the pan was ready to be slid into the hot oven, and Olivia's part was done. She couldn't wait for Mr. and Mrs. Duggan and Danny to come for dinner. They were due in a half hour and she was excited about helping her mom set the table. It was fun to go through Aunt Peggy's fine things in the dining room: a whitewashed china cabinet full of crystal stemware, china plates, and sterling silverware.

"Just be extra careful with it, honey," her mom cautioned her, and Olivia took care to use both hands when holding each item and placing it on the dining-room table. She understood the hidden meaning in her mother's plea: These things would be very expensive to replace, and the Thomases did not have extra money right now to replace anything that got broken.

Staying in Aunt Peggy and Uncle Jack's lavish house made her forget sometimes that her own family was pinching pennies for now. With her dad laid off from his company for a bit, times were a little tight. Olivia knew that the pizza they had ordered last night was to be their last take-out meal for a while. They planned on eating in as much as possible to save money, and would go out only once in a while to a restaurant as a treat. That worked out for the best anyway, she had told her dad, since Lucy was a bit of a handful at restaurants. Her dad had merely smiled; he had appreciated her positive attitude about the situation, even if he didn't believe her.

She could hear the water running upstairs, and knew that Hayley was taking a shower, getting the sand and sunscreen off from the day. It had been a fun day at the beach. Tonight the girls were planning on staying up late and watching movies on Aunt Peggy's big-screen TV. But since they spent nearly every waking moment together, it was nice to have a little time apart, too.

"Are you sure we are allowed to use Aunt Peggy's fancy stuff?" Olivia wanted to know.

Mrs. Thomas paused, wine glass in mid-air. "Well, she did say everything in the house was ours to enjoy," she said. "I'm sure the everyday dishes would be fine to use, but…" her voice trailed off.

"You want to make a good impression, don't you, Mom?"

Her mom cocked her head and smiled a little. "I guess so, Olivia," she admitted. "Although I'm not sure why."

"I think I know why," Olivia said as she placed a linen shell-themed napkin across a plate, like her mother had done. "I feel the same way sometimes."

"You do?"

"Yeah. Especially when I meet new kids, like the kids Hayley and I met on the beach yesterday. They're rich kids."

"Does that matter to you? That they're rich?" her mother asked, eyes raised.

Olivia paused before saying, "No."

"Well, don't get overly impressed by that, Livvy," her mom said. "God doesn't care about superficial things like that and I hope you don't, either."

"Oh I know," Olivia said, too quickly. "I just mean that I felt like I wanted to look good in front of them."

"Well, there's nothing wrong with wanting to make a good impression, but for the right reasons. The fact that we are putting out Aunt Peggy's pretty dishes is just something we do because company is coming, and you always want things to be a little extra special for company. We aren't trying to be showy."

Her mom paused, thinking, and then continued. "I want to do something really nice for Aunt Peggy and Uncle Jack when we get home, to thank them for letting us stay here. Can you think of anything?"

Olivia shook her head, placing another napkin down. "I don't know, Mom, but it's a good idea. I'm sure we'll think of something."

Grandma entered the room and began to help, putting dishes at each place setting.

Olivia's mom remarked, "What puzzles me is why we don't use our good china at home. It only comes out for Easter, Thanksgiving, and Christmas." Olivia thought of her parents' beautiful wedding china, sitting at home in the glass china cabinet, tucked away for the next holiday dinner.

Grandma chuckled and said, "Not Aunt Anna! She made up her mind when she was in her sixties to use her good china every day. Even if it was just a bologna sandwich with some chips, out came the good china. I always admired that about her. She told me once that every day is special and a gift from God, so every day deserved the good stuff."

"She was a smart lady, Grandma," Mrs. Thomas said as she closed the china cabinet door. "She had a very wise way of looking at things."

"Aunt Anna was very spiritual, even through her chronic illness," said Grandma, remembering. "She had a great devotion to Our Lady. The first thing she did every morning was pray the rosary. And the last thing she did before she went to bed at night was pray the rosary. I sure do miss her."

The smell of lasagna gently started to waft through the house, filling it with the warm scents of oregano, basil, and cheese. Olivia's mouth began to water.

Soon after, the doorbell rang, and the beach house was filled with the sounds of laughter and the kind of pleasant commotion you can only get when guests come for dinner. Danny cried for a bit because he was crabby and dinner was later than usual, so Olivia took him for a snack and to play in the other room so Mr. and Mrs. Duggan could enjoy their visit.

The lasagna was delicious. "Olivia, I am impressed that you can cook this well at such a young age," Mrs. Duggan commented. "It was so tasty that I've had enough for more than two," she said, patting her protruding stomach. "I'd better stop."

"Dad helped me," said Olivia, setting her napkin down. "He's a great cook."

"Well, I owe it all to Grandma," her dad said, smiling at Grandma.

Grandma laughed. "Oh, I've had lots of practice over the years. We didn't have fast-food or take-out places all those years ago. If you didn't have dinner made, it was sandwich night. There were no rotisserie chickens to take home from the grocery store, or frozen dinners." She looked at Mrs. Thomas, eyes raised.

Olivia's mom just smiled. Grandma was always reminding everyone how much harder she had it raising kids than more recent generations did. Olivia supposed she would be telling her the same thing when she got married and had her own kids, though. It was the cycle of life.

"I always thought you should've had your own restaurant, Mom," said Olivia's dad to Grandma. "Or a catering business. You could've called it *Mama's Home Cooking.*"

"Who had the time? Raising you active kids was a full-time job!" Grandma pointed a wrinkled finger good-naturedly at Mr. Thomas as she said this. "But it would have been some nice extra income during the lean years, that's for sure."

Mr. Duggan laughed. "Well, then, Olivia, maybe it's up to you to start a new family tradition and go into the restaurant business!"

Olivia froze. What a fabulous idea! She could earn the extra money she needed by doing something she loved: cooking! Her mind raced as the people at the table continued their after-dinner conversation. What could she make? Baked goods? Her chocolate-chip banana bread was out of this world, or so Chad had said one day at lunch. And Jenna absolutely loved her frosted pumpkin cookies. The possibilities were endless. The lasagna was obviously a big hit, and Hayley loved her creamy lemon bars. She had said they were "dreamy and creamy." What a great name for her new business: *Olivia's Dreamy Treats.* She remembered that

St. Thérèse, being French, loved chocolate éclairs, but was not allowed to have them in the cloistered convent. Maybe she could learn to make those, too, in honor of her.

But who would buy food made by a kid? Therein lay the problem. Weren't there rules about that sort of thing? Child labor laws? She remembered learning in history class about the industrial revolution in 19th-century America, when kids her age were forced to work in factories until new laws came about to protect them from that sort of thing.

Too bad. A dream deferred, all because of the federal government and its child labor laws.

"Something the matter, Livvy?" her mom asked as she got up to clear away the dirty plates. Hayley also got up and began to gather the napkins for the dirty laundry.

"Nothing, it's just that Mr. Duggan had a great idea. I'd love to earn some extra money and cooking is my favorite thing to do. It's too bad I'm too young."

Mr. Thomas patted her on the back. "Don't worry, honey. All in good time. Don't rush growing up."

Mrs. Duggan looked at Olivia. "Hmm. Olivia, you're in middle school, aren't you?"

"Yes ma'am."

Mrs. Duggan smiled at the polite southern expression that northerners unfortunately aren't used to hearing from children.

"Well, I wonder. I've been getting so exhausted lately. Carrying a baby can really make you tired, especially in the late afternoons when Danny wakes up from his nap and is raring to go. Would you like to help me out with him a few days a week? I'd pay you, of course." She looked at Mr. and Mrs. Thomas. "If it's all right with you."

Olivia lit up. "Mom and Dad? Can I? Please?"

Her parents exchanged surprised glances. "I don't see why not, if you really want to, Olivia."

"Have you been a mother's helper before, Olivia?"

"No, but I have plenty of experience with Lucy," Olivia offered.

"Well, Danny really seems to have taken to you," Mrs. Duggan said, glancing at Danny, who by now was asleep on a cushy blanket on the floor. "And of course I would never leave the house."

"Then it's settled," Mr. Duggan said, and turned to his wife. "I'm glad you will be able to have some time to rest in the afternoons while I'm at work, honey."

Olivia grinned from ear to ear. This was exactly the opportunity she had been looking for!

Everyone left the dining room to relax with dessert in the living room. Grandma and Olivia swept up crumbs from the tablecloth.

"See? I told you our friend St. Thérèse would come through for you with an answer to your little money problem," Grandma said with a wink. "I've been asking her to help you out ever since you told me. St. Thérèse comes through for anyone who asks, especially those who love her and love God." Grandma kissed Olivia on the top of her head. "You're going to make a great mother's helper, Livvy."

Grandma went into the kitchen, leaving Olivia alone with her thoughts in the dining room. As she scraped up the last of the crumbs with her hand, she felt a deep sense of guilt. St. Thérèse had been helping her, praying for an answer to her problem, and what had she been doing in the meantime? Lying to the kids next door and pretending to be someone she was not. After all, she hadn't really disclosed the whole truth to them.

Oh well, she told herself. *It's not like I'm going to keep up the lie forever. I'll tell them the next time I see them. Really, I will.*

She picked up a pretty crystal wine glass and brought it into the kitchen, admiring it. Aunt Peggy had such lovely things. She vowed that when she grew up, she would have the best of everything, just like her aunt.

ELEVEN

"I know from experience that the only happiness
on earth consists in being hidden and in absolute
ignorance of created things." —St. Thérèse

The next day was Sunday. Everyone busied themselves getting ready for Mass. Olivia rummaged through the closet, looking for a dress or a skirt to wear, and finally settled on a pink skirt with a matching sweater. She and Hayley bumped into each other in the hallway.

"Oops!" Olivia said, laughing and rubbing her shoulder where the two had collided. She glanced at Hayley's outfit but did not say anything.

"What?" Hayley asked, a little perturbed as she looked down at her T-shirt, which read, "Don't hate me 'cause I'm cuter than you." "Something wrong?"

"Well, it's just…" Olivia did not want to start something, but Hayley's tight and obnoxious T-shirt was not going to pass muster with Grandma, she just knew it. "We dress appropriately for God's House," Grandma always said.

"I think you might want to change. You know…Grandma," Olivia said sheepishly.

"Oh come on," Hayley laughed. "I look fine."

"I know, but…" Olivia said slowly.

Hayley waved her off. "I look fine," she said as she passed Olivia and headed for the stairs.

Olivia shrugged her shoulders and went to the bathroom mirror to finish getting ready. She knew what would transpire downstairs when Grandma got a look at Hayley's shirt and shorts outfit.

A few moments later, Hayley, red-faced, walked back upstairs, went to her room, and closed the door. She emerged wearing a skirt and modest top instead.

"Don't…say…it," Hayley warned Olivia with a half smile.

"Grandma got ya, didn't she?" Olivia said, stifling a giggle.

"Yeah, something like that," Hayley murmured, still embarrassed from getting an earful from Grandma. "Geesh, your grandma is no one to mess with."

"Tell me about it!" Olivia laughed finally.

With the help of Aunt Peggy's written directions, the family found the local Catholic church in Keane Harbor, Our Lady Star of the Sea. It was a very old church, with lots of stained glass and statues, "Just the way I like a Catholic church to be," declared Grandma with a whisper upon entering. "Now make a wish, all of you." Grandma was full of superstitions, mostly harmless.

"Why is that, Grandma Rosemary?" Hayley wanted to know as she took in the vastness of the church and its beautiful surroundings.

"My grandma says that every time you enter a new church for the first time, you should make a wish," Olivia whispered. "It's kind of a family tradition with us."

Hayley closed her eyes and thought for a moment. Olivia did the same thing.

"Don't tell me," said Olivia hastily. "It won't come true."

The family walked to the aisle, genuflected, and entered their pew reverently. Lucy settled in with some baby books about saints and was quiet for a little while, until she started to fuss during Mass. Olivia offered to take her in the back, since there was no cry room. She tried to occupy Lucy for a bit as quietly as she could, hoping against hope that Lucy wouldn't let out a huge squeal or yell.

"Hi there, Olivia," came a whisper from near a candle rack. To her surprise, it was Abby. She was dressed in a white and yellow floral dress with a matching yellow sweater and white sandals. The material was really well made and beautiful. Olivia suddenly felt very embarrassed in her simple skirt that she had gotten from the discount store. She had been excited to see it in the clearance rack and had loved its bold floral pattern, but next to Abby's simple, classic dress, she felt a bit frumpy. Her own sandals looked a bit scuffed up, since they were last year's, when her mother had bought them a little big. Mrs. Thomas was happy Olivia could squeeze another season out of them this summer. Abby's long brown hair looked pretty and straight, while Olivia's hair had been hurriedly shoved into a ponytail in the car on the way to church.

And Abby had sandals with a little heel on them, like a teenager would wear. Olivia's own shoes were flat-soled.

Baby shoes, Olivia thought with horror. *Oh, who cares about those dumb things anyway...right?* she asked herself.

"Hi Abby," Olivia said, hiding one of her feet behind the other so only one dingy sandal would show. "What are you doing here?" Then she realized what a stupid question that was.

Abby didn't seem to mind. "We usually go to the ten o'clock," she said. "I was just in the bathroom. You look like you have to go, too," she said, bemused at Olivia's awkward stance.

Olivia blushed and straightened her pose. "Who are you here with?" she asked, curious, as she picked up Lucy to bounce her on her hip.

"I've been getting a ride with the Duggans every week since I've been here. They are renting on the other side of your place," she said, and pointed to the far left of the church. Mr. and Mrs. Duggan sat there in the pew with Danny, listening to the priest's homily.

"Oh, that's nice. I didn't see them." Lucy started to squirm and begged to be let down. "This is my little sister, Lucy."

All of a sudden, for no reason at all, Olivia was reminded of her freckles. Her ugly, blotchy freckles. She looked at Abby's face and couldn't count even one.

"Hi Lucy. You're cute. Well, I should get back. They might start to worry where I went," Abby said.

"It was nice seeing you, Abby."

"You too, Olivia. I hope you come back here again. It's a nice church, and in a few weeks they are going to have an ice cream social after all of the Masses. You should come."

"I'll tell my parents," Olivia said, happy to have met Abby in the vestibule there at church. She felt like they had something in common, both of them being Catholic.

"Bye, Olivia."

Olivia pulled Lucy gently away from the rack of pamphlets and pried a booklet out of her hand, placing it back on the rack where it belonged. In response, Lucy let out a huge wail, to Olivia's horror.

"Miiiiiiiiine!!!!"

Olivia turned red from embarrassment. Everyone in the congregation turned to look around, and a few older people murmured under their breath, obviously agitated at the noise.

"Nooooooo!" Lucy cried.

The priest paused and smiled. He didn't seem to mind the interruption.

A few of the older people had disgusted looks on their faces, obviously thinking *their* children were perfect angels in Mass decades ago.

"James 2:13—I'm paraphrasing here, but to show mercy is better than to judge," the priest said with a grin. "I'm sure many of you have been in that little girl's situation back there at one time, trying to corral a young child."

A few uncomfortable laughs surfaced, and the priest smiled. "Now, where was I? Oh yes…" He then went on with the rest of his homily.

Olivia turned scarlet. She was appreciative of the kind priest's reaction. He was reminding the adults not to judge, to think back over the years to when they had little ones to control during Mass. Especially at Lucy's young age, it could be trying sometimes. But she was also mortified at being called a "little girl," especially in front of Hayley and Abby. And Mr. and Mrs. Duggan, who had hired her to be a mother's helper! Would they reconsider their choice, especially after seeing her not being able to handle Lucy today? She felt like a little kid.

She grabbed Lucy a little too harshly, wishing her sister were not so young and were old enough to sit still during Mass.

Embarrassed, she slunk back to their pew. "Don't worry, Livvy," her dad said. "I'll get her next time. Thanks for taking her, but your sister is a feisty one to handle sometimes, especially for a kid."

Ugh. There was that word again: *kid*. When was everyone going to learn that she was not a kid anymore? That she was growing up? Maybe she was just a little kid after all. A little kid who didn't even wear the right shoes. She sunk down in her seat, unable to listen to the rest of the homily, completely dejected. She stared at her scuffed-up sandals for the rest of Mass, very self-conscious of them now that Abby had seen them. Maybe her mom would buy her some new sandals if she asked. Ones with a little heel. That would make her feel better, she decided.

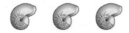

Later on that day, Olivia approached her mom, who was reading a magazine on the gorgeous back deck. She lay on a teak lounge chair with a big, soft cushion, her legs crossed at the ankles, soaking up the late-afternoon sunshine.

"Hi, honey," she said to Olivia, and motioned for her to sit down. "These chairs are so luxurious." She drew out the last word for emphasis. "I've seen these in fancy catalogs and always wanted to try them out."

Olivia nodded, noticing that they looked very classy when compared with their own aluminum lounge chairs at home. These were made out of real wood.

"Mom? I was wondering...do you think we could go shopping and I could get some new sandals?"

Her mom put her book down. "What's wrong with the white ones? Don't they fit anymore?"

"Well..." Olivia knew she had to be honest. "They fit just fine."

Her mom breathed a little sigh of relief. "Oh, good. Aren't they comfortable?"

Again, Olivia could not lie. "Actually, they're very comfortable, it's just…" *It's just that I want shoes like Abby's.*

Her mom looked at her expectantly. "You wanted another color?"

"No, it's just that they look kind of scuffed-up," she said finally.

Her mom cocked her head to the side and smiled. "Oh, they're not that bad, Livvy. And summer's half over, you know. Just try to get some more use out of them and next summer you can get a new pair. You'll have grown out of them by then."

Olivia's face fell. Her mom was totally missing the point. "Um…ones with a little heel? Maybe some will be on sale."

Her mom smiled, understanding now. "You've never worn heels before, honey."

"I know," Olivia said. "I just want a little, tiny heel. It looks dressy." Olivia looked down at her feet and said nothing. Money was tight and here she was, asking for something she didn't even need. But she wanted them so badly!

"If your shoes didn't fit, or hurt you, we could, but if you say they fit well and still look halfway nice…"

Olivia got up. "It's okay; I understand."

"Dad heard from his boss last night, and he said he just didn't know when Dad can come back to work," her mom said suddenly.

Olivia froze. "I thought he was supposed to go back next month."

"That's what we all thought, even his boss, but now it looks like it could be longer. I'm sorry, Livvy. We just can't afford any extras right now, what with Dad's job being up in the air."

Up in the air? Could Dad possibly lose his job for good? Olivia was not about to ask her mother. She wasn't sure she wanted to know the answer.

The two were silent for a little while, the afternoon sun on their faces, taking in the ocean.

"The economy is kind of bad right now, honey," said her mom quietly as she stared out at the sea. "It means that many people are out of work or will lose their jobs soon. I'm sorry, Livvy."

"It's okay, Mom," said Olivia. She thought of Tina, a girl from school who had to leave St. Michael's.

She remembered the last day of school, her heart heavy. They had celebrated Mass as a school and afterward, all of the kids were in a jovial mood as they waved goodbye to friends and teachers in the parking lot. The students all carried backpacks stuffed with old folders and school papers from the year, clearing out their classrooms for the summer.

"Oh, Mom, I forgot something!" Olivia had cried to her mom as she buckled Lucy into her car seat. "I just have to run back inside to bring this library book in," she said, eyeing the book on the car seat. She didn't want to forget it all summer. Her mom handed her the book to take inside. "Okay, just meet us back here at the car when you're done."

Olivia dashed back into the school, which was emptying out quickly. Everyone, it seemed, was eager to start their summer vacations. She heard loud "goodbyes" and "have a nice summer" exclamations from teachers, parents, and students alike. She smiled as she walked down the hallway to the library with her book. She was excited too. Just think: sleeping in every morning, warm summer days with friends, and pushing her uniform skirts to the back of her closet for a few months. But she knew she would miss her teachers, friends, and Sister Anne Marie.

After placing her book in the return basket in the library, she decided to stop by Sister Anne Marie's office to say goodbye and to wish her a happy summer. By this time the hallways were starting to get deserted. The classrooms looked barren since the teachers had already cleared off the bulletin boards and there were no art projects on the walls of the hallway.

She stopped when she got to Sister Anne Marie's office. On the wall next to her door was a framed print of St. Michael the Archangel, patron of their school, stabbing the demon with his mighty sword. Olivia had walked by that picture many times in her two years at the school. She liked the expression on St. Michael's face, like he wasn't going to let evil triumph over good. Sister Anne Marie liked to lead the school in a prayer to St. Michael from time to time.

The door to the principal's office was ajar. Normally it was wide open. She wondered if she should go in or knock. As she was deciding what to do, she heard voices coming from inside.

"Mr. Griffin, I hope you know we wish you all the best and will keep you in our prayers," came the voice of Sister Anne Marie.

"Th…thank you so much, Sister," said a man's voice, trembling. "I'm sorry to choke up now. My wife and I will really miss St. Michael's."

"Well, you know we will always have a place for Tina here, I can promise you that," she said.

"I wish the financial aid you offered would have been enough," he said, sniffing. "You were so generous to offer, but with my wife and I both being unemployed right now…" his voice trailed off.

"Keep praying, Mr. Griffin. God has a plan for you and your family, and you may not know what it is at the moment, but just know that He is working on it right now. Have faith in our heavenly Father."

Tina's dad sniffed again, and Olivia knew he had been crying. "We tried so hard, we really did. I don't know how we will break this to Tina. She will be very sad; she loves this school."

Olivia froze in the hallway. She felt guilty overhearing this private conversation with Tina's dad and felt terrible for poor Tina, who had been attending St. Michael's since kindergarten. She quickly turned away and walked in the direction of the school doors.

She bumped right into Tina.

"Oh, hi Tina," Olivia said, blushing.

"Hi, Olivia. Can you believe school's out already? It will be so weird not to see everyone for three months, won't it?"

Olivia gulped and said nothing. So Tina didn't know she wasn't coming back yet. Her parents must have been doing everything they could up until the last minute, but to no avail.

Tina didn't seem to notice Olivia's discomfort. "I'm just looking for my dad. He said he had to come into the building for a minute. Have you seen him?"

"Um, no, I haven't *seen* him," she said, which was actually true. She had only heard him. She knew she was stalling for time. She didn't want Tina to overhear her dad's conversation with Sister Anne Marie.

A couple of seventh-grade boys came noisily walking by, and Tina and Olivia stepped aside so they could exit.

"See ya in September!" one boy had called happily to the other as they parted ways.

Tina smiled. "Well, I'll just go look for him. Bye, Olivia!" She started to walk away.

"Bye, Tina," Olivia mumbled, watching her go.

"See ya in September!" Tina echoed from the hallway, laughing and waving.

"Yeah," Olivia said, trying to sound as cheery as she could. "See ya, Tina."

Olivia frowned, remembering that last day of school and wishing with all of her heart that she hadn't overheard Tina's dad's conversation with Sister Anne Marie. She wondered how Tina took the news, and if she had resigned herself to it by now. She sure hoped so.

She thought about how she would feel if she had to leave St. Michael's and go to another school. Even though she had only started a couple of years ago, she already felt a part of the family atmosphere at her school. She had had an uneasy start to her first year when meeting new friends and trying to fit in, but once she had smoothed out the rough spots and really gotten to know her new friends, she loved St. Michael's. Olivia felt sorry for Tina, having to leave her friends, teachers, and especially Sister Anne Marie behind. She was sure Tina would find another nice school to go to, but where could you find another loving, compassionate, and special principal like Sister Anne Marie? Olivia didn't think it was possible.

"Come and sit," said Olivia's mom, noticing her sad face. "Look how pretty the water is today. It's sparkling like glass."

Olivia looked out at the vast water and studied the lighthouse in the distance. How long had it been there? Abby said she loved reading about lighthouses and owned books with stories about individual lighthouses and their history. Olivia thought it was great that Abby had a hobby with her dad, much like she and her dad had cooking in common. She spied two pretty sailboats with brightly colored stripes and big black numbers on them, bobbing up and down in the sunshine. She wondered who owned them, and if they even gave a thought to buying new shoes.

"Are you looking forward to starting next door, Livvy? Mrs. Duggan said you could begin watching Danny in a few days."

Olivia nodded. She was, indeed, looking forward to the challenge of her first job.

Suddenly, Olivia had an idea. "Mom, maybe I could get some new shoes with the money I'll earn from Mrs. Duggan."

Her mom looked thoughtful. "You could, Livvy. Of course it's up to you, but remember your plan about sponsoring a child? I know that means a lot to you."

Olivia frowned. If only she didn't need money for so many different things! Wouldn't life be so much simpler if money wasn't so important? Maybe that is why her grandma always said that the love of money was the root of all evil.

Her mom saw the look on her daughter's face and said gently, "It's your money, of course, but you have to make some hard decisions about what you want to do with it. It's about making choices."

Choices. It would be so much easier if she didn't have to decide between what she wanted at the moment and what she knew she had been striving for, for a higher purpose.

"But Mom? If we did have the money, would you let me get sandals with a little heel on them?"

Mrs. Thomas mulled it over and gave a half smile. "I was your age once, remember? And I asked my mother the same thing. It would depend on the shoe, but I don't see a problem with it." She took Olivia's hand, wanting to make her feel better. "I'll keep an eye out for some shoe sales in town, okay? We might get lucky. You never know."

Olivia nodded, happy her mother was giving permission for her to wear heels, but knowing no shop in Keane Harbor would have discounted sandals at the height of tourist season.

TWELVE

"I have always been satisfied with what the good God has given to me—even with the gifts that seemed less good or beautiful than those of others." —St. Thérèse

The next day, the doorbell rang after breakfast. Olivia opened the door to find Brandon, Abby, and Brooke standing on the front porch.

"Hey, we haven't seen you and Hayley for a while. What have you been up to?" Brooke asked. She was wearing a graphic T-shirt with the words "spoiled brat" on it.

Olivia stepped aside so the kids could enter the foyer. "We did a couple of touristy things, and went to see the boats at the pier."

"Fun," Brooke said, taking in the house and its contents.

"Great shirt," Olivia said to Brooke, thinking it would be fun to have a trendy shirt like that.

"My sister always has to be saying something to the world. This one happens to be true. Where's Hayley?" Brandon wanted to know as Brooke sneered at him.

"Feeding Lucy," Olivia said, still feeling guilty for the lies she had told them on the beach. She hated not telling the truth and was not proud of it, but she just could not help herself. *I'll tell them soon*, she said to herself. *I really will. Just...not now.*

"Did you hear about the aquarium?" Brandon wanted to know. "You should go. They've got sharks and dolphins in tanks. It's really cool."

Olivia nodded, knowing all about it.

"Just stay away from Mondays, when it's free admission. It's so crowded you can barely move. Who'd ever want to go then?" He asked this with a scoff.

"Yeah, really," Olivia agreed, thinking of how her family had been planning to go next Monday.

"Paying full price is definitely worth it. Plus, you don't get all the riff-raff."

Olivia bristled at his disparaging comment. What did "riff-raff" mean, anyway? And did that mean that her family and Hayley were "riff-raff" too?

Abby shot Brandon a look. "Brandon, you can be such a snob sometimes."

Brandon held up both hands helplessly. "I'm just saying..."

"Yeah, we all know what you're saying," Abby said. "Anyway, Olivia, we're here to invite you to the big Fourth of July party on the beach. You and Hayley should come and hang out with us. We're going to have a catered barbecue. It'll be fun."

Just then Hayley came into the foyer. "I thought I heard the doorbell. Hi, guys."

"Hey Hayley," said Abby. "We just came to invite you and Olivia to the Fourth of July party tonight. Keane Harbor puts on fireworks and there's a live band. It's really fun."

Hayley raised her eyebrows at Olivia, excited at the prospect of going to a beach party. "If your parents say it's okay, it sounds great to me. Who's all coming?"

"Well, all of the neighbors go, and we'll be there with our *au pair*, Nina." At the mention of Nina's name, Brandon rolled his eyes.

Olivia looked confused. "Your who?"

Brooke sighed, exasperated. "I know, it's totally stupid to have an *au pair* at our age. She's okay, but a little strict."

Olivia had no idea what an *au pair* was. An aunt? The name sounded French. She didn't want to admit that she didn't know, but the curiosity was killing her. It sounded fancy, whatever it was.

Hayley stepped in, unembarrassed, and dying to know. "What on earth is an *au pair*?"

Brandon opened his eyes wide in shock. "You've never heard of one?" He glanced at Olivia. "Don't any of your friends have one?"

Olivia thought of Jenna and Chad at home, and how they'd get a kick out of this conversation. She smiled to herself, thinking of what Chad's clever retort would be.

"Um, they're not really all that popular where we live," Olivia said quietly.

"Oh, it's just a live-in nanny from another country," Abby offered. "They're usually in their early twenties and come to work in the United States for a couple of years. Nina is from Brazil."

"Yeah, and her English is terrible," Brandon added.

"But why do you need an *au pair*?" Olivia asked, trying out the new term. "Your parents are here."

Brandon scoffed. "Well, yeah, they're here, but they're socializing at the Beacon Yacht Club. They golf eighteen holes, go have lunch there and then come back for the afternoon to 'relax.'

At night they go out with their friends for dinner. We're not old enough to stay by ourselves all day and evening, which I think is pretty lame since I'm thirteen years old!"

"Mom and Dad just don't trust you, and I don't blame them," sneered Brooke.

Olivia and Hayley did not know what to say to this. Olivia had heard of people having sitters when their parents worked, of course, but to have sitters so their parents could socialize all day and evening when they were on family vacations? It was just... different.

Brandon ignored his sister's comment. "Luckily, Nina lets us go to the beach alone during the day while she watches TV. Who watches you guys all day if you don't have an *au pair*?" Brandon wanted to know, genuinely confused.

A voice came behind them. "You're looking at her, young man. And Mr. and Mrs. Thomas, of course, who are upstairs. I'm Grandma Rosemary." She held out her hand. "Come on in and sit down, all of you. Livvy, don't leave your guests standing here in the foyer," she admonished her.

Embarrassed, Olivia led the gang to the living room. She saw Grandma frown when she noticed Brooke's T-shirt.

"Oooh, the house is so pretty," Abby said, looking around. "I knew it would be."

"Thank you," Olivia said proudly, and Grandma gave her a funny look.

After the introductions were made, Grandma leaned forward and looked at Brandon. "What's this I hear about a beach party?" Grandma was not one to mince words.

"Everyone in the neighborhood will be there," he said, seem-ing surprisingly a bit nervous under Grandma's intense gaze.

Grandma had an air of authority about her. As Hayley liked to joke, "You don't mess with Grandma Rosemary." Grandma got the biggest kick out of that remark, saying that she wished someone would make a T-shirt with that slogan on it.

"And your parents?" Grandma asked pointedly. "Will they be there?"

"Well, no. They'll be at the yacht club. There's a big party there for the adults. But Nina will be with us."

"Well, seeing as we all just met," Grandma said, "the girls would be happy to come as long as one of Olivia's parents goes with them."

Olivia reddened. How embarrassing! Why did Grandma have to make her feel like such a baby? Hayley simply looked down at her feet, also embarrassed, but not wanting to cross Grandma, either.

"Great," Abby said, breaking the awkward tension as she stood up to leave. "Come about eight. They're serving a late dinner. You're welcome to come too," she said to Grandma.

Grandma frowned. "Thank you, Abby, but I don't get to the beach much."

Olivia glanced at Grandma and felt bad. If only there were a way to get Grandma down to the beach. Would she ever get over her fear of the water?

"Can Olivia and Hayley bring anything? I could whip up a Jello mold or something," Grandma offered, then said, "Oh, I wish I had my copper fish mold here. It would fit in at the beach, don't you think?" Then she laughed, amused at the thought.

Brooke smiled graciously. "Thank you very much, but there's no need to; it's a catered event."

"Oh, my goodness, well, we didn't know that. I am sure there's a fee to cover the meals. What should I give you?"

"It's covered in the association dues by the neighborhood families," Brandon said, with a questioning look on his face, as if they should have known that, being the owners.

"Well, that sounds very nice," Grandma said, already having in mind a shopping list of lime Jello and cream cheese. As if she, Grandma Rosemary, were going to send Olivia and Hayley to a party empty handed! Not a chance!

A few hours later, Hayley and Olivia sat cross-legged on Olivia's bed. Olivia was bracing herself for Hayley to attack her about not yet coming clean for the lies she had told. To her surprise, however, Hayley looked nervous, like she had something else to talk about.

"The party sounds fun," Olivia said as she inspected a mosquito bite on her leg.

"Yeah. Um, Olivia? Think we could lose your parents for the night? I mean, it wouldn't look very cool to have them at the beach party. Know what I mean?" Hayley stared at Olivia with a hopeful look on her face.

Olivia knew exactly what she meant, but could see no way out of it. "Just be glad Grandma isn't coming," she whispered, loving her Grandma to pieces, but thinking of all of the pointed remarks and observations Grandma was capable of making at such an event. When the trio had left earlier that day, Grandma had made a remark about Brandon needing a haircut. It was all Olivia could do to shoo the kids out of the house before Grandma commented about Brandon's shark-tooth necklace. "Whoever heard of a boy wearing a necklace without a religious medal or cross?" Olivia had closed the front door just in time.

"And it's just my dad who's coming. He won't say anything uncool."

"I know," Hayley moaned, "but still." Then she had an idea. "Hey, maybe you could ask your dad to stay on the deck! He could still watch us, but he won't be right there."

Olivia raised her eyebrows, unsure. "I don't know, Hayley…"

"Oh come on. He'll be able to see our beach blanket from where he is. We'll stay right by the deck."

Olivia had to admit, it was a perfect idea.

Mr. Thomas agreed to the plan, as long as he met the new friends and Nina first, and as long as they all agreed to stay in sight of him at all times, without wandering off down the beach.

Hayley, obviously relieved, brought everyone over to meet Mr. and Mrs. Thomas later that evening.

"Wait, before you go," Grandma said excitedly as the girls were out the door with their beach blankets and chairs. She hurried into the kitchen and came out a moment later with a glass dish, covered in foil. "Try to keep it cold," she said as she handed the dish to Olivia. "I'll get you an ice block from the freezer to put underneath it."

Brooke and Brandon tried to hide a smirk, and Olivia noticed. "Oh, Grandma, what'd ya do?" she laughed nervously. "You didn't have to go through all of this trouble, *really*."

"Oh, come now." Grandma said, dismissing her with a wave of her hand. "You can't go to a party empty handed, now can you? You're always supposed to bring a covered dish to parties. If I'd had more time I could've made salami rollups, too," she said with a wink. "But my Lime Jello Surprise sure is a crowd pleaser."

Reluctantly, Olivia took the lime Jello from Grandma. She thought of St. Thérèse and her Little Way and managed a smile.

"Don't forget to bring the dish back!" Grandma called happily as the group walked down to the beach. Brandon softly giggled as they walked.

Olivia wanted to tell him to put a sock in it, but she decided against it, seeing as it probably wouldn't be part of the Little Way.

The sun was beginning to set and the beach was filled with well-dressed neighbors and their friends, all laughing and having a good time as they assembled their blankets and beach chairs. Olivia noticed all ages: teenagers, adults with young children, and older folks, all getting set up on the sand. She was excited to be at such a fun-looking party, right on the ocean. Far out on the water, a big barge was floating, readying the fireworks for when the sun went down. People were lighting tiki torches and small bonfires in the sand.

Olivia's dad waved to her from his seat on their deck. He sat in one of the teak chairs with a small lamp so he could read his book and still keep an eye on the kids.

Olivia smelled grilled chicken and her stomach rumbled with hunger. Large tables with red, white, and blue linen tablecloths were set up along the sand, covered in large silver Sterno servers, their blue flames flickering underneath, keeping the food warm. People in uniforms were setting up another table, which was devoted to huge silver bowls filled with ice, soda, and bottled water. The tables were absolutely groaning with food.

"Who's going to eat all of this food?" Hayley wondered aloud.

"I know. There's more food than people," Olivia noted, thinking of Maria and her family in Guatemala all of a sudden. This was more food than they'd probably ever see in their lifetimes. She glanced down at her grandmother's dish in her hands.

"So, um, where should I put this?" Olivia asked, feeling awkward.

Hayley shrugged her shoulders. "Let's go ask the helpers," she said.

The two girls walked up to one of the food tables and set the dish down amid the flickering candles. Olivia spied a beautiful tray of chocolate éclairs and had to smile—they reminded her of St. Thérèse. Thérèse was not allowed to have them while in the convent, even when she was very sick and dying. The Carmelite order was very strict, and refused her request of an éclair when she felt an astonishing surge in her appetite one day. Perhaps they thought that, in her very ill state, she wouldn't be able to digest it. Still, it made Olivia very sad that poor Thérèse was not able to have the favorite treat she craved in her darkest hours.

"Oh! What are you doing?" asked a stern young woman in a crisp, white uniform, her hands on her hips.

"Um, we brought this dessert," Olivia said nervously.

The woman glared at the girls as if they were committing a crime. She furrowed her eyebrows.

"Young lady, this is a *catered affair*," she said condescendingly. "You can't just bring a dish like *this*." She gestured distastefully at Grandma's foil-covered dish.

"But my grandma…"

"No, no, please take this away," she said harshly. Then, curiosity got the better of her and, with one finger, she lifted the foil off of the edge.

"It's *green*!" she shrieked. "It looks like mold! If Miss Dottie sees this shabby dish, she'll have my head on a platter!"

Olivia cringed. She didn't like this lady one bit.

"Who is Miss Dottie?" Hayley asked, eyes narrowed.

"Why, she's the owner of this catering company, Dottie's Delights, the finest on the eastern seaboard! Now shoo, the both of you, and take this—whatever it is—with you! Get!"

Olivia, angry now, picked up the glass dish and shot the lady a look. "It's a Lime Jello Surprise," she said sharply, "and my grandma made it."

"Hmmph!"

"She's a better cook than Dottie ever will be!" Hayley said through gritted teeth as the two trudged away in the sand with Grandma's Jello.

The two girls settled onto their blankets and set the dish down in the sand.

"Now what?" asked Olivia as she stared sadly down at the dish. "What am I going to tell Grandma?" She didn't want to hurt her feelings, after all of the love Grandma must have put into her dessert.

Grandma had always told Olivia that whatever you cook, you should always put love in it or it will not turn out well. Olivia could recall a few times when she was in a hurry or her heart wasn't into what she was making at the time, and it never tasted as good as when she took her time and tried her best. Imagine if Grandma found out that her beloved dessert wasn't good enough for the rich crowd gathered on the beach. Olivia shuddered at the thought.

"You certainly can't tell her that Difficult Dottie won't put her Jello on the serving table," Hayley said. The two looked at each other and slow smiles spread on their faces, and before they knew it, they were giggling and laughing so hard that they were on their backs, gasping for air.

"Dottie doesn't delight in delicious desserts!" howled Hayley.

"Don't you dare damage Dottie's dinner!" cried Olivia.

"I double dare you, darling!"

"Don't be disobedient and demand that your dreadful dish be dined on!"

The two laughed so hard, they didn't even notice when Brandon, Brooke, and Abby came up behind them.

"We were just talking to Nina and some of her friends over there," Abby said, confused to see Hayley and Olivia falling all over themselves with laughter. "What's so funny?"

"Oh, nothing. We were just thinking of something," Olivia said, wiping her eyes.

Brooke replicd, "Well, the band's setting up and we should go get dinner. It's nearly dusk."

At the mention of yet another "d" word, Hayley and Olivia fell into a chorus of loud giggles.

Brooke, a little put out by a joke she did not understand, rolled her eyes.

Some adults on nearby blankets looked over to see what the commotion was.

"You girls are so strange," Brandon said, shaking his head and smiling. Embarrassed by this, Hayley immediately stopped laughing and tried to compose herself.

Olivia felt a little guilty about making fun of Dottie and her helper, but she felt even worse about Grandma. She loved Grandma. The earlier look of joy and happiness on her face contrasted with the possible look of hurt feelings from a returned dish full of Jello, and it made Olivia very sad. But they couldn't very well eat the whole dessert, all of them. And she didn't want to waste the food by dumping it into a garbage can, but it was looking like that was the only option. Olivia felt very uncomfortable about this whole situation.

"Hayley," she said as she looked down at Grandma's dish, "Grandma is going to feel so bad if we bring this all back."

"I know," Hayley moaned as she shooed a fly away from her dinner. "Here, scoop me a big serving and I'll eat some."

"Good idea," Olivia said, and did the same thing with her plate. It didn't seem to make much of a dent. The dish still looked full.

Abby came and sat down next to Olivia, peering at her food. "What's the green stuff on your plate? I didn't see any of that up there."

"It's...my grandma's Jello mold," Olivia said cautiously, afraid of Abby's reaction. Olivia didn't know if she could bear yet another person making fun of her grandma's dessert.

"Yum! I love Jello. Can I have some?" Abby asked.

Surprised, Olivia slowly scooped some from the serving dish onto Abby's plate. When Abby took a bite of the cool, sweet dessert, her eyes lit up. "Is there pineapple in here? I need this recipe!"

"Really?" asked Olivia happily. "I mean, I know it's great, but..."

"Oh yeah," Abby said, taking another bite. "It's perfect for a barbecue. Let's see if some of the other people want some." And she picked the dish up from the blanket and an unused plastic spoon and began to walk from blanket to blanket, offering Grandma's Jello to the partygoers on the beach.

"Oooh, I taste pineapple!"

"Yum, I didn't expect the cream cheese. Who made this?"

One by one, guests helped themselves to Grandma's lime dessert, scooping it onto their plates next to lobster and fruit, exclaiming that it was so refreshing and delicious. It was the hit of the party.

"I haven't had this since I was a child," one lady in a fancy linen skirt and large hoop earrings remarked. "This brings back memories."

"My mother used to make this!" exclaimed a man in an expensive golf shirt. He closed his eyes and a smile came over his face as he remembered.

When Abby brought the dish back to where Olivia was sitting, it was completely empty. And the caterers were none the wiser.

Olivia gave Abby a look of gratitude. Pretty Abby, who knew just what to do. "Thanks, Abby. My grandma is going to be so happy that everyone liked her Jello."

"No problem," she said with a smile. "Those caterers are crazy. I mean, who doesn't like Jello? My grandma makes the kind with mandarin oranges. It tastes like an orange ice cream bar."

Brandon and Brooke wandered over in the increasing darkness, balancing drinks and plates piled high with crab cakes, gourmet potato salad, and shrimp cocktail. Hayley motioned for them to sit down beside her.

"Aw, man," moaned Brandon as he spotted the empty serving dish. "The Jello's all gone!"

Olivia laughed, secretly pleased that stuffy Brandon would want some of her grandma's Jello. "Sorry, Brandon. You snooze, you lose!"

THIRTEEN

"Jesus Christ alone is singularly to be loved, who alone is found good and faithful above all friends."—St. Thérèse

The fireworks lit up the sky over the Atlantic Ocean in a multitude of colors. As the brilliant starbursts splashed the dark sky, Olivia's heart pounded with each thud. The show was breathtaking, and no one said much as they enjoyed the display, because they were so riveted at the enormous, flashing lights. After the sparkling finale, the crowd murmured their approval with oohs and aahs, staying put on their blankets. No one wanted to leave.

The band played for a bit more, the lead singer singing reggae and island songs to a steel-drum beat. Some of the guests cleared away their belongings so a makeshift dance area could be made on the sand. Olivia and the friends danced, acted silly, and enjoyed themselves with the fun, spirited music. It was a perfect night to be on the beach, having fun with friends amid the glow of tiki torches and candles.

The band even played one of the Tyler Twins' new hit songs, "LOL, I Love You," to which Olivia and Hayley screamed with delight at the beginning bars of the song, dancing happily and laughing as they jumped around.

Out of breath from fast dancing, Olivia and Hayley tumbled onto their blankets to rest for a while when the band started to play a slow song. Many of the adults got up to slow dance, keeping an eye on their sleepy children at the same time. Olivia looked over at the deck and was surprised to see that her dad was no longer sitting in his chair. *Where did he go?* she wondered.

Nina came trudging through the sand in the dark, carrying cans of soda.

"I've got Cokes, guys," she said.

Brandon took two Cokes from Nina and handed one of them to Hayley. "Want one?" he asked her.

Even in the dim lights of the tiki torches and bonfires, Olivia could see Hayley blush. "Sure, thanks."

Brandon took a couple of swigs of his drink, then abruptly turned back to Hayley. "Wanna dance?"

Olivia stopped drinking, the soda pop can mid-air. Brandon asking Hayley to dance? What would Hayley say? Neither of them had ever danced with a boy before.

Hayley didn't even flinch. "Why not?" she asked as she got up and brushed some sand from her clothes. Brandon grinned and the two walked over to where couples were dancing.

Brooke giggled. "He's got a huge crush on your friend," she whispered loudly in Olivia's ear over the music and the roar of the ocean. "It's so obvious."

Olivia frowned. Her dad was not going to like this one bit. She looked for her dad up on the deck. Was he watching?

She watched Brandon and Hayley dance. They looked a little awkward, Olivia noted. For all of Hayley's cool exterior, Olivia knew that Hayley was probably terribly nervous, this being her first time dancing with a boy. The band finished and started another slow song, and Hayley and Brandon continued dancing in the sand. Olivia couldn't believe it. Another dance?

"Having fun, Olivia?" Abby asked as she opened her can and took a sip.

"Sure, no big deal," Olivia said, and then added, "we go to lots of parties like this at home."

"Really? I don't," Abby said softly, and Olivia instantly felt bad for lying.

Just then she saw her dad coming toward them from the sand dunes, making his way toward the dance area in great strides. He walked up to Hayley and Brandon. "Hello there, you two," he said with a small smile. Shadows from the flickering candles and torches danced across his face. "Making room for the Holy Spirit?" he asked, as he gently pried them apart some more so there was a good ruler's length between the two dancers. "There, that's much better."

Watching this, Olivia buried her head in her hands.

UGH! How mortifying! Her face burned with embarrassment. Hayley was really going to lay into her tonight for this, she just knew it.

"Finish the song, and then it's time to come in," her dad said to Hayley and Brandon, and then came over to where Olivia was sitting. He took Hayley's blanket and beach bag and began to gently shake it out. "Did y'all have a good time?"

"Dad, there you are," Olivia laughed nervously. "I didn't see you just now on the deck."

"Yep, time to come in. It's getting late, so I came over to get you. The fireworks were great, weren't they?"

The slow song ended and Hayley reluctantly came over with Brandon.

"Hi Mr. Thomas. Brandon said it's okay if I stay behind with the girls and Nina for a little bit," she suggested hopefully.

Olivia bit her lip. Poor Hayley didn't know what she was getting herself into with this request. She could already tell that her dad was tired and ready for bed, and this little proposal was not going to help the situation. Olivia knew not to push it when her dad was crabby, and at this point, he was borderline crabby. Any small nudge would tip the scales in the wrong direction.

"Did he now?" Mr. Thomas asked tersely. "Well, seeing as Nina has spent most of her evening hanging out way over there by the sand dunes with her friends instead of keeping an eye on all of you, I'm thinking it's best we all went home now. It's been a fun night, but time for bed."

Olivia got up quickly and gathered her things, wasting no time.

"Oh come on, Mr. Thomas," asked Brandon, pushing the matter. "Some friends of mine heard there's a turtle's nest around here somewhere. We were hoping to find it."

"Young man, Hayley is under my charge for the next month, so you can just think of me as her dad until we leave. The party's over for them. Say goodnight, girls." He took Olivia's things from her and started slowly back.

"Um, we had fun," Olivia said, balancing Grandma's empty dish under her arm. "See y'all later, I guess."

Hayley sighed. "Bye everyone, thanks for inviting us." She looked at Brandon with a dreamy look on her face. "Bye, Brandon."

Then Olivia and Hayley reluctantly followed after Mr. Thomas.

A while later, teeth brushed and lying in bed, Olivia found she couldn't sleep. The music of the evening was still playing in her head, and she kept seeing the fireworks in her mind's eye, not to mention the image of Brandon and Hayley slow dancing in the sand. She wondered if she'd ever dance with a boy. With her freckles, it really didn't seem likely.

She tossed and turned, sleep eluding her. She threw off the covers and stepped quietly into the hallway. The only sound was her father snoring in her parents' bedroom. The rest of the house was dark and quiet. She tiptoed down to Hayley's door and knocked softly.

"Come in," came a muffled voice from behind the door.

"It's just me," said Olivia, and went over to the edge of Hayley's bed. "Are you still up?"

Haley sniffed then, and Olivia realized she had been crying. In the soft, yellow glow of the nightlight, she could see Hayley's red, blotchy face and puffy eyes.

"Hayley, are you okay? What's wrong?"

Hayley wiped some of the tears from her eyes. "Brandon's never going to want to talk to me again," she sniffed, her voice catching.

"What do you mean?" Olivia asked, concerned for her friend. "Why on earth not?"

Hayley looked at Olivia through the moonlight that came through the slits of her blinds. Her window was open and the sounds of the ocean gently crashing ashore was calming and soothing.

"It's your dad, Olivia! He was so awful! I'm totally embarrassed!"

Olivia felt bad. She knew Hayley was referring to the episode at the end of the evening.

"Hayley, it's just that he's sort of responsible for you while we're here, you know? I don't know if your mom would approve of you slow dancing."

"Oh, she wouldn't care," Hayley rushed to comment. "Um, I don't think. I mean, I'm twelve years old."

Olivia felt bad that her dad had embarrassed Hayley, and didn't know what else to say. Of course, she wanted to be a good friend to Hayley and sympathize with her, but it was hard because it was her dad. She found herself in a tricky spot. Deep down, she knew they were both too young to be trying to catch the eyes of boys. But she also knew that with Hayley, that explanation wouldn't fly. She decided to try a different tactic.

"Hayley, come on. Brandon's not even your type. He's such a phony snob. You hear how he talks."

Hayley looked up angrily. "He isn't all that bad," she said hotly. "And he had lots of nice things to say while we were dancing."

"Oh really." Olivia was not convinced.

"Yeah, really. And just because you're too much of a baby to be interested in boys, why ruin it for me? It sounds like you're taking your mean dad's side over mine!"

Olivia was stung. Her feelings hurt, she folded her arms and said nothing. Yet another person calling her a baby: her best friend, yet! She couldn't stand it! Here she was trying to help Hayley, and all Hayley could do was insult her and her dad. She got up to leave.

"My dad's not mean, Hayley. He cares a lot about you and doesn't want you to get hurt."

Hayley turned her back toward Olivia. "Just go, Olivia. I don't want to talk to you."

"What?"

"You heard me. In fact, I want to go home, back to Michigan!"

Fuming, Olivia stomped back to her own bedroom and closed the door a little too loudly. She didn't feel like getting back into bed, so she walked to her window and stared out at the darkness over the ocean. The waves, at low tide, were pulled back, far away from the sand. Below, she could see them crashing under the glow of the moon. The sound reassured her somehow, and she sank into a chair by the window, continuing to watch.

Would Hayley really go home? How would she get there? Would Mrs. Stewart have to drive all this way to pick her up, or would they have to cut their own stay short?

What a mess this was. They had been having such a fun time, too.

Now would be a good time to pray, she thought. Grandma always said in times of trouble, when you don't know what to do, you can always talk to God. He never sleeps, and is available twenty-four seven. It reminded her of the nightshirt Grandma had given her for Christmas last year that said, *Can't sleep? Take your problems to God. He's up all night anyway.* Every time Olivia wore that shirt to bed, she felt comforted somehow. She wished she had packed it for this trip.

Dear Jesus, she prayed. **I'm glad you're up, because I am too. I just don't know what to do about Hayley. You were my age once; what would you have done? She is so mad at me, and Dad too. She wants to go home. This is so crazy; a big misunderstanding. Please help us be friends again, and make her want to stay. Amen.**

Then she wondered: Did Jesus listen to liars?

ϜOURTEEN

"While on this earth, we must be attached to nothing, not even to the most innocent things, for they will fail us when we least expect it." —St. Thérèse

The next day, Hayley would not talk to Olivia at all. She kept her silence at breakfast, not even bothering to look up at Olivia while she ate her cereal, keeping her head down in her corn flakes. Hayley said a few words to Lucy, who was eating oatmeal, then rinsed out her bowl, put it and the spoon in the dishwasher, and went to the living room with her MP3 player.

The sky looked cloudy and rain threatened to come in, adding to her sour mood.

Olivia took a bite out of her toast and put it back on her plate.

"Aren't you hungry this morning, Livvy?" her grandma asked, taking a seat beside her to help Lucy finish her breakfast. She got a wet washcloth and began to wipe Lucy's mouth.

"Not much, Grandma," said Olivia, pushing her toast around.

"Oh, come on. I'll make you a framed egg or some pancakes. *Mangia!* Eat!" she urged, like any Italian grandma worth her salt.

Olivia shook her head. "Toast and orange juice are fine, Grandma, but thanks."

"Your dad said you had a fun time last night at the party," Grandma said, wiping Lucy, who squirmed and fussed.

"It was fun," Olivia said. *Until Dad came to get us*, she thought.

Grandma's face brightened. "I saw the empty dish. Looks like my Jello was a hit," she said knowingly. "Not that I'm surprised; who doesn't like a Jello mold?" She hummed to herself as she continued to clean up Lucy.

Olivia nodded. "Grandma, I think I'm going to go upstairs and make my bed," she said.

Olivia kissed Lucy on the top of her head and went off to her room. As she was walking down the hallway, deep in thought, she heard a muffled beeping sound coming from Hayley's room. Curious, Olivia peeked her head in. Hayley's bed was unmade, covers in a heap. Where was the beeping sound coming from?

Then she heard it again. It sounded like it was coming from the bed. Olivia stepped into Hayley's room and went through the covers until she found the source of the noise: Hayley's cell phone. She was getting a text message.

Olivia peered through the doorway to see if Hayley was coming, but she wasn't. Olivia held the phone in her hand, tempted. Could it be from Mrs. Stewart? No, Hayley's mom wasn't big on texting. Maybe it was her brother Ryan, checking up on her.

Quickly, she pressed the button that said, "read message." She had to hurry in case Hayley came upstairs.

Had fun @ parT. Meet me @ 11 thurs. nite? B @ end of pathway. Can C turtle nest w/ friends.

Olivia froze with the phone in her hand. It was from Brandon—she knew it. Would Hayley really go? Would she sneak out to meet him and his friends Thursday night? This was terrible. She had to talk to her, to try to stop this. But how? Hayley wouldn't even speak with her.

You must tell your parents.

Olivia sighed. It was St. Thérèse, she knew, advising her what to do. Why did St. Thérèse have to be so persistent?!

"I want to, St. Thérèse, I really do," she whispered, "but think of how more mad Hayley would be. I would lose my best friend."

Besides, she didn't even know if Hayley would go through with it. This was just Brandon asking her to go. Maybe Hayley would decide against it. *No use getting Mom and Dad involved when there really isn't a problem yet,* Olivia thought. *And Hayley is a good girl. She loves God and St. Thérèse too now. She wouldn't do anything as bad as this.*

Feeling better, Olivia stuffed Hayley's phone back under the blanket where she found it and quickly left the room.

With Hayley not wanting to hang around her, there wasn't much to do. Olivia was very bored. She wished she could start her new job today. She looked through some of the books she had brought, finding fault with each of them: this one was too long, the other too boring, and that one she had read a dozen times and knew the ending by heart. Sighing, she put the books back on her dresser. She thought about home for the first time since they'd arrived in Keane Harbor. She missed Jenna right now. Jenna would have some words of wisdom about the situation. She also missed Chad. He'd have just the right things to say to make her laugh. She had promised to send him some postcards, and she hadn't even found one yet. *Maybe Mom will take me shopping today*, Olivia thought, and went downstairs to find her.

"That's a great idea, Olivia," said her mom, eyeing her pink nose and cheeks. "It looks like rain anyway. You should take a little break from the beach."

When her mom asked her if Hayley would like to go too, Olivia shook her head. "I think she just wants to hang around here by herself today," she said sadly. Her mom, who sensed the new tension between the two, just left it at that.

A while later, Olivia and her mom were in the car, headed into town. Olivia clutched her purse, which contained all of her savings. She wanted to bring her money in case they found a shop that sold children's shoes. She looked out the window and watched the scenery change as they approached the edge of town, when souvenir stores, ice cream shops, and hotels appeared.

"So many crowds, even in this hot, muggy weather," her mom remarked as she drove slowly through town. "I hope I can find a spot." They found a parking spot right off Ocean Boulevard, the main street.

"Look at all of the fun shops," Olivia remarked. "Lots of touristy stuff. I need to find some funny postcards for Chad."

Olivia and her mom walked into a store called "Treasures of the Sea," which was filled with cheap souvenirs like alligator teeth, I ♥ Keane Harbor keychains, and salt water taffy.

The store was packed with beachgoing tourists loading up on overpriced sunscreen, souvenir coffee mugs, bumper stickers, and magnets.

"I promised Chad some taffy," Olivia said as she chose a watermelon-flavored package for him. Then she found the postcard rack and spun it around, looking at all of the different pictures.

Some were inappropriate, so she quickly took her eyes off of those, just like her parents had instructed her to do one time when they were in a bookstore and they had come across some unholy books. Others were too babyish or just boring scenic pictures of the ocean. Feeling bad that Chad could not come to Keane Harbor with them, she decided that she needed something really fun for him.

Then she found it: a postcard with two dogs digging through the sand on the beach. One dog said to the other, "What part of 'Bury the bone in the *back yard*' did you not understand?"

Olivia laughed out loud, amused. This one was perfect for Chad.

"Olivia, hi! What's so funny?" said a voice. Olivia looked up from the postcard and saw Abby and Brooke standing there, each holding a box of fudge. She instantly felt shabby in her jean shorts in front of them.

"Hi y'all," Olivia said, holding the postcard, trying to look casual. "What are you doing here?"

"We thought it looked like rain," replied Abby, "so we thought we'd come into town for some fudge. And a little shopping."

"Where's Brandon?" asked Olivia, feeling a little sick to her stomach at the mention of his name.

"He's a little tired from last night," Brooke said with a glint in her eye. "Must've been all that dancing with Hayley."

Olivia didn't know what to say, so she adjusted her purse on her shoulder and said nothing.

"Hi girls," said Mrs. Thomas, coming up behind Olivia and holding a bottle of iced tea. "Funny running into you here. I was just getting a cold drink."

"Hi Mrs. Thomas," the girls said together.

"Nice to see you both again. It's great that Olivia and Hayley met some friends to hang out with while we're here."

"Where is Hayley?" asked Brooke.

"She's kind of tired today, too," Olivia said, wondering if Brooke knew about her brother's text message from this morning, and if so, what she thought about it. She guessed that Brooke would be all for his plan.

Abby had an idea. "Mrs. Thomas, can Olivia come shopping with us today? We were just about to head to The Shoppes By The Pier. It's a couple of blocks from here."

"It's upscale shopping," Brooke put in for everyone's information. "Not like this tacky stuff here."

Mrs. Thomas looked wary. It was starting to drizzle, and the idea of walking a couple of blocks did not appeal to her.

"Oh please?" Olivia asked, wanting so much to go to The Shoppes By The Pier, wherever it was. Even the name sounded fancy.

"Well, who is with you?" her mom wanted to know. "Your *au pair*?"

"Nina's outside," Abby said, gesturing to a young woman sitting on a bench on the sidewalk, talking on a cell phone.

Mrs. Thomas was unimpressed, especially after the stories she had heard from the night before. Nina seemed more interested in her cell phone than in watching her charges.

"Okay," Mrs. Thomas relented. "Olivia and I will go with you."

Olivia brightened. "Great!"

Abby took Brooke's small box of fudge and put both boxes in her large purse.

"I hope it doesn't melt in there," Olivia said.

"Oh, the stores are air-conditioned," assured Brooke. "Not like *this* place. We just came here for the fudge. Let's go."

The walk to The Shoppes By The Pier wasn't too bad. Everyone chatted and Olivia asked lots of questions about Boston. "Maybe

I'll go there someday and see the *USS Constitution* and the Boston Tea Party exhibit," said Olivia, who loved history.

"I guess," Brooke said, shrugging her shoulders. "If you like that touristy stuff. We've seen it all a million times on field trips."

"I think you would like Boston, Olivia," Abby countered. "Especially if you like early American history."

Abby and Brooke were so different, Olivia mused. She wondered how they had enough in common to stay friends. Although she guessed that someone might very well have said the very same thing about her and Hayley, especially a couple of years ago. She suddenly felt bad for judging.

The Shoppes By The Pier, though outside, were lovely, with a gorgeous water fountain in the middle and pretty flowers and landscaping. They all felt relieved to get out of the rain when they entered each air-conditioned store.

"This one is my favorite," said Brooke, as they entered a store called *La Bonne Heure.*

"What does it mean?" asked Olivia, who did not speak French.

"Don't you take French?" asked Brooke, shocked. "We take French at our school. It's required since kindergarten. We're all pretty fluent," she bragged. "It means *the good hour.*"

What the name had to do with the summer sweaters and Capri pants Olivia saw hanging on the racks she had no idea, but it sure sounded impressive.

Abby leaned over to Olivia and whispered, "I think it's a dumb name, personally, but it is a nice store."

Olivia giggled.

Nina and Brooke went over to the counter and proceeded to look at jewelry. Abby wandered over to a stack of embellished T-shirts in the teen section.

Olivia glanced at her mother at the other end of the store, who was already longingly eyeing a gorgeous beaded purse that looked very expensive. Olivia knew it wasn't something they could afford and felt bad for her mom.

Watching her mom made her suddenly feel guilty about Hayley's text message. Should she follow St. Thérèse's advice and tell her parents? She knew her parents would have a fit if they knew that Brandon was even texting Hayley, much less planning a secret meeting at night! *But there's nothing to tell*, Olivia told herself. *Hayley might not have read the text message, or she might even decide to ignore it. Hayley knows right from wrong... right?* But deep down, the nudging she felt was growing stronger. Her conscience was telling her she should tell her mom about the message, if only to alert them to possible trouble. Her parents had always told her to listen to her gut, that God sent warning signs to people in this way.

Oh, St. Thérèse, she thought to herself irritably. *I'm so sick of worrying about Hayley. I'm not her caretaker. I have my own life to live, my own problems! I can't be worrying about someone else all of the time! You understand, don't you?*

"Look at this," Nina said in her thick Brazilian accent as she held up a spray can. "It's *L'Eau de Suisse*."

"What is that?" asked Olivia.

Brooke came over and took the can from Nina's hand. "Oh come on, tell me you're joking. You haven't heard of it? It's so refreshing," she said. "It's water from a spring in the Swiss Alps. You spray it on your face to feel refreshed, like this." She reached for a can that said "tester" on it and spritzed her face a couple of times. "Ahh!" Her face looked misty from the water.

Olivia took the can from Brooke and gave it a try on her own face. It sure felt good, especially on a muggy day. "Mmm. I like this," Olivia said, giving the can a once-over and trying to read the label, which was in French.

"You should buy one and take it to the beach," Abby said brightly as she perused a rack of belts. "We've got some at home and it's perfect for a hot day."

Abby used *L'Eau de Suisse*. Pretty, perfect Abby, who had long eyelashes and zero freckles. Olivia turned the can over, looking for the price. She found it on a little sticker on the bottom of the can: $12.95.

"$12.95 for a spray can of water?" Olivia shrieked. "I can just put water in a spritzer from the dollar store." Suddenly, her face turned red at Brooke's horrified expression.

Brooke possessively took the spray can from her, as if Olivia did not deserve the water if she was going to be criticizing it. "Olivia, it's water from *Switzerland*," she said. "It's not *tap* water."

"I know," she said, embarrassed and reaching for it back. "I was planning to buy it; I was just kidding around."

Not knowing what else to do, she took the spray can up to the register and slowly took the money out of her wallet. It was painful to be buying something so expensive, especially when she had been saving her money for so long. She thought instantly of Maria, the girl from Guatemala. Thinking of Maria walking so far for water every day while she spent so much for a can of imported water shamed her. If Maria could see her right now, what would she think?

She couldn't believe she was actually doing this, spending almost thirteen dollars for a spray can of water to refresh her face with, but then again, it *was* imported. And it did feel really nice on her face. She thought of how wonderful it would feel at the beach, how fun to casually pull the pretty pink and white canister out of her beach bag.

She smiled as the lady wrapped it in lavender tissue and placed it in a fancy bag with rope handles. *Wait 'til Hayley sees this*, she mused, thinking of how much fun they'd have spritzing it on themselves and laughing at the absurdity of expensive spritzer water. Then she stopped herself. Hayley was still mad at her and probably wouldn't care.

After the transaction, her mom came up to her, surprised. "Oh, you bought something?" Olivia could read between the lines: You bought something *here*? What about the money you are saving?

But Mrs. Thomas said none of those things. She merely smiled and peeked inside the bag. "Water?"

"It's supposed to have minerals and be good for your face," Olivia whispered hurriedly, so as not to be further embarrassed in front of everyone.

"Sounds nice," her mom said, having no idea how much the water was. Knowing how hard Olivia was saving her money to sponsor a foreign child, Mrs. Thomas merely assumed it was a fun, inexpensive purchase.

As they left the store, Olivia clutched her pretty bag tightly. She was secretly looking forward to using the fun water spray. She couldn't wait to bring it to the beach. Wouldn't she look rich and fancy, spritzing herself with it as they all sat on their towels? What an impression she would make on Abby and Brooke! She would look just like one of them!

⸏FIFTEEN

"If there is a mansion in heaven for great souls, for the fathers of the desert, and for martyrs who were penitents, surely there is one for little children. Our place is waiting there if we love our Lord—Him and our Heavenly Father and the Spirit of Love." —St. Thérèse

The following morning, Olivia woke up to a torrential rainstorm. The angry rainclouds hovered over the dark, agitated sea. Olivia turned the blinds on her window to shut out the gloomy view. She had been hoping to spend the morning at the beach, before she went to help Mrs. Duggan with Danny.

She paced around her room a bit, wanting to stay in her pajamas all day if this was what the weather was going to be like. The weatherman on the radio said the rain would not clear up until tomorrow.

She heard a soft knock on her door. "Come in."

It was Hayley, dressed in shorts and a black graphic T-shirt that had "I ♥ vampires" written on it.

"Your grandma sent me up here to tell you that Mrs. Duggan called. She wants to know if you can come this morning instead of this afternoon."

"Why?" asked Olivia, staring at the words on Hayley's T-shirt. She'd never seen it before. She wondered if Hayley's mom even knew she owned it.

"I don't know," Hayley said, a little agitated. "I'm just the message giver."

"Are you still mad at me?" Olivia asked, already knowing the answer.

"Why shouldn't I be?" she retorted.

"Hayley...there's something I want to talk to you about," Olivia said slowly. She walked over to shut the door so they could have some privacy. She didn't really know where to begin. What if Hayley got even more mad at her?

"What is it?" Hayley asked, arms folded.

"Well, yesterday I sort of...heard a noise coming from your room and..."

"Ooh, a ghost?" Hayley asked, her voice dripping with sarcasm.

"No, a text message," Olivia answered evenly, annoyed now at Hayley's demeanor. Did she think this was easy for her?

"I saw what Brandon wrote. You're not going tomorrow, are you?"

Hayley's face turned angry. "You've been reading my texts?" she asked incredulously. "How dare you touch my phone, Olivia!"

"I didn't mean to," Olivia said, trying to defend herself. "It just sort of happened when I was—"

"You were snooping! You have no right to come in my room or look at my phone!" Hayley turned to go. "And if I *do* go, it's none of your business."

"Hayley, I don't think it's a good idea. You could get into big trouble."

"With your dad? He's not *my* dad," Hayley answered hotly,

hands on her hips. In Hayley's eyes flashed pain and raw anger.

Olivia suddenly felt bad, knowing Hayley's dad had died when she was small. Hayley had once told her that the pain of losing a parent never goes away completely, and that she still felt sad seeing other girls with their dads.

"Listen," Olivia said, softening her tone, "that Brandon is no good."

"No good? Not a very Christian thing to say, Olivia."

"You know what I mean, Hayley! Stop turning things around on me. Not only is he a fake, he's too…mature...for you."

"That's because you're still a baby, Olivia. So just stay out of my business and I'll stay out of yours!"

"Hayley, you can't go meet him. It would be wrong. You'd be making a huge mistake," Olivia pleaded. She realized her voice was getting too loud. She didn't want her parents to overhear them, so she lowered her voice to a whisper. "Besides, sneaking out would be like lying to my parents."

"Oh, and this coming from the girl who deliberately lies to her new friends?"

This comment stung Olivia, who blushed in embarrassment. Hayley had her there.

"I guess somehow *that's* okay." Hayley folded her arms and looked at Olivia with a very satisfied look on her face.

Olivia held her fingers to her lips, signifying for Hayley to keep it down. Hayley, however, was too angry and offended to notice.

"You say Brandon's a fake and a snob? You're so busy trying to impress the rich kids that you can't even see what a fake *you* are. You're no better than Brandon, huh?"

"Hayley—"

"And Brandon's actually pretty nice, you know," Hayley said hotly. "He volunteers at a nursing home back home with his class, and he even helped some little girl out at the beach who lost her boogie board in the surf. He's not the cruel person you make him out to be." And with that, Hayley stormed out of the room and into her own, slamming the door behind her.

Olivia winced. If her parents or her grandma heard the door slamming, they'd surely come up and investigate. Door slamming was a big no-no in their household; Olivia had learned that by experience not too long ago. Her father had taken the door off the hinges for the day to teach her a lesson.

Luckily, her parents and her grandma were downstairs watching television, and the loud noise did not travel. With Grandma being a little hard of hearing, the volume on the television was turned up.

Frustrated and dejected, Olivia did not know what to do. She couldn't tell if Hayley was going to sneak out on Thursday night or not. She hadn't said yes and she hadn't said no. She worried that she may have made the situation even worse, and that, if Hayley had been undecided before, the fact that Olivia was so against it might make Hayley decide to go for spite.

God, please help me know what to do, she prayed, knowing full well she was going to rely on her own judgment, not God's.

Reluctantly, Olivia got dressed and went downstairs to tell her parents that she was going to go next door to watch Danny.

"Have a good time," her dad said, smiling. "Your first job. I'm very proud of you."

Olivia looked down and said nothing. How could she tell her dad he was one cause of the strife between her and Hayley? She didn't really feel like talking to him right now.

"Thanks, Dad," she said shortly, and grabbed an umbrella from the rack in the foyer.

"Want to make some pizzas tonight? We've got all of the ingredients."

Olivia shrugged her shoulders. She wasn't really in the mood, but she didn't want to be rude. "Sure."

"Great. When you come back we can start making the dough."

"See ya, Dad."

Olivia hurried next door, trying to forget her dad's disappointed expression. She knew he was wondering why she seemed so unexcited and distant; normally she jumped at the chance to create something in the kitchen with her father.

Mrs. Duggan answered the door with dark circles under her eyes. "Hi, Olivia, I'm so glad you're here." She ushered her inside. "Come in out of the rain!" She took her umbrella and set it to dry on the floor. "I was up all night with Danny. He's been so fussy. I think he's cutting new teeth or something. Thanks so much for coming early. If I don't lie down for a bit, I'll bump into the furniture!"

Olivia managed a small laugh and went inside to the living room, where Danny was playing on a mat with some small toys. He looked up at her with a big grin.

"He's had a morning snack already and really just wants to play. I'm going to go rest for a bit, but if there's anything you need, don't hesitate to get me. Do you have any questions?"

Olivia couldn't think of any, so she waved Mrs. Duggan on. "Go ahead, please. We'll be fine."

"There's an ABC video here he loves to watch, too," she said. "And this stacking toy should keep him busy for a while."

Olivia laughed. "We'll be fine, Mrs. Duggan. I do this all of the time with Lucy. Don't worry!"

Mrs. Duggan grinned tiredly, relieved that she could count on Olivia. "Mommy's going to rest now, Danny. Play nice with Olivia."

The time went by quickly for Olivia. She found she was having much more fun playing with Danny than with Lucy. She wondered why that was. Danny laughed at her silly faces and peek-a-boo games. Then she put the ABC video in and Danny cuddled with Olivia and a blanket on the sofa.

Danny got bored with the video after a while, and wandered over to a basket filled with large picture books. He dug through the basket, spilling its contents all over the floor, and happily held up a hardcover book with a picture of a sea turtle on its cover.

"Read!" he demanded as he scrambled onto Olivia's lap with the book.

Olivia laughed. "Yes, sir!" she said with a little salute as her charge settled in for a good read. She studied its cover. "'I'm a Baby Sea Turtle,'" she read. "Oh, this sounds like a good one, Danny."

"Read!" he repeated, and stabbed his chubby forefinger at the book.

This little boy sure knows how to get what he wants, Olivia mused with an eyebrow raised.

"'My name is Tommy,'" she began, admiring the lovely photographs of sea turtles on the pages. "'I'm a Loggerhead Sea Turtle and I live in North Carolina. This is my story.'"

Olivia smiled down at Danny. "Hey, that's where we are right now: North Carolina."

Danny nodded, not understanding, but liking being snuggled up with Olivia on the couch with one of his favorite books.

The mention of sea turtles made her think of Hayley sneaking out with Brandon and his friends to see a turtle's nest. *Why on*

earth would Brandon care about something like that? she wondered. *He doesn't seem like the type who would care about animals. He's too insensitive,* she thought wryly, then felt guilty for
passing judgment.

She continued, "'I hatched from an egg that my mother dug
in the sand. It took her almost an hour to dig a hole with her back
flippers. The eggs sit under the sand for about two months until it
is time for us to hatch and climb out of our sandy hole. I was one
of over 100 eggs that hatched one summer night.'"

Olivia turned the page. There was a photograph of a baby sea
turtle, newly hatched and crawling toward the ocean in the moonlight.

"'See how I crawl with the rest of the hatchlings toward the
water? I'm only two inches long but I can move quickly!'"

Danny giggled and stroked the picture of the cute turtle with
his hand. "Baby tuh-tuh," he said. He stuck his thumb in his
mouth.

"Yes, a baby turtle. Isn't he cute?" Olivia said, and suddenly
she thought of Chad. He would love to see this book. He collected all kinds of books about interesting animals and species: tree
frogs—because of his pet, Jumper—toads, and even chameleons.

"I have a friend who would like this book," Olivia said as she
flipped through a couple more pages. "But it's a little babyish for
him."

"No baby! Read Tommy!" demanded Danny.

Olivia sighed, knowing she was beaten by a two-year-old.
"Yes, Mr. Turtle Boy. 'My kind of sea turtle is on the threatened
species list,'" she continued reading, "'because every year fewer
turtles lay eggs on the beaches. Sometimes the lights confuse
baby turtles, and we go in the wrong direction and wind up on

the street. Other times, we get caught in fishing nets. People work very hard to help save sea turtles and make sure that dogs or people don't dig us up and harm us.'"

That was sad to think about, people or animals digging up the eggs. Animals she could understand; they didn't know any better. But people? *Animal cruelty is a horrible thing,* she thought.

Olivia finished reading about Tommy the turtle and started another book about a talking rabbit when Mrs. Duggan appeared in the doorway, looking rested and refreshed. "How is my boy doing?" she asked Danny happily.

Danny responded with a big grin and a "Mama!"

Mrs. Duggan laughed. "Looks like you two had a good time. I feel so much better," she said with a stretch. "I should probably change Danny now. Want to see his room?"

They all went upstairs to Danny's room.

"This is a pretty house," Olivia remarked, looking around as they walked.

"It is, but we're just renting it," Mrs. Duggan said. "Someone at my husband's company rents it out to people. We've stayed here for a few years now."

Danny's room had a portable crib and a bunch of toys. "We tried to make it homey for Danny," she said. "The owners let us hang a few pictures so the room would look more cozy for him."

Olivia wandered around the room, looking at the delightful little touches Mr. and Mrs. Duggan had introduced to the otherwise adult room.

On the dresser was a beautiful little statue of the Infant of Prague.

"My mom has this statue on her dresser at home," Olivia said, gently touching the delicate robe of the Infant.

"Oh yes, I've received many graces from the Child Jesus," Mrs. Duggan said fondly.

"The Child Jesus…" Olivia scrunched up her face, thinking hard. "Oh, that was one of the names St. Thérèse used for herself: St. Thérèse of the Child Jesus."

"She had a such a devotion to the Child Jesus," Mrs. Duggan said. "You're Catholic, Olivia—I remember now that Abby said she saw you at Mass!"

"I am, and St. Thérèse is a special friend of mine. My grandma taught me all about her and her Little Way."

"That's wonderful. I pray to her all of the time, and I especially love her devotion to the Child Jesus. I read that she used to place flowers near the statue in the convent, and used to kiss it. She loved him so."

Olivia peered closer at the statue and noticed that the crown on the Infant's head was chipped badly.

"What happened here? Did it fall?"

"Oh, I know," Mrs. Duggan sighed. "Not too long ago, Danny grabbed it and it accidentally fell on the floor." She picked up Danny and kissed his little head. "It's okay; it was an accident, sweetie."

"That's too bad," Olivia said sadly. It was such a beautiful statue.

"I wish I could find another one," said Mrs. Duggan. "I especially love the white lace robe on this one, but I haven't been able to find one just like it."

"Oh look," said Olivia, admiring a colored framed print with a saying on it hanging on the wall. "'A person's a person, no matter how small.' That's from Dr. Seuss."

"Yes," Mrs. Duggan said quietly as she set Danny in the crib. "I love that saying. It's very dear to my heart. It makes me think of God and how much He loves us. Just think about the love God had when He created each one of us, and the plans He had for us as He waited for us to be born, all in His perfect timing."

Olivia looked closer at the picture. "There's a name on here: Gabriel. Who is Gabriel?"

Mrs. Duggan looked out the window at the rainy day, at the

waves crashing angrily ashore. She didn't speak at first, and Olivia didn't know what to do in the silence, so she just stood there awkwardly.

"Gabriel is Danny's brother in Heaven," she said, still looking out at the sea. "God took him before he was born." She turned to look at Olivia and gave her a small smile. "This was four years ago. We named him Gabriel after the angel that visited the Blessed Mother."

Olivia did not know what to say, so she just said, "I'm so sorry, Mrs. Duggan."

Mrs. Duggan grabbed a diaper from the stack and fluffed it open gently. "Thank you, Olivia. We think about him every day and pray to him every night. We want Danny to know about him." She went on to explain that, before she was born, St. Thérèse had siblings that had died very young and used to pray to them all of the time, too, as intercessors from Heaven.

She patted her belly. "If it's a girl we're going to name her Gabriella."

"That's such a pretty name," Olivia remarked, still sad.

Mrs. Duggan noticed Olivia's frown and gave her a little hug. "It's okay; Gabriel is not dead; we believe he's with God now, Olivia, surrounded by the angels and saints, alive in Heaven. He's home and he's safe, for always." Suddenly her eyes got wide. "The baby's kicking! Want to feel?"

Olivia shyly placed her right hand on the spot that Mrs. Duggan was indicating. She felt a series of gentle bumps and kicks and shrieked with delight. "Wow, Mrs. Duggan! This is amazing! She's really doing somersaults in there!"

Mrs. Duggan laughed. "Or he! But I think I have a budding gymnast at any rate, eh?"

Olivia was fascinated. She vaguely remembered her mother letting her feel Lucy kick, but it seemed like such a long time ago. She imagined the little baby, moving around and tumbling, safe and warm inside his or her mother.

"Mrs. Duggan, if you need any girl advice, you can ask me," Olivia said proudly. "I know all about 'em."

Mrs. Duggan laughed again as she started to change Danny's diaper. "I'm sure you do, Olivia! If I think of any questions, I'll let you know."

Mrs. Duggan put Danny on her hip and started out of the room. "There are some cookies and fruit in the kitchen if you're in the mood for a snack," she said, and walked down the hallway toward the bathroom to wash her hands.

Olivia turned to leave the room, but before she did, her eye caught the framed picture once again. She stood there for a minute, staring at Gabriel's name and the Dr. Seuss quote. She thought about the tiny new baby God sent Mr. and Mrs. Duggan, and how, even though the baby was not born yet, he or she was still a human being, with individual fingerprints, toes, eyelashes, and a beating heart—still a person made in the image of God. She said a little prayer for Gabriel and the new baby. Closing the door gently, she left the room.

SIXTEEN

"Charity took possession of my soul and filled me with the spirit of self-forgetfulness, and from that time I was always happy." —St. Thérèse

The next morning, Olivia woke up extra early to the sunshine spilling through the blinds on her window. It was so bright that the window covering could not contain it. The sun sparkled over the Atlantic Ocean, greeting everyone taking early-morning walks on the beach with a bright hello. Olivia watched them from her bedroom window, glad the weather had cleared up. She badly wanted to go to the beach and spend the day at the water.

Olivia read in bed for a little while, wondering what Hayley was doing. She felt the urge to knock on her door to see if she was still asleep. Maybe they could sit on her bed and talk about nothing at all, which is what she loved to do most with Hayley. They always seemed to have fun conversations that made her laugh. But she knew that was not going to happen today. Maybe not ever again; that was how it looked to her.

She tossed her book aside and felt restless. She decided to go downstairs to see who was up. Her mom and dad were in the kitchen starting the coffee maker.

"Morning, Olivia. You're up early today," her dad winked. "Must be the sunshine. Thank goodness it looks like it's going to be a great day."

Olivia nodded and managed a smile. She still felt bad about hurting her dad's feelings yesterday.

Grandma came into the kitchen, holding a newspaper.

"I just went to get the morning paper, and guess who I ran into?" she asked with a grin. She didn't wait for an answer. "That nice girl Abby from next door. We talked for a bit about the ice cream social and rummage sale that the church is having soon."

"Oh, we'll have to make a point of going," said Olivia's mom as she placed an empty cereal bowl and a spoon in front of Olivia at the table. Olivia just stared down at the table. The very mention of going to church made her feel ashamed.

"That's not all," said Grandma. "She invited you and Hayley to the fancy yacht club to go swimming and have lunch today," she said. "How's that sound?"

Olivia looked up quickly at Grandma.

"Who's going?"

"Not Brandon; he's going boating with some other people," Grandma replied with a shrug. "I'm not quite sure about that young man, so all's the better. Do you even want to go?"

Olivia smiled slowly. How fun it would be to spend the day at a fancy yacht club! She wondered what it would be like…should she dress up? Would Hayley even want to go? Were they still friends?

"Who will take us?" wondered Olivia. "Are you and Dad invited?"

"Abby mentioned that Brooke's parents would be staying there all day. What do you think, Steve and Claudia?"

Mr. and Mrs. Thomas talked it over and decided that the girls were old enough to be dropped off at the yacht club for a few hours, but they would have to meet the parents first.

A half hour later, Olivia's mom and dad came back from the house next door.

"Well, I guess that settles it," her mom said. "I sure am glad today's a sunny day."

"They seem like a nice family," her dad said, pleased. "I'll drive you and Hayley there in about an hour. Why don't you go pack your towels and things? I bought some new sun lotion yesterday and I left it in your room."

Olivia was excited. "Great, Dad! I'll go upstairs and tell Hayley. It sounds like she's getting out of the shower."

"This will give you girls a chance to mend things," her mom whispered. "You haven't spent much time with her."

Olivia nodded, hoping her mom was right. As she walked upstairs, she felt a sense of sudden dread, however. She hadn't talked to Hayley since yesterday, and she was nervous to approach her now.

Hayley was coming out of the bathroom with her hair wrapped in a turban and wearing her bathrobe.

"Hi," Olivia said tentatively.

"Hi," said Hayley, her eyes narrowed. "Can I please get by?"

Olivia sighed. "Hayley, come on. It's me. Can't we just forget this?"

Hayley said nothing.

"I promise I won't say anything about…the text," Olivia said hurriedly, to Hayley's surprise—and her own. *What am I saying? Have I decided to just let it go and not tell Mom and Dad?*

"Promise, Olivia?"

"Um…sure. I promise."

"No, I mean *really* promise. Like you mean it."

Olivia rolled her eyes, exasperated. "I really, really promise, Hayley. I give you my word as a friend. I won't tell."

"Good." Hayley smiled slowly, and in that moment, Olivia knew she was forgiven.

She breathed a sigh of relief and quickly told Hayley about the day's plan. "We're leaving an hour from now."

"Great; I'll get my stuff."

"Brandon's not going, though. He already had plans."

"Oh, yeah..." Hayley hesitated, disappointed that Brandon wouldn't be going too. "I guess I forgot that he mentioned going boating. But that sounds slightly fun, actually."

Olivia beamed, relieved that Hayley seemed to be softening up a bit toward her. "Good! My dad's going to drop us off. He just wants you to be sure to bring your cell phone in case we need to call."

Olivia hummed happily to herself as she packed her pool bag with the things she'd need for the day. She spied the lavender shopping bag from *La Bonne Heure* lying on its side on the floor of her closet. Her Swiss spring water! She would definitely have to bring that to the fancy pool today. Happy that she remembered, she stuffed it into the bottom of her bag with her towel and other necessities, her excitement growing stronger. She didn't want her mom to see the expensive water; she'd be full of questions.

She had a nagging feeling she couldn't describe, like she was forgetting something. She double-checked her bag and found everything to be in order: fun misty water, coverup, towel, lotion, swimsuit, and a book. What could she be forgetting? She let out a yawn. She wished she had time for a little nap before going. She was still tired from playing with Danny.

She decided to toss her wallet into her bag, just in case she needed some cash. As she grabbed her purse, she froze, suddenly realizing what the nagging feeling was: Mrs. Duggan had her lined up to work today! In all of the commotion with Hayley, she had totally forgotten that she was due next door to watch Danny in an hour! Her heart sank.

The thought of missing a fun day at Brooke and Brandon's fancy yacht club was devastating. Abby had said they were going to have lunch by the pool and everything! She let out a loud, heavy sigh and sat down on the edge of her bed. She buried her head in her hands and felt like crying. It wasn't that she didn't want to play with Danny and help Mrs. Duggan out, but compared to a luxurious day at the yacht club, well…the choice, unfortunately, was obvious.

But what to do about it? She would feel horrible canceling on Mrs. Duggan at the last minute. Deep down, she knew Mrs. Duggan was counting on her to come. She thought back to the conversation they'd had the day before. Mrs. Duggan's doctor had told her that she should be getting more rest. She had been so relieved to find out that Olivia was free to come and watch Danny so she could nap.

Olivia's heart felt heavy. She knew she had to honor her commitment with Mrs. Duggan, but things had been going so wrong lately. It would be so nice to get away from everything and get a change of scenery to cheer her up. She began to feel a little sorry for herself. This vacation wasn't turning out to be very fun at all. Sometimes she found herself wishing she hadn't even come. She trembled a little and felt tears begin to sting her eyes at the thought of missing a fun day at the pool. Maybe they would be invited over again, she tried to console herself.

She heard a knock at the door and looked up to see Hayley enter.

"Hi," she said shyly, her hand on the doorknob. "Um, do you have room in your bag for a couple of my things, do you think?" she asked with a small smile.

Olivia didn't know what to say. Her heart warmed to see Hayley being so nice to her. She would feel just terrible if she had to admit that she couldn't go now, just when they were slowly starting to patch things up.

"Oh, and I'll bring some nail polish so we can do our toes," Hayley said hopefully. "If you want."

This sealed the deal. She was back in Hayley's good graces for sure now.

Olivia grinned. "Sure!" she said happily.

When Hayley left to get her things, Olivia started to fret. She absolutely hated to do this to Mrs. Duggan, but she couldn't possibly miss out on a fun time at the yacht club now. She thought of telling Mrs. Duggan the truth, but the truth sounded so shallow when she practiced it in her head that she dismissed that idea. Somehow, "I know I told you I'd help you out today, but I'd rather go to the pool with my friends" sounded self-centered, now matter how she worded it.

Hayley came back to Olivia's room and put a towel and some sunglasses into her bag.

"Hayley, can I use your phone for a sec?" asked Olivia. She didn't want to use the house phone in her parents' room, just in case they overheard her conversation. She absolutely did not want them to hear her call Mrs. Duggan and cancel. If they knew she had a prior obligation, there was no way they would let her go to the pool. They had always taught Olivia to keep her promises and honor her commitments.

Not too long ago she had pleaded with her parents to let her play the flute. Her mom had found her a nice teacher and prepaid for weekly lessons. Olivia tired of the flute after six weeks, complaining that she didn't like to practice. Her teacher finally told Olivia that she was wasting her parents' money if she refused to practice, and that he wouldn't come over anymore if that was going to be the case. Olivia had begged her mother to let her quit, but Mrs. Thomas made her continue until she had finished all of the lessons she had paid for, telling her she just needed to give it time, that she wanted to give up too early.

And she couldn't forget the soccer team she'd joined and grew tired of...well, she was starting to notice a pattern, unfortunately. Which made her feel all the more guilty about what she was about to do.

"Sure, who are you calling?" Hayley asked.

"I have to call Mrs. Duggan to ask her something," Olivia said, which was sort of true...well, maybe not quite. She wasn't planning to *ask* her anything, really. More like tell her.

Hayley tossed her the phone and said, "Okay, I'll be downstairs. But hurry up; I can't wait to go!"

Olivia nodded and said she'd only be a minute. She rummaged through her purse and found Mrs. Duggan's phone number and dialed it with trembling fingers.

"Hello?" Mrs. Duggan answered tiredly after a few rings.

"Hi Mrs. Duggan," Olivia said, trying her best to make her voice sound small and weak. She felt very sneaky.

"Oh, Olivia!" her voice brightened up. "It's you! I'm very relieved you're coming today. I'm so exhausted. Danny kept me up all night. He had a couple of bad dreams, poor thing, and I could fall asleep right now. But I do have some bills to write and a bathroom to clean while you're here," she laughed. "What's up?"

Olivia swallowed hard. This was going to be harder than she thought.

"Oh no, well...um...the reason I'm calling is that...I'm sort of sick," she said. The lie felt horrible coming from her own voice. She gulped again and let out a little fake cough to prove her point.

There was a long pause, and then a disappointed sigh. "Oh dear, I'm sorry to hear that, Olivia. Did you catch a cold?"

"Yes...Yes, I think I did," she said, and coughed again for good measure.

"Oh, well…you do sound bad. Maybe it was from all that rain we had," she said sadly. "A change in weather can do that."

Olivia was silent, not knowing what to say.

"I suppose you're calling to tell me you can't come," Mrs. Duggan said, disappointed. "That's okay, dear. You stay home and rest. Maybe sit on the deck. The sunshine will do you good, I'm sure."

This was torture. Mrs. Duggan was being so nice, and genuinely cared about her. The lie she was telling felt dirty and wrong. But she was ensconced in it now; there was no turning back.

She coughed again, for lack of a good response.

"Oh I bet you feel lousy," Mrs. Duggan kept on talking. "You take good care of yourself, Olivia, okay?"

Olivia said she would do that and hung up.

Mrs. Duggan was right. She did feel lousy.

SEVENTEEN

"*Jesus, the Doctor of all doctors, teaches without
words....I have never heard Him speak but I know He is
inside me. At each and every moment, He guides me to do
what I must do.*" —*St. Thérèse*

The Beacon Yacht Club stood out like an antique jewel against
the Atlantic Ocean. As they approached the club, Olivia marveled
at the majestic bell tower rising into the deep blue sky.

"It must be a navigational aid for boaters," her dad said, obviously impressed. "What a beautiful old building."

Mr. Thomas pulled the car into the gate and stopped at a guard
shack. He rolled down his window to speak to the attendant.

"These girls are guests of the Danshurys," he said, and, after checking his clipboard, the guard nodded, letting them drive
in. As they pulled up to the circle driveway, Olivia and Hayley
gasped at the sight of the main building, with its beautiful red tile
roof. Behind the main building she could see a marina with large
yachts bobbing up and down in the water.

To Olivia and Hayley's surprise, Brooke bounded out of the
main doors in pink short-shorts, a tank top, and matching flip-

flops. Abby was next to her, wearing a blue and white floral skirt and a white sleeveless top.

Olivia instantly regretted her choice of a white sundress. Hayley, too, looked down at her own outfit, displeased.

"You think we're too dressed up?" Olivia whispered, panicked, wishing she hadn't listened to Grandma earlier. *Grandma's old-fashioned*, she thought. *Nobody dresses up anymore.*

"I don't know much about the country-club set," Grandma had said with tight lips when she saw Olivia on the stairs, "but one thing I do know is that jeans are a big no-no at these places. Eleanor Bingley from the senior center goes to her son's club for dinner sometimes and is always talking about the dress code there. She said one time someone came in with jeans on and they practically threw her out into the street!" Grandma emphasized this with a giant wave of her arm.

Olivia had rolled her eyes. "Oh Grandma, I think you're exaggerating. They can't throw someone out for wearing jeans."

"Oh no? They can't? Well, no granddaughter of mine is going to find out the hard way. How you dress says a lot about who you are and what you stand for. And don't you roll your eyes at me, young lady. Go upstairs and put something else on."

Olivia, who knew when she was beaten, trudged back upstairs to change out of her jean shorts.

"And make sure Hayley's dressed appropriately, too," Grandma had called after her.

Now Olivia sent a silent plea to God so that they'd all fit in and have a good time today, then felt guilty. Talking to God so happily after what she'd done this morning to nice Mrs. Duggan seemed shameful. And what would St. Thérèse, her special close friend, say about her behavior? Thérèse, who went about her daily work without complaint while she was ill, who washed windows while feverish and weak, who made it a point to think of others' needs before her own? What would she say about a twelve-year-old girl who made a commitment to help out a tired, expectant mother and broke it to have fun at a swanky club? She shook her head to get it all out of her mind. She'd have to make amends somehow. She would, really. After today.

"You're here!" Abby cried happily as she opened the car door.

"Hi Mr. Thomas," said Brooke, eycing the outfits of Olivia and Hayley. "Mom and Dad are inside talking to some friends in the Breakers Lounge."

"That's okay," he said good-naturedly. "We chatted this morning." He looked at the girls as they got out of the car.

"So…Brandon went boating today?" Hayley asked of Brooke. "You didn't want to go too?" Olivia shot Hayley a look. *Why does Hayley have to be so obvious that she doesn't like Brooke?* Olivia thought irritably. *Brooke isn't so bad.*

"Nope," Brooke chirped. "I thought it would be more fun to come to the club. I'm bored with boats."

Mr. Thomas smiled at the girls. "Do you have everything? I'll pick you up about five o'clock, okay? Have fun and stay with Brooke's parents."

The girls all waved as Mr. Thomas drove away, climbing the entrance steps.

"You guys are a little overdressed. It's casual here at BYC," Brooke said to Olivia with a small smile.

Olivia blushed. She so badly wanted to fit in today and impress Abby and Brooke. She was mortified.

She wished she could talk to Sabrina back home, who would know about situations like these. Sabrina sccmed to always know how to dress for every occasion. When Olivia showed up in jeans, Sabrina had on dressy slacks. When Olivia chose to wear a skirt, Sabrina would have on cargo pants. She just couldn't win. Something told her that Sabrina would have known exactly what to wear to the yacht club today.

Brooke paused. "I guess you're okay," she said lightly, and glanced at Hayley. "After all, you're only *guests*."

Hayley's eyes narrowed. "Hmm…Brooke, I wonder why your parents didn't mention anything to Olivia's mom and dad this morning when they talked," she shot back. "Seems like *that* would have been the perfect time to inform us poor kids about the dress code."

Olivia's eyes grew wide with embarrassment. "Well, actually, our club back home is much more formal," Olivia lied, trying to cover up—and much to Hayley's shock. "But maybe since we're here at the beach, it's more casual."

Brooke nodded a smile of approval. "Come to think of it, Olivia, it's the same way back home for me, too."

Olivia sighed quietly, relieved to have passed another all-important test. She noticed a funny look come over Abby's face.

Brooke simply chose to ignore Hayley's comment and walked on ahead, leading the way. "Follow me to the ladies' room," she said importantly.

"Hayley!" hissed Olivia, careful to make sure that the rest were out of earshot. What was Hayley thinking, with her "poor kids" comment?

"Stop it!" said Olivia, sounding like her own mother when she was tired and had had enough of Olivia's antics. "Do you want to be here or not?" she scolded, then felt bad for doing so.

"Olivia, you are unbelievable, you know that? The only club you belong to is the Spanish club at school!"

Olivia gave her a sarcastic smirk, but said nothing.

Abby walked back to where Olivia and Hayley were.

"Don't worry," Abby whispered to Olivia and Hayley. "You two are fine. We're going to change into our swimsuits now anyway." She said this with a warm smile.

Olivia smiled gratefully and admired the halls, which were adorned with old maritime trophies and photographs. Glass cases ran along the wall, with nostalgic items and souvenirs from the yacht club's past.

"I've been here a bunch of times and no one cares. You can wear what you want," Abby whispered. "The only place that's formal is this restaurant," she said, pointing to a fancy dining room they were passing. Above the double doors on the wood-paneled room was a sign: The Anchor Room.

Olivia slowed down to peer inside and saw the room decorated with white chair covers, pink and blue linen tablecloths, and arrangements of beautiful flowers.

"Oh," Olivia said, pleased. "Looks like they're setting up for a baby shower." She had been to several of her cousins' baby showers with her mom and grandma.

Hayley stopped for a closer look and tentatively stepped inside, admiring the pretty room that looked out at the marina.

"What a gorgeous view," she said as she looked at the sailboats lined up in their slips.

"Don't you just love babies?" Abby asked. "My friend's mom just had a baby boy named Nicholas," she said as they looked over the beautifully decorated room. "I got to go to the shower and help with the presents."

"Wouldn't it be fun to have a shower here?" Olivia wondered aloud. "It's so fancy and pretty."

An expectant mother walked in just then, carrying a large bag.

"Oh hello, girls," she said as she struggled with the heavy bag and looked for a place to set it down.

"Do you need some help?" offered Olivia, holding out her arms so the lady could hand over the bag.

"Oh, thank you, but it's really kind of bulky. Just some favors for the shower. My mother is bringing in the rest of the things," she said, craning her neck toward the hallway. "I wonder where she can be?"

Brooke came in just then, looking perturbed. "I was wondering where you were," she snapped. "We're not supposed to be in here."

The pretty mom-to-be motioned them all inside further. "Oh no, I don't mind if you have a look around. Isn't it lovely? The club has done such a nice job." She ran her fingers along the napkins, which were folded into flowers.

"Would you like some help setting up the favors?" asked Olivia, who badly wanted to stay.

The lady looked startled at first, then smiled. "Oh, you are so sweet for offering. Actually, I could use a little help with these favors. The shower will be starting soon and it will take me forever on my own and I haven't found any of the workers. Are you sure you girls wouldn't mind?"

Hayley shook her head. "Of course not. I'm Hayley, this is Olivia, and Abby, and Brooke," she said.

"Well, I'm delighted to meet you all. I'm Mrs. Linden, and this is Baby Elizabeth. She's due in six weeks," she said, rubbing her belly. She looked distant and faraway at that moment. "My little blessing."

"Congratulations," Olivia said, feeling touched. "How can we help?"

Mrs. Linden opened the big shopping bag and pulled out a cream-colored candle wrapped in tulle and tied with a pink bow.

"See these candles? One goes at each place setting," she said, putting one to her nose and inhaling deeply. She offered one to Olivia.

"Mmm," said Olivia. "Vanilla, my favorite."

"Me too," said Mrs. Linden with a grin. "I hope everyone likes them."

Brooke sighed, obviously unhappy with the way things were going. She wanted to get to the pool, and helping some lady set up for her baby shower was not part of the day's plans. She reluctantly picked up a couple of candles and set them down on one of the tables.

The girls followed suit, each taking some candles and walking around the room, placing them on the tables. Mrs. Linden slowly walked over to a chair and sat down with a sigh. She looked tired and grateful for their help. It didn't take the girls long to complete the task for her.

An older lady entered the room just as they were finishing up. "Oh, it does look pretty," she said to Mrs. Linden.

"It wasn't me, Mom, it was these four girls who did the work," she said gratefully. "I just met them and I put them all to work! What must they think of me?" she laughed.

"Well aren't you all sweet?" the older lady said approvingly. "My daughter is so tired these days, and it's hard for me to move around with my arthritis," she said. "Are you members of the club?"

"I am," Brooke piped up. "These are my friends and we were on our way to the pool," she said impatiently, eager to secure lounge chairs before it got too crowded.

"Oh, of course. We won't take up any more of your time," Mrs. Linden said graciously as she reached into the bag. "We have some candles left over. Would you each like one? Thank you so much for your little way of helping."

The girls were happy to accept their candles from Mrs. Linden.

Mrs. Linden took Olivia aside and waited for the rest of the girls to leave the room. "Thank you again, Olivia," said Mrs. Linden. Her face had a faraway look just then. "I want you to know how much your little act of kindness means to me. Things haven't been easy. Not too long ago, I found out that my baby has Down syndrome," she said.

Olivia's eyes widened. "Oh, Mrs. Linden...I'm so sorry to hear that..."

Mrs. Linden smiled and stared out the window. "My baby is a blessing. My husband and I have been praying for so long to be parents, and now we are. She's the best thing that's ever happened to us."

Mrs. Linden turned from the window and handed Olivia another candle.

"Thank you for being so nice."

Olivia's face turned red and she was filled with shame. She nodded and said a quick goodbye. Then she hurried out of the room and down the hallway.

"Hurry up, guys," hissed Brooke, who had been waiting impatiently. She started walking quickly down the hall. "We've wasted enough time already."

"I don't think it was a waste of time," said Abby, and Hayley agreed.

Olivia adjusted the bag on her shoulder and tried to keep up the pace as they walked down the hallway.

"Did you hear what Mrs. Linden said?" whispered Hayley, who was trying to forget about their little argument in the hallway earlier.

"What?"

"Little way. She said 'little way of helping,'" Hayley gave a knowing smile and a gentle elbowing. "St. Thérèse likes to pop up in the most interesting ways, huh?"

Olivia stared straight ahead as she walked, thinking of Mrs. Duggan and Mrs. Linden, both about to have babies. She felt even more terrible about ditching Mrs. Duggan after hearing Mrs. Linden's story. Mrs. Linden had been so grateful for her help.

She thinks I'm such a nice person, Olivia thought. *What would she think if she knew how I bailed on Mrs. Duggan when she needed me?*

Mrs. Duggan, who was so friendly and who cared enough to give her a chance at her first real job. And she had let her down.

"Oh, I don't know," said Olivia, her good mood gone at the very thought of herself following Thérèse's Little Way. As if the Little Way was something sinners like her could follow—someone who lied to her new friends, disobeyed her parents, and betrayed someone who was counting on her and needed her help. After the terrible things she had done, St. Thérèse certainly couldn't be nudging her now, or wanting to be a part of her life. St. Thérèse was the epitome of goodness and kindness in her mind; a selfless person who never thought of herself. *I, on the other hand, am nothing like her. No matter how hard I try, I'll never be like her.*

Olivia shrugged her shoulders. "It was probably just a coincidence."

Hayley looked at Olivia, confusion and surprise written all over her face.

"Olivia…come on. Coincidence? No way."

Olivia walked faster. "Don't you think we should be trying to keep up with them?" Olivia was angry at herself for the way she was acting, but not able to stop herself.

Hayley frowned. "Yeah, I know all about how you're trying to keep up with them," she said sadly, but Olivia didn't hear her.

ᵉEIGHTEEN

"Joy isn't found in the material objects surrounding us, but in the inner recesses of the soul. One can possess joy in a prison cell as well as in a palace."—St. Thérèse

"What a beautiful place," Olivia said, tremendously impressed as she put up her hair in a ponytail. The girls were sprawled out on pool lounges with soft, navy blue cushions. Abby was painting her toenails a hot pink color and waving her hand to dry them.

"Sometimes when it rains, we go to the bowling alley downstairs," Brooke said, taking a sip of bottled water. "But it's only got three lanes."

Olivia thought that three lanes sounded just fine to her, but said nothing.

Nearby, members played tennis on one of the clay tennis courts. Straight ahead, the view of the harbor was breathtaking, and a large fleet of club-owned sailboats rocked gently to and fro, bearing the initials "BYC," an anchor intertwined with the letters.

It was a glorious, sunny day, and Olivia began to feel at peace for the first time in a while. She closed her eyes and lay back, letting the sun drench her from head to toe, enjoying the faint sounds of tennis balls being hit back and forth and the distant hums of boat motors coming into the marina. She let all of her worries dissipate, imagining the tide sweeping them all away. All that mattered was right here, right now: the sun on her face, the soft lounge chairs, the sounds of the people enjoying themselves at the yacht club.

Olivia casually rolled over, reached into her pool bag, and pulled out her bottle of *L'Eau de Suisse*. She uncapped it and started spritzing her face.

"What on earth?" Hayley asked as she watched Olivia water herself from head to toe. "What are you, a houseplant? My mom has something like that for her philodendron."

Olivia smirked. "Very funny, Hayley. This happens to be spring water from the Swiss Alps. It's very refreshing. Try some," she urged her.

"What's the difference?"

"Oh, there's a difference," Brooke assured Hayley, getting in on the conversation. "Olivia doesn't want tap water on her face. It would ruin her nice complexion!"

"Yeah," Olivia said, running the backs of her fingers along her cheek, feeling proud that Brooke thought she had a nice complexion. "I don't ever want pimples."

"She has peaches-and-cream skin, a natural beauty," Brooke said authoritatively. "She can't jeopardize that."

Yeah, thought Olivia, *I do have really nice skin, don't I?* She blushed with the realization that she could possibly be a natural beauty, like Brooke had said. Why not? She felt very flattered.

Hayley took the can from Olivia and examined it. Her jaw dropped. "Thirteen dollars? You paid thirteen dollars for a can of water?"

Olivia snatched the can back. "A little goes a long way. It'll last a long time," she snapped.

Abby nodded. "It's true," she said. "I still have mine from last summer."

Olivia sighed and lay back on her chair, closing her eyes. *Leave it to Hayley to not understand and ruin everything.*

Hayley leaned back too, and the conversation ended, neither one understanding the other.

Olivia felt very trendy, hanging out at the fancy yacht club pool, spritzing herself with a can of water from Switzerland. A couple of girls about her age walked by in two-piece suits, and she noticed them looking at her for an extra long time as they passed. Olivia smiled and tried to look as cool as she could, enjoying feeling pretty and rich. She wondered if they were also admiring her "peaches and cream skin." She couldn't help feeling a twinge of guilt for being so prideful, though.

She thought back to a story Grandma had told her about the time when Thérèse went to the seaside with her family as a young girl. Passersby stopped to ask her father if the pretty girl running about on the sand was his daughter. Thérèse was pleased to overhear this, secretly believing she was, indeed, pretty. When she studied at a tutor's house as a teenager, visitors would comment on the pretty girl with the light brown hair, which she was happy to hear. An aunt had even given her a beautiful blue hair ribbon to wear, which delighted her until she began to feel guilty for thinking so highly of herself, saying that these things would have made her vain if God had not taken her out of the world and into the cloistered convent.

Olivia started to feel a little guilty about being vain herself, but she was having too much fun to stop. *Besides, if St. Thérèse had once felt the same way, it must be okay*, she told herself.

Brooke needn't have worried about the crowds; the pool area was relatively empty except for a couple of families splashing in the shallow end of the pool. Nearby was a gazebo that housed a snack bar, which served fruit smoothies and sandwiches.

"Are your parents coming outside?" Olivia asked.

Brooke shook her head. "Nah, they'll spend all afternoon in the Breakers Lounge talking about the 'good old days.'"

"What does that mean, the 'good old days'?"

"Oh, when it wasn't so easy to become a member here," she scoffed. "Now they practically let *anyone* in."

Olivia looked down at her unpolished toes. *I wonder if they'd let my family in,* she wondered. *Oh who cares, anyway? We're here to have fun. Just forget about it.*

Hayley opened her mouth to say something, then closed it when Olivia shot her a look to keep quiet. They were, after all, guests of Brooke's.

Olivia reached up to adjust her towel, and accidentally scraped her hand on a little plastic flag atop her lounge chair.

"That's odd," Olivia said. "What is the flag for?"

Brooke rolled her eyes and scoffed. "Don't they do this at your club?" she asked impatiently.

"Brooke!" Abby snapped, then turned to Olivia. "You put the flag up when you want one of the servers to come to you, like this…" and she demonstrated by putting up the flag on her own chair.

It wasn't long before a young woman in a polo shirt and shorts came up to them with an order pad. "Hello, girls. Can I get you anything?" she asked brightly.

Brooke held up her hand, taking over. "I'm thirsty. I could use a Coke," she said, then turned to the rest of the girls. "Go ahead, order what you want. It's on my parents anyway."

The girls gratefully ordered Cokes and lemonades and settled back into their chairs to soak up the hot sun.

"How weird," Hayley whispered to Olivia. "Why get served when there is a snack bar right over there we could just walk over to?"

"I don't know," Olivia whispered back, "but it seems more fun this way." She arranged the table next to her so there would be room for the drinks when they came. "Oh Hayley, isn't this the life? I could do this every day." Olivia grinned from ear to ear.

"It isn't bad," Hayley admitted, looking about at the beautiful, glistening pool with its blue water and kids splashing happily. She lowered her voice. "But I feel sort of weird here."

"Not me," Olivia said as she got out her earbuds to listen to some music. "Actually, I feel right at home."

The server came back with a tray carrying the girls' drinks and set them down on their individual tables. Each drink had a paper umbrella and a wedge of lemon on the side of the glass. "Let me know if you need anything else," she said cheerfully.

Hayley took a sip of her Coke and whispered to Olivia, "Yeah, with rich people it's all about what they feel they *need*," she said with a giggle, hoping Olivia would join in. She picked out the paper umbrella and set it on the table, eyebrows raised.

Olivia stirred the straw in her lemonade and took a sip. "I think I need to do my toenails," she said, wiggling them.

"Okay," Hayley said, sitting so she could reach her bag. "I brought some of my nail polish."

"Or you can use mine," Abby said, holding up her own bottle.

"Sure," said Olivia, happily taking Abby's bottle. She saw Hayley's surprised expression and said, "Well...it's just that I sort of like Abby's color, you know?"

Hayley's face fell. "Sure. This color's kind of dark anyway."

"Hot pink's the new color," Brooke said knowingly as she took a sip of her Coke. "No one wears red anymore."

Olivia and Abby laughed as Olivia painted her toes hot pink. Hayley, having had enough, excused herself to go to the ladies' room.

"Let me know when you get bored," Brooke said. "We can walk around the pro shop."

"Oh, what do they have there?" Olivia asked interestedly.

"Lots of stuff," Brooke said. "BYC sweatshirts—Oh! You should get one—and purses and clothes."

"It's kind of pricey but they have some nice things," Abby admitted.

Brooke glanced at Olivia's swimsuit. "You know," she said with a smile, "the shop has some really cute swimsuits. You should think about getting a new suit."

"Why?" asked Abby. "Olivia's suit is just fine."

"Well," Brooke said, screwing the top back onto the nail polish bottle. "I mean, it just seems a little grannyish, being a one-piece."

"Brooke!" cried Abby angrily. "That's not true!"

Olivia bit her lip and looked down at her one-piece suit. What a pain it was to have to wear something just because your mother told you to. She remembered asking her mother earlier in the summer for a two-piece, but her mother shook her head, saying they were immodest.

Abby continued, "Olivia, your suit is fine. Don't listen to Brooke."

Olivia appreciated Abby's kindness, but she didn't want a swimsuit that was just "fine." She wanted something really cute and trendy, like the rest of the girls at the pool had. She shuddered, suddenly realizing why the girls who had just passed by had been looking at her for an extra long time. They weren't admiring her "peaches and cream" skin; they were staring at a girl who had the wrong kind of swimsuit!

"It would be fun to look around the store," she said coyly, glad she had thought to bring her wallet along. How fun would that be, to have a new swimsuit and a BYC sweatshirt to wear back home? Her parents would never have to know about the suit; she'd hide it really well. And she'd be the only one she knew who had a real sweatshirt from a fancy yacht club.

Hayley came back and flopped back onto her beach chair, looking thoroughly bored. She let out a large sigh.

"Hey, do you like the Tyler Twins?" Abby asked, trying to change the subject.

"Yeah, I'm listening to them right now!" Olivia cried, and she and Abby started to giggle. "What are the odds of that?"

Hayley frowned. "Yeah," she said jealously, "I mean, they're only the most popular band on the planet; what *are* the odds?"

The other girls didn't hear her, or didn't care. "What song are you listening to?" asked Abby.

"*Ella Don't Cry.*"

"Omigosh! I *love* that song! They opened with that one when we saw them in concert last month."

Olivia's eyes grew wide. "YOU SAW THEM IN CONCERT?"

Brooke leaned over and said, "Yeah, they kicked off their national tour in Boston. Our seats were right up front and my dad got us backstage passes."

Backstage passes? Was Brooke actually saying that…

"Greg, the shorter one, was so nice," Brooke rambled on. "I got my picture taken with them. Wanna see?" And with that, Brooke pulled out her cell phone and lit the screen so everyone could see, holding it up.

Olivia took the phone from her and stared at the photo as if in a trance. There was Greg Tyler, lead singer for the Tyler Twins, with his arms around Brooke, Abby, and Brandon. He looked all sweaty from performing and everyone had huge grins on their faces. Greg's brother Sean was on the end of the group, holding a bottle of water, his long blond hair in his face. In the background were lots of people sitting on sofas in what must have been the Tyler Twins' dressing room.

"He drinks water!" Olivia cried. "What was it like?"

Hayley snorted. "Big deal! Everyone drinks water!"

"Yeah, but he drinks *Rocky Springs* water," Olivia said dreamily. "From now on, all I will ever drink will be Rocky Springs water."

"Good luck with that," Hayley said, laughing.

Abby grinned. "They were really cool," she said. "I didn't expect them to be so nice."

Hayley reached out for Brooke's phone and stared at the picture in awe. "How did your dad ever manage to score backstage passes?"

Brooke shrugged her shoulders. "He knows people. We've seen lots of music stars backstage. Last year I got to meet MacKenzie. No big deal."

Olivia shook her head, not believing she was hearing this: a girl who was able to meet big-name international singers like the Tyler Twins and MacKenzie. And she was so nonchalant about it. It was too much.

"Their new album just came out," announced Brooke.

"Oh yeah, 'LOL, I Love You'!" cried Olivia. "I want that one!"

"Just download it to your laptop," Brooke said simply. "No biggie."

Olivia nodded, as if that was exactly what she was going to do. Except for one problem: She didn't have her own laptop. Well, no one needed to know that.

Hayley handed Brooke's cell phone back to her.

"Who wants lunch?" Brooke asked, pulling her sunglasses on top of her head.

"I'm starved!" said Olivia, and reached over to put her lounge chair flag up.

Abby and Brooke did the same with their flags.

"I could go for a cheeseburger with fries," Brooke said.

"Me too!" Abby and Olivia said in unison, then laughed loudly and pointed at each other. "Jinx!"

Brooke looked over at Hayley. "What about you, Hayley?"

"You know, I'm not all that hungry," she said, hurt in her eyes.

Then she tossed her bottle of nail polish back into her bag. It wasn't like anyone would be wanting it.

NINETEEN

*"I beseech You, my Divine Jesus, to send me a humiliation
every time I try to place myself above others."*
—St. Thérèse

Around dinnertime, the rain came back again, much to the
disappointment of the Thomas family, fiercely hitting the over-
sized windows in sheets. The beach was lonely and deserted.
Even the normally squawking seagulls stayed away, hiding until
better weather came.

"Livvy, want to come help me with dinner?" Grandma asked
as she came into the living room, holding an empty baking dish.
Olivia was sitting on the couch with Aunt Peggy's lap desk, writing out her postcard to Chad. She was wearing her new yellow
BYC sweatshirt since the rain made the day feel damp. The storm
put Olivia in a bit of a funk, and she was finding it hard to disguise her gloomy mood as she wrote to Chad.

"As soon as I'm done writing this postcard," she said. Grandma
nodded and went back into the kitchen, humming an old Italian
song from way back when. Olivia had heard that song hundreds
of times throughout her life, and it always brought a comforting
sound to her ears.

Dear Chad,

We're having a great time! Wish you were here! Ha ha, I know you didn't want me to write clichés. We went to a fun beach party for July 4, next week we're going to an aquarium, and we have been swimming a lot in the ocean. No, I didn't go fishing or run into any sharks—yet.

I got a mother's helper job with a family here. I am watching a one-year-old boy named Danny. Hopefully I can earn lots of money for that idea I told you about. Hey, he's got a book on baby sea turtles you would like! LOL

Hayley says "Hi!"

See you in a few weeks,

Olivia

Olivia reread her postcard and frowned. It wasn't all that interesting or funny, but at least the picture part was. She just wasn't in a funny mood, what with the dreary day and the guilt she was feeling over Mrs. Duggan. Also, she felt Hayley pulling away again. Olivia was confused; she thought things were looking up ever since she'd promised not to tattle on Hayley to her parents. Yet something was up again; Hayley had been distant all day long, especially at the yacht club.

She capped her pen and tucked the postcard into her purse to stamp and mail later.

In the kitchen, Grandma was taking chicken pieces out of the refrigerator and preparing a big baking dish.

Grandma began to unwrap the chicken from the package. "I'm not sure they'd serve my chicken recipe at your posh yacht club," Grandma said with a smirk, "but it would be their loss!"

Olivia laughed. "Oh Grandma, you should have seen it! It was so pretty and fancy," she gushed. "There was a waitress by the pool that waited on us and brought us lunch. I wish we could join something like that at home. Brooke is so lucky," she said wistfully.

"New sweatshirt? It looks nice and cozy."

Olivia blushed. It had cost almost $50. When she saw it hanging in the pro shop, Brooke held it up to her and squealed.

"It will look so great on you!" she cried. "And it's the last one left in your size!"

Olivia stood in the dressing room and admired her reflection in the mirror. She had to admit: She looked super cute in it.

She shyly opened the dressing-room door to show Brooke.

"That's the one, the yellow!" Brooke had cried. "And it goes perfect with your dark hair. Buy it!"

Olivia had nodded with a smile. "I know, I thought the same thing!"

Brooke handed her a pair of short-shorts. "Try these on. Super cute. They have the name of the club on the back."

One look at the shorts Brooke was holding up and Olivia knew they were way too short. The writing was right on the seat of the shorts. Her parents would never approve. But she didn't want to admit this to Brooke.

"Come on, I have the same ones. Try them on," Brooke urged.

Olivia couldn't say no. Reluctantly, she took the shorts from Brooke.

"Don't you care what my opinion is?" Hayley wanted to know.

Olivia didn't want to know because she knew what Hayley's opinion was. It was obvious from the frown on her face.

Olivia tried to close the door so she could change, but Hayley nudged her aside and moved into the dressing room, closing the door in Brooke's face.

"Are you crazy?" she whispered. "Your parents will kill you!"

Olivia waved her off. "They're not going to know," she said, exasperated.

"Who is this strange girl?" Hayley asked the air around her. "Gee, I don't know," she answered herself back.

"You're talking to yourself, and *I'm* strange? And who's planning on sneaking out tonight?"

"Olivia, let's try this again," Hayley said almost too patiently. "Let's think back to fifth grade when you got your ears pierced against your parents' wishes and got grounded for a month. Ring a bell?"

Truthfully, Olivia did have a pit in her stomach at the thought of disobeying her parents. But look what happened when she listened to older people; she had listened to Grandma earlier and had overdressed for the club and felt silly. She knew her parents meant well, but they just didn't get what it was like in her generation. The sweatshirt, though expensive at $49, was really cool and the shorts were trendy and fashionable. Olivia felt like she didn't own anything trendy. It would be fun to have something cool like the other girls wore. How she would actually find a way to wear them was another story...one she'd just figure out later.

She glanced at the shorts. She'd heard enough of the Thomas family "modesty speeches" to know that her parents and grandma would disapprove of them instantly.

"Hayley," Olivia whined, "you just don't get it."

"Oh, I get it all right. And you're going to get it from your parents if they see you wearing those. And guess what? You buy all of this...junk...and you'll have nothing left for The Project. Remember The Project? Don't you even care?"

Her savings were dwindling fast. She'd already spent almost $75 in Keane Harbor so far, and on things she didn't need.

Torn, Olivia held the sweatshirt in her hands and felt the soft, velvety fabric between her fingers. It was so soft, and she knew she'd love to wear it on cold days and in the winter. And what a nice souvenir it would be! Then she picked up the pair of shorts and admired them. They were just like all the cool girls were wearing, with sayings on the bottom. This pair said, "BYC Diva" in pink glittery writing. It would be fun to be a diva, right? But what did it mean?

"You've bought enough souvenirs already," Hayley said, reading her mind. She began to tick them off on her fingers: "Taffy, a shell necklace, shell earrings, that shark keychain, and that dolphin magnet…"

Olivia had glared at her, annoyed at her photographic memory. "What are you, my mother? And the taffy isn't for me; it's for Chad, so you can't count that. It's a present. You sure remember everything I've bought so far. What about you? You've gotten tons of stuff."

Yeah, what about you, Hayley? Olivia thought angrily. *You're so high and mighty about disobeying my parents; look what you are planning to do by sneaking out tonight!*

"I've bought stuff, but it's all stuff I can *afford*!" Hayley said, and then realized her mistake too late.

That did it. "Out," Olivia shooed Hayley out of the room. "So I can change."

Then she felt that voice she was beginning to know so well.

Your dignity is a gift from God.

A few moments later, Olivia brought the sweatshirt and shorts to the counter and handed them both to the young salesgirl.

"You're lucky; you got the last pair of these shorts," the lady chirped as she admired them. "Shall I put this all on your club tab?" Once again, Olivia felt St. Thérèse gently whisper in her heart. **While on this earth, we must be attached to nothing, not even to the most innocent things, for they will fail us when we least expect it.**

It was from one of the books she owned that contained quotations from St. Thérèse. She'd read it many times and truly believed it, until now, when all of the lovely things in the store beckoned her.

Olivia shook her head. "Um, no thank you," Olivia murmured as she peeled out bills from her wallet—money for The Project. "I've got cash."

But now, back at home with Grandma and her parents, her purchases didn't seem to make a whole lot of sense. There was absolutely no way her parents—or Grandma—would let her walk around in short-shorts with writing on the behind. Olivia winced, remembering, but then ran her hand along the appliqué on the sweatshirt. It was an anchor entwined with the initials BYC. She thought wistfully of the fancy yacht club. "I'd give anything to belong there."

"Huh." Grandma rinsed the chicken pieces under running water and cocked her head. "Wish you were rich, hmmm?" Grandma's wrinkled hands patted the chicken dry with paper towels and set them aside on a plate. Grandma was very methodical while she cooked and never seemed to get flustered.

Olivia thought about that for a moment. "Sure, why not?" she shrugged her shoulders. "Everyone wants to be rich."

"Well, that all depends," Grandma said, picking up a chicken leg.

"On what, Grandma?"

"On what your definition of 'rich' is. I'd say the child for whom you're saving money to help in Guatemala would think you're the richest, luckiest girl in the world, wouldn't you?" Grandma cocked an eyebrow.

Ouch. If Grandma only knew that she had spent all her money. "I guess so," Olivia conceded. "So that means we're rich?"

"What do you think?"

"Not really, Grandma," Olivia scoffed. "I mean, I don't have everything I want. It's not like I'm a spoiled brat." She knew a few people who would fit that description perfectly.

"No, you're not a brat, Livvy, but you *are* spoiled," Grandma pointed out.

Olivia was stung. How could her own grandma call her spoiled? What about the new sandals she wanted? Didn't that sacrifice count for something?

"Grandma, how can you say that?"

"Oh Livvy, if you'd seen some of the things I've seen in my lifetime, you'd understand. Have you ever been hungry?"

Olivia shrugged her shoulders nonchalantly. "Sure, lots of times."

"No you haven't. I'm not talking about having an appetite for dinner, or the fact that you skipped lunch. I mean *hungry*. You haven't eaten for two days because there is no food to eat. That kind of hungry."

Olivia said nothing.

"These kids next door. Would you say they're luckier than you are?"

That was an easy one. "Of course."

"Really? Do they sleep better than you at night in cozier beds?"

Olivia shook her head. No, they didn't.

"Do they have more food than you to fill their tummies?"

"No."

"Do you lack a loving family who cares for you and teaches you about God?"

"No."

"Do they go to a better school than you do?"

Olivia thought about St. Michael's School and Tina. Tina, who could not afford to come back in the fall, and did not know it yet.

At Olivia's silence, Grandma smiled softly. "Hmm. Well I'd say you *are* pretty rich, after all."

Olivia looked down and began to busy herself by wiping up the countertop to disguise her shame.

"I'm glad you had fun today, Livvy. There's nothing wrong with that. But just remember this: There's always going to be someone with more money than you. You just be content and thankful for what God gave you. It all belongs to Him, anyway."

Olivia said nothing.

"The Lord wants us to find true happiness; not the kind that can be found in a store or a country club. Once you have that, you'll always be joyful, whether you're eating a peanut butter sandwich or a fancy steak. The trick is to get rid of the clutter in your heart and be satisfied and grateful no matter the circumstances."

In her heart, Olivia knew Grandma was right. It was just hard to hear at the moment.

Grandma gave Olivia a sideways squeeze. "Your good friend Thérèse once advised to avoid all display, to love our lowliness, to be affected by nothing. 'Then we shall be poor in spirit and Jesus will come to seek us.' There are some things I wish I had when I was younger, too. But you know what? I know they wouldn't have made me truly happy in the long run. I've known people who have chased after the next, greatest thing their whole lives. They could never catch up—always out of breath, waiting for the next thing to come that would make them happy. They could never enjoy the moment."

Olivia smiled. "Okay, Grandma. Let's enjoy the moment."

"That's my Livvy. We can start by working on getting dinner together. Wash your hands now."

Olivia did as she was told, but deep down, she felt horrible. All of the money she had wasted at the store being 'in the moment' was money that could have been used to help a poor child. She felt sick at her display. One thing she had not been at the gift shop was poor in spirit.

Grandma handed Olivia a bottle of olive oil. "Sprinkle this generously on the bottom of the pan," she said, gesturing with the bottle. "Then tip the pan all around to coat the bottom evenly with oil."

Olivia did as she was told, staring out at the window at the gloomy day. It matched her mood. "Think it'll ever stop, Grandma?"

"Oh, the good Lord only knows," Grandma said as she rummaged through the drawers, looking for something. "Those weather people don't even know, but they act like they do." She began to collect some spices from the cupboard: pepper, garlic salt, and parsley. "All of that fancy-schmancy weather equipment and nobody knows anything. Hopefully it will let up so you and Hayley can go back to the beach tomorrow."

She thought about tonight. If it kept on raining like this, Hayley wouldn't try to sneak out, would she? Olivia knew she herself wouldn't; but then again, she wasn't the sneaking-out type. Plus, she was a little afraid of the dark. Would Hayley think to bring a flashlight? She shook her head, trying to drop the very idea of it all. There was no way Hayley would do such a foolish thing. She decided to concentrate on Grandma's chicken.

"…after you've rinsed it and blotted it with paper towels, then you add the chicken to the pan and dredge both sides in the oil like this—Olivia, are you paying attention?"

Startled, Olivia looked up, a little dazed from her thoughts. "Yes, Grandma."

"Good, because if you know how to make Italian baked chicken, you'll always have a delicious go-to dish." Grandma bustled about the big kitchen, getting frustrated. "These fancy kitchens are something else. Why, when I was raising your dad and his brothers, I didn't have all of this high-falutin' stuff like a wine chiller and—what's this?" she pointed to a large appliance on the counter.

"I'm pretty sure it's a food processor, Grandma," said Olivia, inspecting it.

"Land sakes alive, what on earth does that thing do, split the atom?"

Olivia laughed. "It grates cheese and purees stuff."

"A cheese grater that plugs in and takes up so much space on the countertop? What's wrong with a simple box grater for the *parmeggiano* cheese?" Grandma asked. "Just crazy if you ask me!"

She drizzled some extra olive oil on a chicken breast, took Olivia's hand, and motioned for her to rub the oil in.

Olivia winced. "Maybe they have a pastry brush for this."

Grandma scowled. "Nonsense. Your hands are the best tools in the kitchen, always remember that, Olivia. You can have all of these confusing kitchen gadgets Aunt Peggy's got shoved in the drawers. Your hands can do all of the work they can, and better."

"Plus, no tools to wash," Olivia said, getting in the spirit of things as she massaged each chicken piece with olive oil.

Grandma's eyes lit up. "Now you've got it, my Livvy!"

Next it was time to sprinkle dried oregano, garlic salt, and some freshly ground pepper over the chicken. Grandma covered the entire pan in foil and placed it in the oven. "A little while later, we'll take the foil off so the chicken skin can crisp up and brown," Grandma said as she went over to the sink.

"Now, would it be too much to ask for a dishtowel in this palace?" she asked, turning around in the immense kitchen.

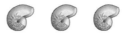

Later that evening, Olivia bumped into Hayley in the bathroom as she was brushing her teeth at the sink.

"Oops, sorry," Olivia said.

"Nice sweatshirt," Hayley said sarcastically.

"Thanks. I'm glad I bought it."

"Gonna wear those short-shorts tomorrow?"

"Probably," Olivia said, nose in the air. "Are you gonna wear that dumb T-shirt?"

"Probably. Are you completely broke now?"

"I still have plenty left," Olivia said, thinking of the money she'd earned from Mrs. Duggan the other day, then realizing she'd already spent that too.

"You'd have even more if you would have babysat today like you were supposed to," Hayley snapped.

Ouch. That hurt. How did Hayley know she had lied to Mrs.

Duggan today? *She must have been listening in the hallway when I was on the phone,* Olivia thought irritably.

Hayley kept brushing her teeth. Olivia noticed that she had shoes on, and her hair looked freshly brushed. Her heart sank. This could only mean one thing: Hayley was getting ready to go out tonight! Olivia retreated back to her room to wait for Hayley to finish, and to frantically ponder what to do. *Boy, she's so preachy to me, and look at her planning to sneak out tonight! But I promised her I wouldn't tell on her,* Olivia thought regretfully. *I can't go back on my promise. What kind of friend would do that?*

Her mom appeared in the doorway, holding a pair of Lucy's pajamas.

"I'm putting Lucy down for bed," she said. "Want to come in and say prayers with her?"

"In a minute, Mom," Olivia said, trying her hardest to look like she was concentrating on choosing her own pajamas for the night.

Her mom came in and gently closed the door. "Olivia," she whispered, "what is going on with you and Hayley? You two barely spoke at dinner."

Olivia didn't say anything. She just continued to rummage through her dresser drawer.

Her mom tried again. "You're arguing, aren't you? What is it about?"

"Oh, I don't know," Olivia said, trying to think of something she could say. "Maybe it's just too much togetherness on the trip."

"Maybe," her mom said, but looked doubtful. "Did you have some sort of disagreement?"

Oh St. Thérèse, Olivia prayed quickly, *now what? I can't tell her what I've done, buying immodest clothes and a $50 sweatshirt.*

And I can't tell her what I know about Hayley; it would destroy everything. Hayley would absolutely hate me! And what if Hayley decides to get back at me by telling Mom and Dad about how I've been lying to the kids and what I've been spending my money on? Then I'd get into trouble and my fun summer vacation would be ruined!

You know what Jesus asks you to do, Olivia. Hayley is doing something very wrong, and could get hurt. Forget yourself and your wants; you must help your friend.

There was St. Thérèse, guiding her again, but Olivia was not in agreement with her. As much as she loved her saintly friend, she really didn't think St. Thérèse fully understood the situation. It had taken Olivia so long to truly befriend Hayley, and she didn't want to mess up a good thing. Well…it wasn't exactly a good relationship now, but they'd clear this up, she knew they would. And telling her mom about Hayley's plans would mess it all up; they'd never have that chance again to be friends.

"I'm kind of tired, Mom," Olivia said closing the drawer with her leg and tossing the chosen pajamas onto the bed. "I don't really want to talk about it. I think I'll just read in bed."

Am I being selfish? Olivia thought. She knew God would think so. After all, wasn't she putting her own concerns above Hayley's safety?

"I can help, you know," her mom said hopefully. "I've had lots of experience with this kind of thing."

I bet not like this, Mom, Olivia thought sadly.

Olivia sighed. "I'll try to turn things around tomorrow with her, Mom," Olivia said, and gave her mom a hug.

"That's my girl," her mom said, her voice muffled in Olivia's hair. She pulled away and looked at her.

"Your dinner was great, Olivia. Best chicken I've ever had. And you've got your first job, too. You're becoming quite a young lady now, aren't you? I'm proud of you."

Her mom got up and left Olivia to her book. She opened it up and tried to settle in for a good read. She frowned. Her mom was proud of her. Would she be proud if she found the short-shorts hidden in a bag in her closet? That she had been lying to the kids about being a rich kid? That she had let Mrs. Duggan down when she needed her by lying about being sick?

Any other time, she would have been thrilled to have the compliment of being called a young lady. But not tonight.

Tonight, she knew, she was acting like a selfish child.

TWENTY

"O my God, I wish to console You for the ingratitude of wicked men, and I beg You to take away from me the liberty to displease You." —*St. Thérèse*

T he rain was still falling in a slight drizzle when Olivia looked at her bedside clock at 10:57 p.m. "Spitting rain" is what her grandma called it. *What would Grandma think if she knew what I'm about to do?* Olivia thought, trying to brush the thought from her mind. She knew exactly what her grandma would think—and say. And it wouldn't be pretty.

Olivia sighed, knowing she would soon be out in the damp night. She had made up her mind to follow Hayley, just to see what she was up to. *At least it's letting up*, she thought as she put on some clothes and tennis shoes and grabbed a rain jacket from her closet.

She opened her door a crack and listened. Hayley's footsteps creaked slightly on the carpeted stairs as she tiptoed down. Olivia heard the soft opening and closing of the front door. Hayley had left.

She heard Lucy make a soft moan as she slept. She could also hear her dad snoring from her parents' room. The whole house had luckily gone to bed early that night.

Olivia gently crept downstairs, following Hayley's footsteps out the front door. She didn't need an umbrella, but she tugged at her hood and covered her head. She pulled a mini-flashlight out of her coat pocket, then thought better of it. She didn't want to be seen. Hayley would be livid if she caught her following her. She stuffed the flashlight back into her pocket and decided to see her way by the porch and pathway lights from her house and the neighbors'. She hurried quietly to catch up with Hayley, who was by now at the walkway to the beach. In the darkness, the rain dripped on her softly and moistened her face so she had to wipe the drops off her cheeks. Anyone who saw her would think she had been crying. Truly, she felt like crying. What on earth was she doing out at 11:00 at night, following Hayley in the rain?

To keep her out of trouble, Olivia reminded herself for the umpteenth time, trying to reassure herself that she was doing the right thing. *To see what that troublemaker Brandon and his friends have in mind. It's better than getting her into trouble with Mom and Dad.* She thought of her parents' faces if they could see her now. But she told herself that this was the perfect compromise: This way nobody—not her or Hayley—would get into trouble. The more she thought about it, it really was the perfect plan. She gulped. *Well, hopefully this will all be over soon. Who knows? Probably 15 minutes from now we'll all be back in bed.*

The soft glow of the orange path lights leading down to the beach illuminated Hayley's figure as she walked. Brandon's text message said they were supposed to meet at the end of the path. Olivia looked around to find something to hide behind. If she were spotted, everything would be ruined. She crouched down behind a clump of reeds and watched. Soon her legs started to get sore, so she reluctantly sat on the sodden ground. She winced as she felt the wet seep through her pants, wishing her coat were longer or she had something waterproof to sit on. Oh well. Brandon should be here any minute. She studied Hayley as she stood at the edge of the path. Hayley was shifting back and forth, looking around nervously. She was too far away to read the expression on Hayley's face, but she could tell by her stance that she was nervous and afraid.

Olivia felt a little nervous and afraid herself. She was glad she at least had the foresight to put her watch on. Five minutes passed, then ten. Where was Brandon? Wasn't he coming? Olivia shifted on the wet ground, trying to get comfortable. She felt something on her check and wiped it away, thinking it was another raindrop, but the rain seemed to have finally let up, thankfully. She felt something else on her hand, and realized that the mosquitoes were starting to come out after the rain. If she stayed here much longer, she would get eaten alive!

She was covered from head to toe, but her face and hands were still exposed. If she stood up, she would most certainly be seen, so she stayed put. She yanked on her hood to cover her head more. She was absolutely miserable. She hoped Hayley would someday appreciate this, how she valued their friendship so much that she risked getting grounded for life by her parents and being eaten alive by mosquitoes in the dark.

Oh Lord, please make something happen soon, she prayed silently. She listened to the soft waves on the beach crash ashore and wondered again what she was doing here at night by herself.

Finally, she heard faint footsteps and laughter along the wet pathway, and she could see Brandon walking with some other kids. She crouched lower into the reeds and held her breath, biting down on her lower lip. When they passed her, she stole a glance. She recognized Brooke, another girl, and a boy walking toward Hayley. She wondered why Abby wasn't there.

Visibly relieved, Hayley waved at them.

"Hey," Olivia heard Brandon say.

"Hi, guys," Hayley said, relieved that they had finally come. "Brandon, what took you so long?"

Brandon shrugged his shoulders, complacent. "Josh was busy getting something we're going to need," he said.

"Well, are we going to see the turtle's nest or not?" asked Hayley impatiently, who was getting more uncomfortable about this whole situation.

Olivia could see Hayley's face illuminated by the path lights. She looked nervous and afraid.

"Relax," said the girl in the group. "You act like we're doing something bad. We're just going for a walk on the beach to see some stupid turtle's nest. Personally, I can think of more fun things to do, but you know Brandon…"

Olivia could hear the other kids laughing in agreement.

"Fine, let's go," said Brandon, and the group walked farther along the boardwalk until they were on the sand.

I've got to follow them, Olivia thought frantically. She didn't feel right about this at all. It was getting later and later and she started to panic, picturing her mom or dad checking on them and finding them both gone.

She crept behind the group at a distance until Hayley stopped in the sand to take off her flip-flops and turned around and saw her.

"Olivia!" she hissed. "What are you doing here?"

Olivia did not know what to say. "I'm following you," she said simply.

"Well, that's obvious," Hayley retorted. "Go away before they see you!"

"I'm not leaving you," she said. "Not alone with them."

"Hey, who's back there?" Brandon said, shining a flashlight in their direction. The light landed on Olivia's face, illuminating it in the darkness. "Oh, it's you. Where'd you come from?"

"Um..." Olivia stammered.

"Whatever, I don't care. You can come. Just keep quiet and don't make a sound," he warned.

Hayley looked at Olivia, disgusted. "Yeah, Olivia, you can come if you don't ruin our fun."

Olivia sighed and continued to follow them along the wet sand. The rain let up slowly, and by the time they had walked for a few more minutes, stopped completely. *Well, there's one good thing*, she thought wryly as she trudged along.

What are we doing out here? she wondered as she wiped the last of the misty rain off of her face. It was hard to see. She could see the faint glow of the moon as it tried to come out from behind the dark clouds, signaling that the rain was now over. She felt chilled and damp, and longed for her soft, warm bed. It was surreal to even be here, out in the dark late at night, looking for a turtle's nest on a dark beach. She hadn't even known that there was a turtle's nest nearby. She thought back to the book she had read to Danny and wondered what he would think about her getting to see turtle eggs. As her soaking wet tennis shoes dug into the sand, she remembered something, though. Danny's book said the eggs were buried about 20 inches deep. How were they supposed to see the eggs if they were below the sand?

"Hayley!" she whispered loudly, but so the others could not hear. They were up ahead a bit and laughing.

"What? Do you want to go back?" Hayley asked, acting tough, but Olivia knew she was half hoping Olivia would say yes so she'd have an excuse to leave.

"No, it's just...this is a waste of time, Hayley. We're not going to be able to see anything. The eggs will be buried under the sand."

Hayley thought about this as they walked. "Well...I don't know. Maybe they're hatching or something," she said impatiently. "Brandon seems to know what he's talking about."

Olivia mulled this over. "Yeah, but..." Olivia could see Hayley roll her eyes in the new moonlight, and knew she was thinking that this was just another way Olivia was babyish and immature.

"I highly doubt Brandon and his friends would come all the way out there to look at a mound of sand. There must be something to see."

Olivia shrugged her shoulders and then suddenly the group ahead of them stopped, their flashlights aiming at an orange sign with tape surrounding a small area of sand.

Loggerhead Turtle Nesting Area, the sign read under the glow of the group's flashlights bouncing on it in the dark.

Eggs, Hatchlings, Adults, and Carcasses Are Protected By Federal and State Laws.

"Well what do you know?" Brandon sneered. "Maybe we'll do some time in the big house. NOT!" At this, Brandon and his friends laughed cruelly.

Olivia was confused. What was he talking about? Why would looking at a turtle's nest on the beach send someone to jail? This was more serious than she had imagined.

Hayley looked at Olivia, wide-eyed.

"Josh, get the shovel from the bushes," Brandon ordered.

The two other girls giggled stupidly. "Let's make a sandcastle!" Brooke cried.

"No, I need you to shine the flashlights over here," Brandon said, gesturing toward the nest. The girls obeyed.

The two boys climbed over the orange plastic tape and within seconds she heard the rhythmic scraping sound of the shovel.

"What are you DOING?" Hayley hissed at the boys. "You can't dig up those eggs!"

Scrape, scrape, scrape. Brandon's shovel dug deeper and he flung sand all around him, not caring. Hayley climbed over the tape, tearing it in the process, and roughly grabbed the shovel from Brandon and flung it into the bushes.

"Hey, what are you—" but then Josh laughed it off and the two boys began to use their hands to continue digging.

"Bull's eye!" cried Brandon as the flashlights bounced all around him in the dark, illuminating a hole filled with a pile of small white eggs. Olivia could not believe it. There must have been over 100 eggs in the hole the mother turtle had dug months ago.

"Found 'em!"

Olivia's heart started to beat wildly. This wasn't right. They weren't supposed to be doing this. She thought back to Danny's book. The eggs were supposed to stay covered until they were ready to hatch, right? They shouldn't be disturbing them in this way.

"Okay, you found the eggs!" she pleaded, desperate. "Now cover them back up and let's go!"

The boys said nothing as Brandon picked up one of the eggs and held it in his hand. "Looks like a ping-pong ball," he said with a grin. "It's squishy. Wanna hold one?"

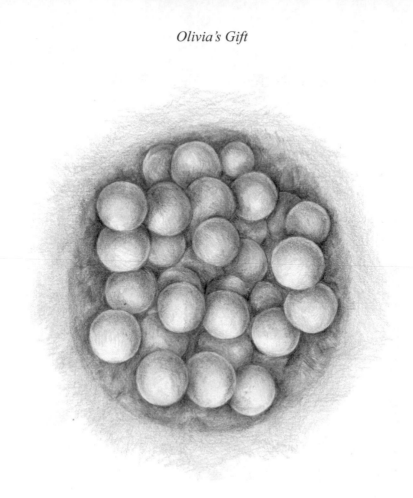

Olivia stared at him in the moonlight. "No way. Put it back."

Brandon stood up. "Come on; it won't bite. Here." He gently placed it in Olivia's palm. She stared down at it in shock, her eyes wide. She breathed heavily. This felt totally wrong, yet, after reading Danny's book, she was curious. Was there really a baby turtle in there? She lifted her hand and peered at the tiny egg for a closer look. It was leathery and soft.

Okay. I looked at it. Time to put it back. She started to lower her hand and give it back to Brandon, but something stopped her.

It moved.

Olivia's heart skipped a beat as she watched the tiny egg

tremble back and forth in her hand. It rolled around a couple of times, then stopped.

The baby turtle was inside and it was moving!

Oh Lord, she cried inwardly. *What have I just done?*

*Oh God, Oh God, Oh God, Oh God…*her mind raced. She suddenly thought of Mrs. Duggan and her baby moving and kicking inside her belly.

Doing somersaults. Alive.

"I don't want this! Put it back. It moved! Put it back and cover them back up!" she demanded frantically. She gave it back to Brandon, trusting that he would do the right thing once he knew the truth: that there was a live baby turtle inside.

Next to her, Hayley gasped. "She told you it moved! Brandon, they're alive! Put them back NOW!" cried Hayley.

Brandon held up the egg with a sinister look on his face. *This was not about to happen. This was not…*Olivia's face grew white with horror.

Instantly he tossed the egg behind him. It made a tiny thud as it landed in the dune vegetation. Everyone laughed while Hayley and Olivia stood there, speechless.

Olivia felt like she had been punched in the gut. "You will NOT do that again!" Olivia warned Brandon.

"I won't?" he sneered, picking up one more, this time hurling it toward the ocean. It landed at the edge of the water and bounced into the surf.

"You're killing them!" Olivia cried, remembering from Danny's book that the eggs would not survive in the water. They had to hatch on the sand.

"Oh come on! It's just an egg. It's not alive yet!" Brooke retorted, rolling her eyes.

Disgusted, Olivia turned toward Brooke. What was the matter with her? *How could I not have seen her true colors*? Olivia wondered sadly.

Brandon picked up three eggs and pretended he was on the pitcher's mound, throwing them overhand out into the surf.

"Hey, who's the pitcher on our baseball team, you or me?" Josh challenged as the two boys laughed uncontrollably. Then Josh picked up a few of the eggs and began to toss them around. "Look, I can juggle!"

The two girls got into the act as well.

"I want to try!"

"Give me some!"

"Noooooooo!" Olivia cried, running toward the turtle's nest. "Stop!"

"Be quiet!" yelled Josh. "Do you want someone to hear us?"

"YOU BET I DO!" yelled Hayley at the top of her lungs.

"Yeah, yell a little louder," Josh said, full of sarcasm. "Then the cops will come and haul you in with us! Do you want that?"

Within seconds, Brandon, Josh, and the two girls were hurling the eggs into the bushes and onto the wet sand, laughing as quietly as they could.

"You're killing them! All of you, STOP! Oh God, please make them stop!" Olivia was beside herself.

The four grabbed as many eggs as they could and wrapped them in the bottoms of their shirts, moving down toward the shoreline.

"Let's play catch!" one of the girls suggested.

The boys came back and scooped more eggs out of the hole.

Hayley grabbed Olivia's arm. "We have to do something!" She looked around wildly. "Grab as many as you can. We'll take them down the beach and bury them where they can't find them!"

Without thinking, Olivia ran over to the turtle's nest and reached inside, hoping to find a handful she could carry in the bottom of her shirt.

She shoved her arm into the sandy hole and moved her hand around, hoping to find something, anything…

One. There was one egg left in the hole.

She grabbed it and the two girls dashed as quickly as they could down the beach. They ran until they were out of breath and the beams from the group's flashlights were distant yellow pinpoints enveloped in the blackness.

Exhausted, Hayley collapsed onto the sand. "They're far away," she breathed heavily as she looked back. In between gasps, she said, "I'll…dig…a hole."

Olivia stood by helplessly as Hayley dug, cradling the egg gently in her hand, not wanting to harm it. It was already a little dented from the kids grabbing the other eggs. *You'll be okay*, she said inside as she looked at the wiggling egg. *Just hang in there, little turtle.*

"Okay," Hayley said, looking up at Olivia in the moonlight, wet sand sticking to her hands. "It's deep enough. Put it in. Hurry!"

As Olivia knelt down, her mini-flashlight tumbled out of her coat pocket, but she didn't care. She softly placed the egg into the sandy hole Hayley had dug. With two hands, she covered the hole with the sand and patted it on top.

Hayley and Olivia looked down at the covered hole in silence. Neither could think of anything to say at that moment. Olivia imagined the egg underneath, fighting for its very survival. She wondered if it would live. *Oh God, please.*

The two girls, with tear-streamed faces, looked at each other in the moonlight.

"Our Father…" began Olivia.

"Who art in Heaven…" continued Hayley.

As the ocean crashed gently ashore, the two girls bent over the sand and begged God to let the turtle live.

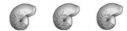

They scrambled to the house without saying a word and slipped inside, taking care to get out of their wet coats and shoes in silence and hanging up the coats in the closet so they would be undetected in the morning. When the girls were satisfied that they had covered her tracks, they stole quietly upstairs. When they got to their bedroom doors, they simply looked sadly at each other. Then they went inside.

Olivia jumped into bed and, still shivering from the cold, rainy night, covered herself under her sheets.

She tried to get comfortable in bed, but she just couldn't. After a few minutes, she heard low, muffled sobs coming through the wall.

Olivia turned over in bed, staring at her darkened window, listening to the drizzle, with tears slipping down her cheeks. "Saint Thérèse," she whispered, "what have they done?"

Life is a gift.

Olivia reached over to the nightstand, where her St. Thérèse chaplet was sitting next to the clock radio. She grabbed it and clutched it tightly, praying in her head.

She didn't fall asleep for hours.

T WENTY-ONE

"We have only the short moments of this life to work for God's glory. The devil knows this, and that is why he tries to make us waste time in useless things."
—*St. Thérèse*

She dreamed of turtles: Mother turtles nesting on the shore, deep holes filled with eggs, baby turtles struggling to survive, their mothers keeping watch. She dreamed of hatchlings scurrying toward the tide as fast as their flippers could carry them. When they finally reached the water's edge, giant sharks appeared and swallowed them whole in one single gulp.

Olivia sat up abruptly in bed, breathing heavily and covered in sweat. Her pajamas clung to her and her hair was stringy and damp. *It's just a bad dream,* she told herself. *It isn't true.* She turned her pillow over and fell back into it.

But it was true. And Brandon and his friends were the sharks.

It was true. Except for one. Did he make it?

The next morning, Olivia changed into shorts and a T-shirt, went downstairs, and poured herself a bowl of cereal. She rubbed her eyes, feeling sleepy as she got the milk out of the refrigerator. She had barely slept all night.

Her dad walked into the kitchen and plugged in the coffee pot. He filled it up and switched it on, glancing at the clock. He watched Olivia chew her corn flakes for a bit in silence.

"You look pretty tired, Livvy," he said, noticing Olivia leaning on her elbow as she ate. "I wonder if you're coming down with something. Why don't you go back to bed?"

Her mom walked into the kitchen just then. "Up so early?" she exclaimed as she kissed the top of Olivia's head. "Even Lucy is still asleep. You're not usually up now."

"I couldn't sleep." It was the truth. She tried to look cheerful. It wouldn't do to have her parents notice her long face. They would get suspicious.

"Grandma's still asleep. She was up late last night, I think." Her mother bustled about the kitchen, getting orange juice out of the refrigerator.

Olivia's head jerked up. How late? Did Grandma see her and Hayley come home?

"I promised Hayley I'd take her into town later to go to the drugstore," Mrs. Thomas continued. "Do you want to come? Want to get a candy bar or something?"

Olivia shook her head. "Nah, I'm okay."

"Want me to get you a Fudge Chewie?"

"Um…sure, thanks." Olivia was consumed with fear. If Grandma had seen them come in, would she tell her parents? Would she lecture them on the side? With Grandma, there was no way of knowing.

"Come with us," her mom urged. "You can get a word search book or something," she suggested hopefully.

Olivia continued to eat her cereal in silence. She was about to think up an excuse when her dad asked, "What do you say we take a stroll on the beach?"

The beach? Oh, little did her dad know that was the *last* place she wanted to be right now!

He saw her hesitation. "Oh come on, we've already been here a week and we haven't taken a walk together on this trip, just you and me. Throw on some shoes."

Olivia found herself with no choice but to go back down to the beach.

Because it was still so early in the morning, very few people were out to greet the morning sun as it shone brightly, casting a glistening glow on the water. A few lone runners dashed by, earbuds in their ears, smiling hello as they passed Olivia and her dad, leaving deep footprints on the wet sand.

Her dad took a deep breath and stretched out his arms, taking it all in. "Don't you just love the ocean air?" he asked. "I think coming on this vacation was the best thing we ever did," he said. "What do you think?"

"Sure, Dad," Olivia said, trying to be agreeable.

Father and daughter walked down the sand, enjoying the view. Seagulls were everywhere, looking for bits of food or dead fish along the shore, picking through the sand, trying to find breakfast.

"You're not worried about my job, are you?" he asked her, concerned. Olivia had been saying so little. "Because you don't have to be."

"What made you ask that, Dad?" Olivia bent down to pick up a red and white scalloped seashell. She examined it and found a little hole at the top, perfect for putting some cord through. It would make a cute necklace, so she put it in her pocket.

"Oh, I don't know. Mom told me you were asking her about it. You seem a little...preoccupied lately."

Olivia looked up at her dad and squinted. She wished she had her sunglasses or a hat. She shielded the sun from her eyes with her hand and replied, "No, not really. I just...have some things going on with Hayley."

Her dad was silent before responding, "I see. Do you think it was a mistake to bring a friend along on the trip?"

"No," Olivia rushed to say, remembering how much fun they'd been having until the turtle tragedy. She thought of how they giggled until late at night, ate popcorn and watched movies on TV, and spent lazy hours lying out on the beach, listening to the Tyler Twins. She thought of how they had worked together to frantically save the life of one tiny turtle in its egg, and wondered for the umpteenth time if it had survived. She supposed there was no way to know.

They continued to walk, talking about the Navy ships they saw way out on the horizon, making guesses about where they were headed. After a time, they came upon a large group of seagulls, milling around and squawking loudly.

"Wow, looks like these guys found a breakfast buffet," her dad laughed. "Wonder what they've got there?"

They walked closer, but the gulls were not scared away. They were greedily feasting and screeching as they called out to one another in the morning sun.

With interest, Olivia studied the white birds and what they were devouring, when suddenly she knew.

With a pit in her stomach, she knew.

In the melee of the flock of hungry birds, she saw the empty white shells, scattered about violently, with the remains of the turtle carcasses being picked apart to bits. Up toward the dunes stood the orange sign, its plastic tape broken from the night before and sagging into the sand.

Tiny turtles, chewed apart and left for dead by cruel people who did not care.

Who could have such little regard for life...any life?

Then she saw a black flip-flop lying on the sand, and she knew.

The scene of complete destruction was too much for Olivia. The screeches of the seagulls and the sound of the waves threatened to deafen her, closing in on her. The sand suddenly felt like quicksand, pulling her down, down, until she fell into it on her knees and held the back of her neck with her hands. A sudden dizziness overcame her.

She heard her dad speaking to her as if she were in a tunnel, muted sounds that were faint and far away.

Her stomach pushed up, up, up...until Olivia felt herself stiffen. She bent over and vomited into the sand.

When it was over, she fell backwards onto her bottom and sat there in shock.

"Olivia, are you okay?" her dad was holding her by the shoulders, gently shaking her. "What is it?"

Olivia squinted up at her dad, her mouth feeling acidic and sticky. "Dad, I want...to go back."

Her dad looked concerned. "Sure, let's go right now. Do you need help standing up?"

Olivia nodded and let her dad help her up from the sand. Together they turned around and walked back from the direction they had come. She didn't dare turn back to look.

"You're sick. I'll help you," her dad said soothingly, and smoothed her hair as they walked. "We'll take it slow."

"I'm okay, I'm okay," she told her dad. "It's just...the seagulls..."

Her dad sighed. "I know. It's so sad. I saw the sign about the loggerhead turtles. It looks like someone was purposely destroying the eggs," he said, shaking his head. "Whoever did it should be put in jail," he said angrily. "I'm glad I brought my cell phone. I'm going to call the police right now so they can report it to the wildlife division." He took his cell phone off of his belt and began to punch in numbers as they walked.

As her dad began to inform the police of what they had seen, Olivia felt like she was in a daze. They trudged along the sand while her dad talked.

"Dad...Brandon and Brooke did it..." she said softly.

He looked at her in shock.

"Are you sure?" he mouthed to her, covering the mouthpiece with his hand. "How do you know?"

She nodded, beginning to feel weak again. "I just know. Dad, I don't feel so good," she said, and he nodded at her as he talked, motioning for her to sit down.

"No, I don't think it was an animal that did it," she heard her father say into his phone. "There's a black flip-flop at the scene."

Olivia sank dejectedly into the sand, wondering what was going to happen now. She looked down at her hand as it supported her in the sand, and saw something gleaming next to it. Lowering her head, she saw the object sticking out of the sand.

Her mini-flashlight. The one she dropped last night while they buried the egg.

This could only mean…she looked around wildly, suddenly having newfound strength. This was the exact spot where she and Hayley had buried the egg! She turned this way and that, desperately searching for their hole. There was no way that she'd find it—

Until there it was: a tiny eggshell, opened and empty, near the little hole they had dug.

Olivia panicked. Could a seagull have gotten it? Did it make it to the shore?

Oh please God, let me know if he made it…

And then she saw the tracks: a tiny sliding pattern, crookedly making its way down toward the ocean, where it disappeared in the wet sand of the water's edge.

A surge of relief and happiness welled up inside her and she buried her head in her dirty hands, not caring that her face and hair were getting covered in sand. Tears streamed down her cheeks, but she didn't care. Somehow, in that moment, nothing else mattered—not Brooke, not new sandals with heels, not her dad's job.

The baby turtle had made it. He had lived.

And now he was home.

Twenty-Two

"Remember that the dear Jesus is there in the tabernacle expressly for you, for you alone. Remember that He is consumed with a desire to come into your heart....Jesus has not put this attraction into your heart for nothing. He comes to find an empty tent within us...that's all He asks."
—St. Thérèse

Olivia spent the rest of the afternoon babysitting Danny. It was hard for her to concentrate on doing puzzles with him and playing with bricks. She was grinning from ear to ear and could not contain her excitement. As sad as she was about the events of the night before on the beach, she couldn't stop feeling jubilant about the little turtle that had survived. She kept imagining him swimming out to sea to begin his life in the salty waters. She marveled that the baby had survived in her and Hayley's desperate rush to bury it in the sand. She couldn't believe it was possible that their hasty efforts to protect the egg had been successful.

She gave Danny a big hug when it was time to leave.

"More play!" he shouted.

Olivia laughed. "I'll be back, Danny." She looked up at Mrs. Duggan hopefully. She had shown no sign of irritation when

Olivia had shown up to babysit earlier that day, no outward appearance that she was angry with Olivia for bailing on her before so she could go hang out at the yacht club; for that she was grateful. Apparently Mrs. Duggan bought the story that she had been sick the previous day. Embarrassed, she blushed and looked down, but Mrs. Duggan did not seem to notice.

She handed Olivia some cash. "I got a lot done today, thanks Olivia. I even got a nice nap in. I'm so glad you're feeling better."

Olivia gratefully accepted the money and put her hand on the doorknob. "Mrs. Duggan?"

"Yes, Olivia?"

"I just wanted to, um…"

She couldn't do it. She couldn't admit to her what she had done. Not yet.

"Yes?"

"…let you know that I left Danny's empty sippy cup in his room."

"That's okay; I'll get it. Bye, Olivia!" she said happily, and closed the door behind Olivia.

Well. It didn't quite go as expected. Well, maybe that was the way it was supposed to be. Maybe she didn't have to apologize. Mrs. Duggan didn't know what she had done; maybe she didn't have to ever know. With a renewed spirit, Olivia happily headed back to the house.

"Where've you been all day?" asked Hayley, who was sitting on the front porch, bouncing a basketball. Her sunglasses were perched on top of her head and her bare feet and legs were sandy from the beach.

"Babysitting," Olivia said, slipping off her flip-flops and joining her on the front porch. "Danny was extra active today."

Hayley tossed the ball to her and she put it on the ground and balanced her bare feet on top of it.

"You were asleep when I woke up," said Olivia.

"Your mom took me to the store," replied Hayley, "then I went down to the beach with her and Lucy."

"Did you run into anyone?" Olivia wanted to know, staring at her feet as she rolled the ball around. She wasn't sure she wanted to know the answer.

"No, and I'm glad."

Olivia breathed a sigh of relief.

For a while, neither of the girls knew what to say until Hayley broke the silence. "I want you to know that I'm so over Brandon."

Olivia looked at Hayley, who was playing with a blade of grass she had picked and was slowly tearing into tiny pieces. "Really? I'm glad."

Hayley threw the pieces of grass into the lawn and reached over to scratch a mosquito bite on her leg. "Yeah, I don't even know why I liked him."

Olivia rushed to her defense. "How were you supposed to know that he would be so…"—she struggled to find the words— "cruel?"

Hayley nodded. "How stupid was I? But no more. Now I know what he's really like. He has absolutely no respect for life." She picked up another blade of grass and began to pick it apart. "None of them do."

"But Hayley," Olivia said, anxious to tell her the good news, "you'll never guess. Our turtle survived! He hatched!"

Hayley jerked her head up. "Seriously? How do you know?"

"Because I saw the tracks this morning. Hayley, he hatched and crawled toward the water!"

"But how do you know it was our turtle?"

"Because last night I accidentally dropped my flashlight in the sand where we dug the hole and I found it there this morning by the tracks it made. It *has* to be our turtle!"

Hayley let her breath out slowly and shook her head. The two girls grinned widely and gave each other a hug. "I can't believe we did it, Olivia! We saved our little turtle! He made it!"

"We should think of a name for him," Olivia suggested happily.

The two girls thought about this for a moment.

"I've got it!" Olivia cried. "We'll call him Gabe, short for Gabriel."

"Okay," said Hayley with a giggle. "But how did you come up with that?"

"I don't really know," Olivia said coyly, "but to me it sounds like the name of someone special."

"Yeah, a survivor," Hayley agreed, getting into the spirit of things.

"Right," Olivia said. "Someone who lives."

Grandma held her purse in her hands and waited patiently by the car, watching the girls return from the beach.

"My, Hayley, you've had a lot of sun today. You're a little red."

"I know, Grandma Rosemary. Olivia and I are going in to change."

"Where are you going, Grandma?"

"I'm waiting for your father. He's taking me up to church for Eucharistic Adoration. Why don't you two girls come along?"

Olivia looked at her feet. The very mention of church made her uneasy. She could feel the guilt for all of her sins gnawing at her, deep down in the pit of her stomach. She didn't want to go. She'd feel like a hypocrite.

Grandma, sensing her hesitation, said gently, "It's been a while since you've gone. Jesus is waiting for you, Livvy."

Olivia bit her lip and looked at Hayley, who shrugged her shoulders. "Sure, let me get changed."

Olivia had no choice but to follow her inside and get out of her wet, sandy clothes.

A few minutes later, they were all headed up to Our Lady Star of the Sea church.

"We'll stop for ice cream on the way home," her dad said as they passed a crowd at the Dairy Freeze, and Hayley grinned.

Adjacent to the church proper was a little chapel with ten rows of pews. On the altar stood the ornate monstrance with the exposed Body of Christ. The four of them knelt down in the first pew, made the sign of the cross, and spent time adoring Jesus and praying.

Olivia pursed her lips together. She did not know what to say to Jesus. All she knew was that she felt drawn to the monstrance in a way she could not explain. It was a yearning in her heart to be closer to Jesus. She did not always feel this way when she went to Eucharistic Adoration. In fact, to tell the truth, there were times the only reason she went was because her parents were going and she had to go along. But today was different. She felt far away from Jesus because of her sins, which weighed heavily on her heart, like an anchor on one of the boats they had seen in the harbor on the way to church. She yearned to be closer to Him.

The unexplainable miracle of Jesus in the Eucharist was confusing to her, but Grandma said it was confusing to adults too, even to her. Olivia felt like Grandma knew everything about their faith, but Grandma had just laughed when she had told her that.

"Oh Livvy, I don't claim to know everything, for Heaven's sake. Only God knows all. But I do know that I trust blindly."

"Blindly?" Olivia had asked, confused. To her it had a negative sound, like someone who just went along without knowing any facts.

"Why, sure," Grandma had said. "To have blind faith is not to be closed up in the dark, but to see brightly with your heart."

Olivia shut her eyes tightly and breathed in deeply, looking for blind faith. When she opened her eyes, she saw the beautiful statue of the Blessed Mother in the side of the chapel. She looked at the outstretched hands and felt Mary fill her with love and faith in order to talk to her Son.

Jesus, I'm here to say I love you and that I am really, really sorry for doing the things I've done. I lied to so many people, Lord: the kids, my mom and dad, Mrs. Duggan. I snuck out when I wasn't supposed to, and I've been so jealous of Abby and Brooke. I think that's called "coveting" or something. I let money take over my whole life. I spent most of my savings on junk, some of it immodest, and now I don't have enough for my project. I feel like I've let down a little child in Guatemala. Is it possible to disappoint someone I've never even met?

Olivia buried her face in her hands, and was lost in her prayer. As she poured her heart out to Jesus, she remembered a touching story she had read about St. Thérèse in front of the tabernacle:

One day, as Thérèse was cleaning the altar in the sanctuary, Thérèse seated herself in front of the altar. She gently knocked on the tabernacle door and whispered, "Jesus, are you there?"

Thérèse spent many hours in front of the tabernacle, because it is there that Jesus waits for people to visit and adore Him.

Olivia was so absorbed in talking to Jesus that she did not even notice that her dad, Grandma, and Hayley had finished and had left the chapel. Olivia ended her prayer, made the sign of the cross, and walked back to join them. She felt different somehow, in a way she couldn't explain. She felt loved and safe.

At the Dairy Freeze, the four of them enjoyed their ice cream while sitting at a wooden picnic table. It was a warm, sunny day and the ice cream felt refreshing and cold.

"We're low on milk and bread. I'm going to walk next door," her dad said, motioning to a convenience store. "Anyone want to come?" Hayley, who was finished with her ice cream, got up and said she would go help. Grandma and Olivia were left alone.

"What do you call that again?" Grandma wanted to know.

Olivia held up her cup. "It's a Freezie, Grandma. Vanilla ice cream mixed with candy pieces."

Grandma waved her hand and shook her head. "Whatever happened to an old-fashioned vanilla or chocolate cone?" she asked. "We never had any of those crazy concoctions. It was chocolate, vanilla, or strawberry."

Olivia laughed. Grandma was always talking about how the old days were best. "And Grandpa's favorite was strawberry, right?"

"That's right," Grandma said, finishing the last bite of her vanilla cone. "He never was much of a chocolate fan. It had to be strawberry," she said firmly. "I used to get rock salt and make it for him every June when the strawberries were everywhere," she said, a faraway look in her eye.

Olivia continued to eat the last bites of her candy-bar Freezie.

Grandma wiped her mouth and hands on a paper napkin and crumpled it into a ball. "You were deep in thought at church."

Olivia scraped the bottom of her cup and said nothing.

"Far be it for me to intrude on someone's private prayers, but...anything you want to talk about?"

Olivia shook her head and continued eating. "No, I just feel bad about...certain things."

"Like what?"

"Just...things. You know, things I've sort of...done."

Grandma sighed. "Well, Livvy, if there's one thing I've learned, it's that guilt can eat away at you."

She got up to throw her napkin and Olivia's empty cup into the trash can. Sitting back down again, she covered Olivia's hand with her own, wrinkled one. "And there's only one way to get rid of it, honey."

Olivia looked at Grandma, her big brown eyes brimming with tears. "Grandma, Jesus told me something today at church."

Grandma raised her eyebrows. "He did? In front of the tabernacle?"

Olivia nodded. "It was something I felt in my heart."

"What was it?"

"He told me—I mean, He didn't tell me, it was more like He sort of invited me—to go to confession."

Grandma nodded, then said, "See how kind our Father is? He doesn't demand; He invites. He wants you to want to come."

"I guess so. But I really hate going. I get so embarrassed."

"Well, that's natural, Livvy. I don't suppose that most people actually *enjoy* going, but afterward, they are so glad they did."

"I know," Olivia said softly. It all made sense to Olivia, but she still didn't want to go. She always felt a little sick to her stomach whenever it was time to go to confession, and she didn't really know why.

Grandma cocked her head a little and smiled. "God gave us the sacrament to be closer to Him, to help us live our lives in a good and wholesome way so that when we mess up, which we often do, we can come back to Him and receive a clean heart. Our Father is a loving Father who forgives and forgets, but we have to show Him we're sorry. Sometimes we have to be brave and admit our wrongs, even though we don't think we can go through with it."

The late-afternoon sun was in their eyes by now, and Olivia held her hand over her eyes to shield them. Grandma shifted uneasily on the bench of the picnic table.

"I saw you and Hayley come in last night."

Olivia felt like the wind had been knocked out of her. She looked into Grandma's eyes, searching for more information. How had she heard them, when they were trying to be so quiet? And most importantly, exactly how much trouble would she and Hayley get into?

Ugh. What a trip this had been so far. And they still had two weeks left in Keane Harbor. She wished for the comforts of home: her bedroom, her bike, Sabrina and Chad. Something like this would never have happened at home. Home was boring; nothing ever happened there. Right about now she'd be playing basketball on her driveway or on the phone with Chad. Chad would be talking about catching tree frogs or lightning bugs, and she'd be listening with polite interest. Maybe they'd be marinating shish kebob for grilling, and her dad would be cutting the grass. Lucy would be in her little plastic playhouse in the yard. Life was so much simpler at home.

Grandma shook her head. "Livvy, I don't understand you. Sneaking out of the house at night. You should know better!"

There was not much that Olivia could say. There was no use denying it; Grandma knew they had snuck out. And that would be lying anyway. She certainly didn't want to add yet another lie to her growing list. She craned her neck, looking for her dad and Hayley. She half wished they'd come along just now, just to break up the conversation. On the other hand, though, it did feel good to finally have it out in the open.

"Grandma, it was such a huge mistake." Olivia poured her heart out to Grandma about meeting the other kids, and how Brandon, Brooke, and their friends had killed the turtles on the beach. She also told her about the horrible scene she had witnessed that morning.

Grandma was horrified. "Those poor little things," she whispered sadly. "They were never given a chance. Is it ignorance, or cruelty, or both," she wondered aloud, "to deny life?"

Grandma and Olivia were silent for a few moments, listening to cars whiz by on the street, their destinations unknown. Olivia wondered where they were going. Everyone always seemed to be in such a hurry, even on vacation. Tourists always seemed to be scurrying here and there. She wondered if grownups ever stopped to slow down once in a while and think about important things, not work or paying bills. Different kinds of important things: life and death things…

It seemed as if today's culture placed the value of life below so many other things that have little importance in the long run.

"But one made it," Olivia said. She told Grandma about how she and Hayley had begged the kids to stop, and how they had snatched the very last egg out of the hole and had run off with it, burying it farther down the beach. When Grandma heard about the discovery of the turtle tracks, her eyes glistened with tears.

"I've decided something," Grandma said. "I can see how sorry you are and how much pain this has caused you and Hayley. I can see it in your eyes and hear it in your voice. And I know it's one of the reasons you want to go to confession." Grandma paused, choosing her words carefully. "I think this is one of those things that can be our little secret."

Olivia got up and walked around the table to give Grandma a hug. "Oh, thank you, Grandma!" she said, greatly relieved that her parents did not have to know.

Grandma patted her head gently. "There's no need to spoil the vacation." She pulled away and looked at Olivia sternly. "But listen, missy. From now on, you and Hayley are to behave, you understand? That means no more sneaking out and no more shenanigans."

Olivia laughed. "Grandma, I promise!"

Whatever "shenanigans" were, she didn't want any part of them.

TWENTY-THREE

*"He will forget all our inequities and will never
remember them again. He will even do more than that:
He will love us even more than before our fault!"*
—St. Thérèse

Olivia stared at the door as it slowly opened. A young man walked out with a peaceful look on his face. He nodded at Olivia, indicating that he was done and it was her turn to go inside the confessional.

In her sweaty palm, Olivia held a small piece of paper. She had written down every sin she could possibly remember earlier when she was examining her conscience, which Grandma said you were supposed to do before you went to confession. Earlier, sitting cross-legged on her bed at the beach house, she had thought very hard about what sins she had committed since her last confession, and she wrote them down as they came to her. She didn't want to forget anything.

She slowly rose from her pew. She was the only one left waiting today.

"Afterward, you'll feel like St. Thérèse did—like she was walking on air." Grandma's words came to mind and comforted her as she walked inside the tiny room. She had a choice: She could sit with the priest face-to-face, or she could kneel at the kneeler behind the screen. Confronted with this decision, she did another on-the-spot examination of conscience: Lying to her parents and her friends, sneaking out, a love of money. Yup, better go to the kneeler and be hidden. She was absolutely sure her sins were the worst the priest would ever hear. Better not to see him.

"Bless me, Father, for I have sinned. It has been…" she had to think. How long had it been since her last confession? She started to panic. Did she go during Lent? She couldn't remember. It was all becoming a whirl to her, she was so nervous. She thought back to Christmastime. Was it cold out? Would she have been wearing a coat?

The priest cleared his throat after a long pause. "It's okay, young lady," he said kindly from behind the screen. "You can just continue."

Olivia thought she heard a smile in his voice, and it comforted her. "Um, okay."

There was another long pause. Olivia's mind spun. What should she start with first? Maybe she should go in order, starting with the worst. It was a tough call, though, since they all seemed equally bad in her mind.

"And what are your sins, my child?"

"Oh, right," she said, embarrassed. She groaned. This was not going well at all. She sent up a silent plea to St. Thérèse to pray for her, to help her through this.

Ask the Blessed Mother, said Thérèse in response. **Our Lady knows, and she wants to help you. The more you live in Mary, the more you are united to Jesus. Let Mary carry you and unite you to Him.**

Olivia smiled. Whenever St. Thérèse whispered something in her heart, whatever bad situation she was in seemed to improve. Thérèsc had such a devotion to the Blessed Mother, so it seemed natural for her to advise Olivia to seek her help. Following Thérèse's directive, Olivia quickly asked for courage for her task.

Oh please, Blessed Mother, Olivia prayed silently, *help me do this.*

All the while, the priest waited patiently on the other side.

"Oh, um, sorry," Olivia said. "I was talking to Mary."

"You talk to her too? I talk to her all the time," the priest said.

"You do?"

"Certainly. When I'm upset or nervous, I especially like to say to her, 'Mary, be a mother to me now.' Why don't you try that? It might make you feel at ease."

She felt a little silly, praying aloud in front of the priest. But he was a priest; what better person to pray in front of, right?

"Mary, be a mother to me now," Olivia said. Immediately she felt a sense of calming peace wrap around her shoulders, Mary covering her with her mantle of love.

"Are you ready now?" the priest asked.

"It worked!" Olivia cried, then turned beet red. Had she just shouted in the confessional? Yikes! "Oops, sorry, Father."

The priest laughed. "It's okay. Now let's start over again."

"Okay." Olivia looked down at her list of sins and read them off, one by one. "Father, I lied to my parents, my new friends, my neighbor who hired me to do a job, and my best friend."

"I see. Well—"

"Oh, there's more," she interrupted him sadly. "I bought some clothes I know my parents would disapprove of, and I wasted all my money that I was going to use for a charity. I also became totally obsessed with money and trying to impress people. Well, I guess that's it."

"It's good that you came to celebrate the sacrament of reconciliation. Jesus is happy that you came," said the priest's calm voice from behind the screen.

Olivia didn't much feel like she was having a celebration, but she didn't say that to the priest.

"And it really is a celebration, you know, because you have asked God to forgive you, and He does. It is a good thing, a joyful thing, to be reunited with our Lord in this way. When we lie and aren't true to ourselves, we are telling God that we don't need

Him. The fact that you came here today is proof that you love God and want to make things right. So many people are obsessed with money, and that takes them further away from God and the things that matter. You say you were saving up for a charity?"

"Yes, Father, I am saving up to sponsor a child in Guatemala." Olivia frowned. *Well, that dream is gone now*, she thought.

"That is a very admirable thing for someone so young to do."

"But I wasted most of it by buying things for myself," she said sadly. "Stupid stuff that I can't take back. I sort of became obsessed with money and wanting to look like a rich kid in front of my new friends."

"Well, you are right," the priest said. "Money can become an obsession. I see it all of the time. The thing to remember is that God has given us all gifts, and we should be grateful for everything He has given us. Even when it seems like others have more, we should try our hardest to recognize that God is always looking out for us, and will provide us with what we need. We don't have to worry or obsess about money if we just trust Him for all of our needs.

"Lying and a love of money are sins of pride," he said kindly. "And it is good that you have recognized them for what they are. The evil one is always on the prowl, looking to tempt us with things that are not of God."

Embarrassed, Olivia thought about the pair of shorts she had bought. Those were certainly not of God. She knew God did not want her to present herself to the world as a mere object, but as God's own daughter, someone to be respected. Someone with dignity.

He continued, "God forgives you and He knows you are truly sorry. Don't worry. For your penance, I want you to say two Hail

Marys, but also think of doing something extra nice for someone you know.

"And remember, there's no need to ever be afraid or nervous to go to confession, especially as you grow older. Priests hear confessions all of the time and we don't judge people, ever.

"There's nothing anybody could ever say that could shock us or that we haven't heard a million times before, so it's okay," he laughed. "Now, you can recite the Act of Contrition."

Olivia took a little card on the table next to her and read the words from the card:

> *"O my God,*
> *I am heartily sorry for*
> *having offended Thee,*
> *and I detest all my sins,*
> *because I dread the loss of heaven,*
> *and the pains of hell;*
> *but most of all because*
> *they offend Thee, my God,*
> *Who are all good and*
> *deserving of all my love.*
> *I firmly resolve,*
> *with the help of Thy grace,*
> *to confess my sins,*
> *to do penance,*
> *and to amend my life.*
> *Amen."*

Then the priest said these most comforting words: "God, the Father of mercies, through the death and resurrection of His Son, has reconciled the world to Himself and sent the Holy Spirit among us for the forgiveness of sins. Through the ministry of the Church may God give you pardon and peace, and I absolve you from your sins in the name of the Father, and of the Son, and of the Holy Spirit."

"Amen," Olivia responded. Then she made the sign of the cross and stood up, went to the door, and placed her hand on the handle. "Bye," she said.

"Goodbye," the priest said.

Olivia exited the room and felt lighter somehow. St. Thérèse had once said after one of her confessions, "I felt my soul breathe." Olivia took a deep breath and exhaled, enjoying the peace and calmness she felt, letting her soul breathe as well.

Sitting in the pew was a boy about her age, looking nervous and pale. She marveled at how, only several moments earlier, she must have looked the same way. She gave him a reassuring smile and saw his face soften a bit.

It was time to begin her penance.

She knelt in one of the pews, made the sign of the cross, and began: "Hail Mary, full of grace, the Lord is with thee…"

As she prayed, she felt the Blessed Mother's smile on her and she felt warm all over. She also felt Jesus giving her a hug, showing her His love and compassion.

When she was finished, she practically floated out of the chapel. It was over! She had told God she was sorry and He, in His divine love and mercy, had forgiven her sins. Her slate was wiped clean. She didn't yet know what she would do for the last part of her penance, but she knew she'd think of something.

Olivia realized she still had the slip of paper in her hand that listed all of her sins. Her *old* sins.

Smiling, she tore it up into tiny bits as she walked to meet her dad in the van, tossing the pieces of paper into a trash can by the front door to the church.

She couldn't wait to go home and tell Grandma and Hayley how great she felt. Maybe Hayley would go, too.

And next time, Olivia knew she wouldn't even need the screen.

TWENTY-FOUR

*"Upon leaving the confessional, I was so happy and so
light, for I had never before felt such joy in my soul."*
—St. Thérèse

Olivia felt the wind whip her hair around as she skated
down the street with Hayley. She was glad Hayley had suggested
they get out their inline skates. It was a perfect day to be outside
and smell the fresh sea air. She felt as light as a feather ever since
coming home from confession a few days earlier, although she
still wasn't quite sure what her penance should be. The priest had
mentioned doing something nice for someone, but she had no
idea what to do…or for whom.

The girls whizzed by Brandon and Brooke's house.

"Wonder what they're doing," Hayley said as she nodded toward their house.

"I don't know; I haven't seen them," said Olivia with a frown
as she concentrated on her feet so she wouldn't fall flat on her
face. She was admittedly no expert on skates like Hayley.

"I overheard your parents talking last night. They said there
were some cars in their driveway. They were official looking."

Olivia looked up. "Really? Like the police?"

"I don't know, I couldn't hear. They were whispering. I did hear Grandma say something about how she never liked us hanging around them in the first place—something about them being a 'bad influence.'"

Olivia thought of her grandma hearing them return home that night. She wondered if Grandma had told her parents. Then again, she had said she wouldn't, and Olivia knew she could trust Grandma to keep her word.

"Olivia…there's something else I heard them talking about," Hayley said slowly, unsure how to continue.

"You can tell me." Olivia hit a stone and wobbled a bit, so she turned her concentration back onto her feet.

"I heard your dad say he wasn't sure if he could go back to work. Olivia, did your dad lose his job?"

Olivia jerked her head up. "No! At least—he never said anything." Could this be true? Had her dad lost his job? But he was supposed to go back to work next month. And he hadn't said anything.

"Maybe he didn't," Hayley assured her. "I just heard them as I was walking by at the house, and I probably didn't hear it right."

"Yeah," Olivia agreed. "He would have told me, I'm sure he would have."

Later that evening, Olivia found her dad outside, checking the air on the tires of their van. The crickets were chirping loudly in the darkness, and she could hear the waves off in the distance behind the house.

"Dad?" she asked, unsure how to broach the subject.

Her dad stood up and stretched. "I knew this front tire was low," he said. "I'll take it to the gas station tomorrow. What's up, Livvy? I thought you and Hayley were watching a movie inside."

"We're taking a break to make popcorn," Olivia said. "Um, Dad?"

"Mmhmm?" Her dad was preoccupied checking the other front tire's air pressure.

"Dad, is everything okay? Do you still um...have a job?"

Her dad stopped and looked at her under the floodlight.

"Sure, honey. Why?"

Olivia sighed in relief. "Well...Mom said that you talked to your boss last week, and that it might be longer than you thought. I just wondered about it."

Her dad put the tire gauge in his pocket and walked over to give her a hug.

"Well, honey, yes—it may be a little longer before I can go back. I just found out that it may be a couple more months. But it's nothing for you to worry about, okay?"

"Okay," she smiled. "You sure?"

He nodded. "I'm sure. Now let's go inside and see if Hayley burned the microwave popcorn again."

The two walked inside, Olivia linking her arm through her dad's.

"Unfortunately," Olivia said as she opened the door, took a sniff, and looked at her dad, "she did."

TWENTY-FIVE

*"Love your littleness and your poverty, it is
that, as well as your blind trust in His Mercy,
which pleases the good God."*
—St. Thérèse

Olivia sat on the deck, watching the people on the beach below. It was relaxing sitting by herself, enjoying the evening breeze. The barbecue grill was still open, cooling off after a dinner of grilled cheeseburgers and corn on the cob. She felt full and happy as she watched a boy dragging a boogie board with its cuff attached to his ankle, heading back into the surf for another ride on the waves.

She thought about the time they'd spent in Keane Harbor so far, and all of the things she'd tell Jenna, Chad, and Sabrina when they got back home in two weeks. Would they believe that Hayley danced with a boy at a beach party? Or that they had saved the life of a baby sea turtle?

And what would happen to Brandon and the other kids? She was relieved that Abby wasn't involved in the killing spree. She wondered if the kids would go to jail. Could kids her age go to jail? Maybe some sort of youth jail? What they had done was serious, she reasoned. Taking the innocent lives of the baby turtles on the beach was unconscionable in her mind. The new life God creates should always, always be respected.

She also thought all of the money she'd squandered, money that was meant for someone else, a young life thousands of miles away. She felt ashamed. There would be no way out of it; they'd want to know why she would suddenly stop talking about The Project. She'd have to admit that she foolishly spent it all trying to impress kids she had just met and would probably never see again. She firmly made up her mind to get the money back.

Somehow, some way, I'll earn it back, she thought. *I know I can do it. It may take a long time, but I'll do it.*

Olivia knew Jenna and Chad would be especially disappointed. She felt closest to them and felt embarrassed at how she had behaved in Keane Harbor. Would Hayley let them know all of the things she had done? She hoped not.

"It's a big one!" Olivia heard the boy call out to his friend as they waited for the next wave to come in.

Olivia smiled as she watched them. It would be fun to have a boogie board. Maybe if she asked her dad—

Oops, there she went again, thinking about money. And with her dad laid off for longer, it was a thoughtless wish. She decided then and there to be grateful for what she had. After all, she didn't really need a boogie board. They were leaving Keane Harbor in two weeks. Not much use for a boogie board in the calm lakes of Michigan. Instead, she thought of another idea: Maybe Hayley would want to go take a walk on the beach in a little while and collect some sand in sandwich bags to take home as a souvenir. Maybe Chad and Jenna would like a bag, too.

She closed her eyes and listened to the surf, thinking about her day. The priest had mentioned something about doing something nice for someone. What could that be? She could apologize to Mrs. Duggan the next time she went over to watch Danny, which was in a couple of days. But she knew, deep down, that it was something she had to do anyway, so that didn't really count.

Her mom interrupted her thoughts. "Hi, honey. Relaxing?"

Olivia turned and saw her mom in the doorway. She had a warm smile on her face. "Mhmmm."

"Grandma told me you looked so happy after you came home from confession the other day. I know how that feels," she said, sitting on the edge of Olivia's lawn chair.

"You do?" Somehow she couldn't envision her mom sinning. To Olivia, her mom was perfect in the eyes of God. She could never picture her parents or her grandma doing anything wrong!

Her mom laughed. "I know what you are thinking, but everyone should go to confession, you know. Me, Dad, Grandma…"

Olivia nodded. Obviously she had seen them go to confession over the years, but somehow she didn't really think about it until just now.

Her mom laughed a little. "Nobody's perfect…even parents!"

Olivia didn't know what to say to that. Maybe she'd best keep quiet on that one.

The smile on her mom's face grew wider. "You and Grandma have a little secret, I think."

Olivia's eyes grew wide. How did she know? Was she mad?

Her mom held up her hand. "Far be it for me to pry. Grandma seems a little secretive today. But I'm not going to ask. It's your business with her. I just want to let you know that if you want to talk about it with me or Dad as well, you can feel free."

She kissed the top of Olivia's head. "Dad and I are taking

Hayley up to the drugstore. She has a cough and I think some cough syrup would help her be a little more comfortable tonight."

"Okay, Mom." Olivia was relieved that her mom wasn't mad—or asking questions. Maybe one day soon she'd tell her everything that happened: Brandon, the turtles, the shorts, the money.

"We're putting Lucy down to bed, but keep an ear out for her, to help out Grandma, okay? She seems pretty tired and could use your help for a bit."

She could hear Hayley coughing in the distance from the open doorwall. She sounded like she had really come down with a bad cold. She felt bad for her friend. What a shame to have to be sick in their last week there.

A few moments later, her mom and dad and Hayley backed out of the driveway.

Olivia reached up to scratch her head, which seemed to have collected some sand in it from earlier in the day. It was getting dark out and everyone on the beach was packing up their things and leaving. *I need a shower*, she thought as she stood up and walked back inside the house.

"Grandma!" she called to the other end of the large house as she walked upstairs to the bathroom. "I'm going to take a shower!"

Grandma didn't answer, but Olivia kept walking, shaking sand out of her hair.

She heard the phone ring and Grandma's footsteps on the tiled floor as she hurried to answer it.

"Peggy! Hello! What? Oh yes, we're enjoying your house so much!" Grandma's voice trailed off.

The shampoo felt good as it worked its sudsy magic on Olivia's scalp. *How do I manage to take the beach with me wherever I go?*

she mused as she stared down at the sand accumulating on the floor of the shower. Stepping out of the shower, she wrapped herself up in a bathrobe and a fluffy towel on her head. Aunt Peggy bought the best when it came to linens and towels. *That's okay,* Olivia thought as she put on her pajamas. *We're lucky to have some pretty, nice things at our house, too.*

The mirror was fogged up, so she took one of the towels and wiped it down a little so she could see. Then she opened the window so it would defog quicker. She stared at her reflection in the mirror, a big yellow towel wrapping her hair up in a turban. Leaning in closer, she studied her face; the sun had given her even more freckles the past couple of weeks at the beach, even though she had used sun lotion every day.

Maybe I need a higher SPF, she thought as she put on her pajamas.

The breeze started to rattle the blinds on the window, making an annoying noise. Olivia absentmindedly started to raise them up and glanced out at the receding tide and moon rising over the water. The ocean sure was beautiful at night. Her eye rested on something on the sand. Had one of the boys left something on the beach? She squinted her eyes and peered harder. The thing was moving!

In shock and horror, she knew what it was: little Danny, walking straight into the water!

"NO! Danny, NO!" she screamed through the window, but the sounds of the waves crashing ashore drowned out her cries.

She ran to the bathroom door and flung it open.

"GRANDMA!" she screamed from the top of the stairs. She scampered downstairs and looked for Grandma. The doorwall was open, the evening breeze coming into the living room. It was the quickest way down to the beach.

Frantically, she looked for Grandma. Not seeing her anywhere, she ran outside to the deck in her pajamas. In her panic,
she tripped over a pair of flip-flops and fell down hard on the
deck. Wincing in pain, she rubbed her ankle. Had she twisted it?
It didn't matter; what mattered was getting to Danny. He was too
little to be able to swim. If he got into the water—

There was no time to think of that. The only thing that mattered was that Danny was in danger. She tried to stand up but her
throbbing ankle made it difficult. Through the slats of the deck,
she could see Danny standing at tide's end, staring at the water.

"GRANDMA! Danny!" she screamed at the top of her voice.
She threw her flip-flops aside and grabbed the handrail on the
deck stairs, the breeze whipping her wet hair around her face.
Wincing in pain, she hobbled down the stairs as quickly as she
could, falling onto the soft sand. She looked up and saw Danny
inching into the water, growing smaller and smaller as he walked
deeper into the surf. The wind was whipping the waves hard. It
would only be a matter of time before—

Olivia was frantic and tried to get up. She looked around the
deserted beach. Where on earth were Mr. and Mrs. Duggan? She
was the only one around who could save Danny. Then she felt the
voice again:

**You're not alone. Ask me. I can help you; I can pray for
you.**

From the back of her mind came something she'd heard her
Grandma say over the years. "Little Flower, show your power in
this hour," Olivia whispered. "Oh God, please save little Danny!
He's so little; let him live, Lord!"

She had to get to him before it was too late! "Oh, Mary, be a
mother to me now! Please save Danny!" she pleaded as she sobbed.

It was then that she heard a sharp voice coming from the side of the house.

"Danny, STOP!" yelled Grandma, striding through the sand with determination toward the water. Her jaw was set and she was hurrying as fast as her elderly body would physically allow.

As Olivia got closer, she saw Grandma inch into the water. In her attempt to scoop up Danny, Grandma stumbled and fell into the water.

Olivia gulped. Grandma couldn't swim! A few seconds later, Grandma's head bobbed up and she was able to stand, lifting Danny out of the surf. Out of breath, she carried him as far as she could out of the water and set him down into the sand, holding him tightly. Olivia hobbled as best she could over to Danny, who was sobbing uncontrollably as he sat in the sand. Olivia knelt down beside Danny and Grandma in the sand, and the three of them embraced and cried.

"Oh, Danny, oh, thank You, God!" Olivia cried.

She opened her eyes and looked at Grandma, whose eyes were fixed heavenward, tears streaming down her face. Her lips were moving but she was not speaking as she cradled Danny's head in the moonlight.

They stayed like that for a long time, hugging and crying and praying.

Eventually, Mr. Duggan came running toward them in the sand.

"Danny! What happened?" he cried, panic-stricken. After Grandma explained what had happened, Mr. Duggan said that his wife had been feeling under the weather. He had put Danny in his crib so he could tend to her needs.

"He must have climbed out of the crib and gotten outside," he said breathlessly. He sighed heavily and squeezed Danny tightly for a long time.

Finally, they all stood up and headed back to the deck. No one said anything.

"I can't thank you enough." Mr. Duggan choked back tears.

"God sent Danny's guardian angel," Grandma said wisely.

They all parted ways and Olivia and Grandma went inside. Grandma rushed to check on Lucy, who was still sleeping peacefully in her room. Although it seemed like hours, in reality they had only been outside for about ten minutes.

When Grandma came back downstairs, Olivia was standing in the living room, still shivering, her arms wrapped around herself. "Oh Grandma, I tried so hard to get to him," she said, the tears coming back. "I couldn't get to him. I couldn't—"

Grandma came over to her and hugged her. "It's okay," she said, her voice shaking. She pulled away and looked at Olivia. "How is your ankle?"

Olivia looked down at her leg and foot, covered in sand. "I don't...I don't know..." she sniffed. "But I don't care. I just care that Danny is safe."

"Come on now," Grandma said as she put some ice in a bag for Olivia. "No harm done. We all had a scare. It's over now."

Olivia sank into the sofa, letting out a huge sigh. She buried her head in her hands and felt relief slowly set in. It was over. Danny was safe. No harm done. Olivia glanced at Grandma's sandy feet. Grandma had been there on the beach to save him. She rescued him from the water and—

She and Grandma stared at each other then, both realizing the magnitude of what had just happened.

"Grandma!" Olivia cried, shaking her head. "You did it!"

"Wha-What? I did what?"

"You went down to the beach! You got back in the water! After all of these years! You did it! You overcame your fear of the water!"

Grandma grew pale then, and her face registered the shock. "I did?"

Olivia limped over to the couch Grandma was sitting on and gave her a huge hug. "You did! You did! You overcame your fear!"

Grandma shook her head slowly. "I can't believe it. I actually did, after all of these years."

"After all of these years!" Olivia laughed then.

"Grandma, I felt St. Thérèse with me. I prayed that little prayer you do when you're nervous. Remember that time we almost got into a car accident and you said that?"

"I do," she said, patting down her still-wet hair.

"I also asked God and the Blessed Mother to help."

"I think He was helping all of us," she said solemnly. "He gave me the faith to have the courage to do what I had to do. Livvy, never in a million years did I think I'd go back in the water."

Then an angry look crossed Grandma's face. "Your grandpa! This was all his idea, getting me back into the water! He knew I would run out there to save that little boy! He knew that was the only thing that would get me into the water again!" Feisty Grandma made a fist and pursed her lips. "The nerve! He's gonna hear it from me, I'll tell you that!"

Olivia hugged Grandma again and the two fell into a chorus of giggles, laughing and crying with relief all at once.

"Oh, Grandma, I'm so proud of you!"

TWENTY-SIX

*"To come near to Jesus, we must be very little. O how few
are the souls who aspire to be lowly and unknown."*
—St. Thérèse

Our Lady Star of the Sea Church was a hub of activity for
its annual summer ice cream social and rummage sale. Little children ran around outside on the lawn, ice cream cones dripping
onto their clothes from Sunday Mass, but everyone was in such
a good mood and it was such a beautiful day that their parents
didn't seem to mind.

Grandma, Lucy, and Mr. and Mrs. Thomas went to check out
the rummage sale inside the activities building while Hayley
and Olivia went straight to the tables serving ice cream sundaes.
Grandma loved rummage sales, white elephant sales, tag sales,
garage sales—anything that sold second-hand items.

"You never know what you might find," Grandma said with a
wink. "And we brought a van, so we can take anything home!"

Olivia saw her parents exchange a glance; their van was
packed to the gills on the way here. She didn't know what her
grandma had in mind, but she was sure her parents wouldn't be
too thrilled to be taking too much stuff back home.

Grandma didn't notice. "You girls make yourself some yummy sundaes. If you need us, we'll be inside." She happily took Lucy's hand and led her into the building.

"Steve, not too much, okay?" Olivia heard her mom whisper.

"Claudia, you know how Mom is. I'm sure it won't be anything huge, just some knick-knacks. You know how much she likes knick-knacks."

Mrs. Thomas sighed. "Yes, dear, I know."

Olivia giggled. If she knew Grandma, she would come out with an armful of used treasures to display in her house.

"We'll have to look around inside after we eat," Hayley said, eying the ice cream, "but right now I'm starving." She looked down at the bag Olivia had in her hand. "By the way, what's in the bag?"

Olivia tightened her grip on the bag. "I have something to donate to the rummage sale," she said faintly.

"Why the secrecy? You can't tell me?"

"You'll find out in a little while," she said. "Come on, let's get some ice cream."

As the two girls stood in line, they saw Abby in the distance.

"Here comes your new best friend," Hayley said, as Abby approached them, waving from the sidewalk. She crossed the lawn, which was filled with children running around as they held bowls of ice cream.

"What do you mean?" Olivia felt stung until she looked at Hayley's hurt face as she watched Abby come nearer.

"Nothing, forget I said it." Hayley turned toward the table and picked up a spoon and a napkin.

"Hi guys!" Abby said, holding a bowl of chocolate ice cream piled high with whipped cream, sprinkles, and a cherry. "I thought I saw you."

"Hi Abby," Olivia said, still confused over what Hayley had said. What on earth was Hayley driving at? For the next several minutes as everyone talked, Olivia's mind was on Hayley's comment. She looked down at her own scuffed-up sandals and was amazed to realize she didn't even care that Abby was standing there in front of them in her expensive outfit.

"I haven't seen you guys on the beach."

"We've been…busy," Olivia said, not wanting to talk about the events on the beach. Although Abby wasn't involved in the devastation of the sea turtles, Olivia didn't know if she even knew about it.

"Been watching Danny a lot?" Abby asked.

"No, not really." Olivia was still feeling bad that Mrs. Duggan hadn't called her as often since the day she'd lied to her. She wondered if Mrs. Duggan knew the truth; she must have known.

But Hayley wasn't one to mince words. "Your friends had quite the time on the beach, killing a nest of baby sea turtles a couple of weeks ago. Maybe *that's* why we haven't exactly been knocking on your door," she scoffed.

Abby looked down at her ice cream. "I know," she said softly.

"We just don't understand how they could be so sick," Olivia retorted, "and how you can call them your friends." At this, Hayley looked at Olivia, shocked at her declaration.

"Let's sit down over there," Abby said, motioning to a picnic table in the shade, away from the commotion and noise.

Hayley and Olivia both got out of line and followed Abby over to the table, where she set down her plastic bowl and pushed it away, letting her ice cream melt. "I am so ashamed of them," she said sadly, playing with the hem of her skirt.

"How could they do that?" Olivia demanded.

"You know, guys, Brandon and Brooke don't come from a great home. I mean, sure, they're rich and have all kinds of stuff, but their mom and dad are nothing like yours, Olivia. The kids are with Nina most of the time, and she doesn't even really care about them that much; she's just doing a job. They're always dropped off somewhere, like camp for weeks at a time, or with a babysitter. Their mom and dad are not mean, but…I don't know…do you get what I'm saying?"

"So because they don't spend much time with their parents, they think it's okay to kill baby sea turtles?" Hayley didn't look at all convinced.

"No, no, that's not what I'm saying at all, Hayley. I'm not making excuses for what they did. I just want you to understand where they are coming from. Their parents really aren't there to teach them things, or love them that much. I think for Brooke and Brandon that it's their way of acting out and trying to get attention they don't ever get from their parents."

"You sound like a psychologist," Hayley smirked. "It all sounds nice, but they still did something really bad, and they should pay for it."

"Oh, they will," Olivia piped up, eager to reassure everyone. "My dad called the police as soon as we saw the eggs. The wildlife authorities are gonna investigate."

"And as soon as I found out what they did, I told their parents. They were really upset."

"Well, I would hope so!" cried Olivia.

"They got into a whole bunch of trouble," Abby continued, "and a couple of officials even came to the house the next day. They had to answer a ton of questions. I don't know what's going to happen. They're in serious trouble."

"Well, I'm glad," Olivia said smugly.

"Me, too," Hayley said.

"I still don't understand why you are friends with them, and go on vacation with them," Olivia wanted to know. "How can you stand to be with them?"

"I don't have a choice," Abby said quietly.

"Sure you do. I had a choice whether I wanted to come here with Olivia's family," said Hayley.

"Well, I didn't. My dad is serving overseas in the Navy, and my mom is really sick. She can't take care of me until he comes back in October. By then she should be in remission."

Olivia stared. She'd had no idea. Here she thought Abby's life was so perfect—Abby with the perfect hair and clothes. She realized, like her dad always said, that things weren't always what they seemed to be. She felt bad that she had rushed to judgment.

"Do you miss your dad?" Hayley asked.

"Yeah. A lot. He's been gone a long time."

"Mine too," Hayley said quietly.

Olivia reached over and patted Hayley's back. "He's watching over you, Hayley."

"I know," Hayley said.

"I'm sorry, Hayley," Abby said, suddenly realizing what Hayley had meant.

"Thanks."

"Mr. and Mrs. Dansbury offered to take me for the summer so my mom could get well. It was really nice of them. They're not all that bad and Brandon and Brooke have their good points sometimes. Their parents have been really nice to my parents, and even helped them pay part of my tuition last year when my mom had to stop working. So it's hard for me to be mad at them, you know?"

"I guess," Hayley conceded. "So how are we going to make sure it doesn't happen again?"

"I can pretty much guarantee it won't," Abby said and leaned in close. "I heard Brandon crying last night in his room."

"No way!" cried Olivia, and she and Hayley exchanged surprised looks.

Abby nodded. "I thought it was just because he got caught, but he looks genuinely sad. I think the authorities got through to him when they came over. Brandon has a couple of pets at home, and I think he finally got it through his thick skull that lives are nothing to be toyed with."

Olivia simply could not imagine a tough guy like Brandon crying about anything. He had such a hard-as-nails exterior, like nothing bothered him, so sure of himself and on top of the world. Picturing him crying alone in his room painted him in a different light. Again, a case of things not always being what they seemed to be.

"Well," said Hayley awkwardly, "I don't know what to say, but I am glad he seems really sorry. I liked him at first, but then when he did that, I lost all respect for him."

"Think we can forgive him?" Olivia asked Hayley. Olivia wasn't so sure she could.

"It's gonna be hard, but maybe..." Hayley said, her voice trailing off.

"I dunno," Olivia said softly, thinking how she herself had some explaining to do as well. It would be pretty hypocritical of her to act all high and mighty toward Brandon's actions when she had done some pretty bad stuff, too. When she went to confession, she also made a promise to Jesus that she would try to do the right thing. Now was the time to do the right thing by Abby. She craned her neck, looking for a sign of her parents and Lucy and hoped they would come over and interrupt so she could be saved from doing what she knew she had to do.

No such luck!

Oh well, I guess it's for the best, she thought. "So, um...I have a little explaining to do too," she said awkwardly.

Abby raised her eyebrows and waited.

"Because, um, I told you some things that aren't true."

"I know," Abby said with a shrug of her shoulders. "You told us before, remember?"

"Well...there's a little bit more."

"Ah," said Abby, who was silent a moment, but then said, "Well, it doesn't matter anyway."

Olivia was relieved. This wasn't so hard. Except that she hadn't got to the biggie lie yet.

"But...the house we're staying in...that's not really *my* house. It sort of belongs to my aunt and uncle."

At this, Hayley grinned her approval. Olivia could read Hayley's mind: *You are doing the right thing.*

"You're the niece of Mr. and Mrs. Pemberley?" asked Abby, surprised. "Then where are they?"

"They're back home in Texas," she said. "They couldn't come this summer so they asked us if we wanted to spend July here."

Then there was that little matter of France. "And I'd like to go to France...someday," she said quietly, thinking of how wonderful it would be to visit Lisieux, where St. Thérèse had lived. "But I don't see that happening anytime soon. My dad is laid off and things are kind of tight right now."

Abby shrugged her shoulders. "No big deal, really."

"Thanks," Olivia said with a little laugh. "I'm nobody special, not rich or anything like I had you all believe."

"Nobody is really what they seem on the outside, not 100 percent anyway," Abby said.

In Abby's brown eyes, Olivia could read her meaning: Things aren't always what they seem to be. But deep down, she felt the true happiness of knowing she did the right thing, and she felt proud of herself.

"So, sad to be going home next weekend?" Abby said, eager to change the subject. She finished her ice cream, licking her spoon.

"Yes and no," Olivia said. "I mean, I'll miss hanging out at the beach and stuff, but I'm kind of ready to go home."

Hayley's head jerked up. Although Keene Harbor was fun and they'd had a great time at the beach, she was ready, too. She was tired of the big, fancy house that made echoes in its vastness, a house she could get lost in with its gazillion bedrooms. She wanted her cozy home, her mother, and her brother Ryan.

"Really?" Hayley asked hopefully.

"Yeah. I miss everybody. Hayley and I have some great friends back home. We want to have fun before school starts up again. And I miss my bedroom and my basketball net."

At this, Hayley looked at Olivia and a slow smile spread over her face. She lost the pain in her heart she'd had ever since Olivia had hung onto Abby and the others like a puppy dog, eager for their acceptance and friendship.

Olivia was hers again.

Olivia gave Hayley a playful shove. "Hayley has a lot of bossing around to do before September, don't you, Hayley?"

"Come on!" Hayley cried happily, glad to have the old Olivia back. "I'm not that bad…most of the time!"

"Nah, not that bad. Come on, let's go get our ice cream before these little kids eat it all up."

"And you say *I* give orders? Right!"

"You guys are really funny," Abby said, watching the two girls play around. "I wish I had a best friend at home like that."

Hayley and Olivia grinned at each other. They were blessed, and they both knew it.

Hayley and Olivia cach ate two hot-fudge sundaes with the works. After about 20 minutes, Hayley had a funny, pained expression on her face.

"Ugh."

Just when Hayley declared that she was starting to feel a little sick, Grandma came over holding a picture frame.

"Look what I found," she declared proudly, her face radiant with her new treasure. She held up the picture, a photograph of two cows in a pasture.

"Grandma, they're cows!" Olivia cried. "Why would you want a picture of a couple of cows?"

"I really have to know, Grandma Rosemary. The curiosity is killing me." Hayley said this somewhat weakly, holding her stomach.

Grandma laughed. "It's not the cows I like, it's the frame. I'm going to take the picture out and replace it with a picture of my granddaughters, sillies."

Olivia was relieved. "Oh, good!"

Hayley, with a hand on her stomach, asked, "I wonder who would take a photo of two cows…and then frame it to hang on a wall?"

"You should go in there and have a look around," Grandma

said. "Lots of treasures to sift through." She looked with concern at Hayley. "Eat too much, honey?"

"Ugh, I guess so," groaned Hayley.

"You look a little green around the gills." Grandma was concerned, and suggested the three girls take a little walk around the church grounds. "It aids digestion," she said earnestly.

The girls stifled a giggle.

"So does not stuffing my face with ice cream," Hayley whispered, and Olivia pursed her lips together and tried not to laugh.

Grandma dug into her purse and gave each of the girls a few dollars. "You go have fun and find some little treasures! I'm going to put this in the van for safekeeping."

"Thanks, Grandma Rosemary. Can I come with you? I left something in the back."

Olivia looked at Hayley, confused. "Are you sure you're okay?"

"Yeah, it's starting to go away. I'll be right back," Hayley assured Olivia. "I'll meet you inside."

Abby and Olivia got up and wandered over to the activities building, where the rummage sale was being held, with Olivia still holding her bag. There was so much to look at that they didn't know what to inspect first. Tables groaned with merchandise and crowds of people perused the items.

Olivia picked up a pair of sequined sunglasses and tried them on. "How do I look?" she asked.

"Fabulous, my darling," said Hayley, who had come back, this time with a bag in her hand. Olivia took the sunglasses off and put them on Hayley instead.

"I think they're yours," she said, while Abby wandered off to the far side of the room to look at a stack of books. "You look like you're feeling better."

"Yeah, a little bit."

"What's in the bag, Hayley?" Olivia asked as Hayley admired her reflection in a small mirror.

Hayley blushed and took off the glasses. "It's your favorite T-shirts," she said. "I'm donating them to the rummage sale."

"Seriously?"

"Yeah. I don't know, it wasn't the greatest thing to be shouting to the world—about vampires, and this one about being 'cute.' Made me feel sort of strange when people would read it," she said sheepishly.

"You know what Grandma would say: 'That's your conscience talking, don't ignore it.'" Olivia grinned, copying Grandma's often-repeated phrase. "But I know what you mean. Look what I'm giving away," and she opened the bag so Hayley could peer inside.

"No way! Your new shorts?"

"Yeah. The thought of someone reading something on my rear end was too weird for me. Plus I know it's wrong."

Hayley held out the T-shirts. "Here, put them with your shorts."

Olivia happily took the shirts and put them in the bag just as Abby came over holding an old rotary telephone. Playing with the dial, she asked, "Ever buy anything at one of these things? You never know what you'll find. One time I found a really pretty purse, practically brand new!"

Olivia shook her head. "No, I haven't, but look at this stuff!" She picked up a strange-looking serving tray with a picture of a large, green parrot on it.

"What on earth?" the three girls exploded into giggles when they read that "Polly want a cracker?" was painted on the tray.

Hayley took it from Olivia and admired it. "Well, you know, if I were having a fancy dinner party with a…bird theme…I'd want this!"

"I think you're supposed to put crackers and cheese on it," groaned Olivia.

"Where do people *get* this stuff?" Abby said as she picked up a cookbook entitled *50 Ways to Cook Asparagus.*

"Olivia, you love to cook; get it! The sticker says 50 cents!"

"A penny for each asparagus recipe," Olivia said as she turned the pages of the book. "What amazes me is that someone, somewhere, bought this book on purpose!"

"Not necessarily," said Abby as she held up a pair of silver hoop earrings, looking for the price. "Maybe it was a birthday present or something, and the person held on to it until she couldn't stand it anymore!"

"Well, all I know is that I don't know how I've lived this long without owning *this*," said Hayley as she held up a record album entitled, *Christmas Disco Hits, Volume III.*

"You mean there were actually Volumes I and II? This place is a riot!" cried Olivia, examining a pair of suede, bright-purple, high-heeled shoes.

"I can't begin to invent a reason for wearing those!" exploded Hayley.

People around them were looking at glassware, old TV sets, books, and DVDs. The room was very crowded, and after awhile, Olivia began to get warm.

"I think I heard one of the ladies say something about a room down the hall with some cool things in it," she said. "I'll be right back."

Olivia walked down the hallway, studying the things for sale on the tables, which were piled high with all sorts of household kitchen items like used pots, pans, and teakettles.

"Can I help you find anything?" a nice older woman asked Olivia as she studied an embellished vanity mirror that had undoubtedly once been on a lady's dresser.

"Oh, no thank you, but I do have something to donate," she said, suddenly remembering her bag. "I hope it's not too late."

"It's never too late; the sale goes on until six o'clock," the lady said, holding out her hand. "What do you have here?"

"It's just…some clothes." She was embarrassed that the older lady was going to open up the bag right in front of her and see the immodest pair of short-shorts with the word "Diva" on the bottom. What would she think?

But she reached inside the bag, ignoring Olivia's silent pleas, it seemed. She held up the shorts. Disappointment was all over her face as she pulled the too-tight "Don't hate me 'cause I'm cuter than you" and "I ♥ vampires" T-shirts out of the bag as well.

"These things look fairly new," she said.

"Oh, I never really wore the shorts," Olivia assured her. "I mean, my mom would never let me wear those. And the shirts, well…my friend sort of got tired of them."

"Well, it's nice of you to donate them," the lady said with a smile. "You are very generous. I'll just take these to Mrs. Foster— she puts the prices on everything. I think she's in the kitchen."

The lady gave Olivia her bag back. "Just in case you buy something today," she said with a wink, and walked down the hall to find Mrs. Foster.

Olivia found the door open to a small room with various knick-knacks. *I wonder if Grandma saw this room*, she wondered. Alone in the room, Olivia was content and happy to be rid of the pair of shorts and Hayley's obnoxious T-shirts. She was so glad that Hayley wanted to get rid of them. They really bugged her, because Hayley was not the type to be so egotistical, and had never once referred to herself as "cute" or liking vampires.

She smiled as she perused the things people had once treasured but had now donated to the rummage sale in order to help the church raise funds. She found a bud vase with little red roses all over it and immediately thought of St. Thérèse. It was marked 75 cents, and Olivia knew it was meant to be hers; it was as plain as the nose on her face that it was a sign of love from St. Thérèse—another one of her roses. She felt her heart skip a beat, as it did every time St. Thérèse sent one of her rose "hellos."

She knew just where it would go, too: right on her dresser at home, maybe with a silk rose in it. It sure was nice of Grandma to give her and her friends a little spending money. She felt guilty spending more money on herself after all the shopping she had done in Keane Harbor, but Grandma wanted to treat her, and she didn't want to appear ungrateful. She also did not want to turn down a rose from St. Thérèse.

Clutching the pretty vase, she turned to walk out of the room when something caught her eye. At first she wasn't quite sure if she was seeing it correctly, so she went over to the table for a closer look. In the rear left corner of a table covered with religious pictures, books, and medals, she saw the beautiful statue and felt her heart skip a beat. It was adorned with a white lace robe and its red crown was perfect, absolutely perfect. Not a scratch or a chip on it.

The Infant of Prague, she breathed. The beautiful Child Jesus, smiling at her as she stood there, open-mouthed, amazed at her find.

And at that instant, she knew: This statue was meant for her to give to Mrs. Duggan. Olivia gently reached over and touched the soft, lacy robe. She couldn't believe her luck...but she knew it wasn't luck that brought the Child Jesus to her here at the rummage sale. She knew that with God, there are no coincidences.

She smiled at God's divine intervention; Jesus helping her to complete her penance of doing something nice for someone else. She picked up the statue and gave it a little kiss, just like St. Thérèse used to do in the convent when she was caring for the holy statue of Baby Jesus in the manger; she loved the Child Jesus so.

Carefully cradling the statue to her heart, Olivia had a peaceful feeling of the love she had in her heart for her Lord and his servant Thérèse. She hurried out of the room, as if afraid somehow the statue would disappear before she paid for it.

She found a young man with a cash box sitting at a table in the hallway.

"Ready to check out?" he asked. "Oh, I see you found the Infant of Prague. Isn't it beautiful?"

"It's amazing," Olivia said with a grin as she looked down at it, then suddenly remembered something important: In her excitement she had not thought to look for a price. "But how much is it?"

The man thoughtfully turned the statue over, but found no price tag anywhere. "Looks like Mrs. Foster forgot to price it." He pondered for a few moments. "Well, let's just call it two dollars."

Olivia could not believe her ears. "Are you sure?" she asked. "It's such a beautiful statue..."

"I'm sure," the man said, nodding and looking thoughtfully at Olivia. "Something tells me this is going to a good home."

"It certainly is," Olivia said, handing the man the money for the statue and the vase.

He leaned in to Olivia. "You know, there's an interesting story about this statue."

"Oh, do you know who donated it?"

"Not personally," he said, "but Mrs. Foster does. She told me that it originally belonged to a priest."

"Oh," Olivia said, happy to hear this.

"That's not all: The priest was *blind*."

The man smiled as he wrapped up Olivia's vase in some tissue paper.

"He was?" Olivia looked down at the statue. She felt the Infant's lacy robe and imagined someone blind appreciating the beauty of the statue without even being able to see it.

"That's true faith," the man said. "To have such a special statue and to cherish it—when he couldn't even see it." He gave her a wink.

Olivia looked lovingly at the statue. She knew someone else who would appreciate this special statue of the Infant of Prague— at least, she hoped so. She also hoped that it wasn't too late to get back in Mrs. Duggan's good graces.

"Thank you very much," she said to the man and handed him the statue so he could wrap it in tissue as well.

"You're welcome. Have a blessed day," he said, handing her a plastic bag with her purchases.

And with a quarter left in her pocket, Olivia went to go find her friends.

She found Abby and Hayley waiting for her on a bench outside. Abby was holding the parrot tray in her hands, a giant grin on her face.

"You didn't!" cried Olivia happily. "Oh, Abby!"

"I wanted something to remember you guys by," Abby said with a smirk. "Every time I look at this goofy tray, I'll remember you and how much fun we had this summer." She gave the girls hugs. "I've got to get going. Mrs. Dansbury said she'd pick me up at three."

The girls waved goodbye to Abby and as she walked away, she held up the tray and they all laughed themselves silly.

After they had composed themselves, Hayley sighed. "Oh, too funny. Hey, Olivia, did you give the stuff away?"

"Yup," replied Olivia. "And wait 'til you see what I found in the other room."

Just as Olivia was about to pull her beautiful treasures out of the bag, she saw Mrs. Foster hurry outside, sopping wet.

"Oh, girls, did you happen to see Mr. Newman, the janitor?"

The girls shook their heads, staring wide-eyed at Mrs. Foster.

"Oh, I know, I look a fright. There was an incident with that huge lemonade dispenser in the kitchen," she said, running a hand through her wet hair. In her other hand, she held the shorts and T-shirts Olivia had given her earlier.

"It started to leak all over the kitchen, and the paper towels were all gone," she said breathlessly. "The people working the ice cream tables must have taken them. The kitchen is a disaster!"

She tsk-tsked and shook her head as she looked with disdain at the volunteers who manned the ice cream tables. "Unfortunately, I had to use whatever I had right there, and it happened to be the clothes you girls donated. Now I'm a sticky mess, and the clothes are, too! I'll have to throw them away!"

"I'm—so sorry," Olivia said with surprise as the sticky Mrs. Foster stood in front of them with Hayley's soggy, dripping-wet shirt and Olivia's shorts in her hand. "Is there anything we can do to help?"

"No, not unless you know where the mop and bucket are kept!" she said in exasperation.

The girls stifled giggles as Mrs. Foster hurried away, looking in agitation for Mr. Newman.

"I don't mean to laugh at that poor lady, but Olivia, the clothes we donated are totally ruined. She's putting them in that big trash can over there!"

Olivia made a goofy face. "What a shame! Now nobody can wear them…which isn't such a bad thing! Hey, I've got a quarter left. We can split some popcorn!"

Hayley groaned good-naturedly. "Are you kidding me? I think I've had enough junk food for one day! I'm feeling better—let's not push it!"

The two girls got up and walked across the lawn, discussing if popcorn was truly junk food. They came to the conclusion that it was not.

Thérèse, I love your sense of humor, Olivia thought happily, carefully clutching the statue to her heart. *You know just what to ask God for in every situation! How do you do that? You're the best.*

"Whatcha got in the bag?" Hayley wanted to know.

Olivia told Hayley about the treasures she had found inside and how she was convinced they were signs from God.

"I really hope Mrs. Duggan likes the statue," Olivia lamented with a frown. "When I tell her about how I lied to her, she might be pretty angry."

"Well, you're owning up to what you did, and that's the important thing. It shows total class, Olivia, and I'm proud of you."

"Really?"

"Yeah, really. You said you're nobody special but I think you are. And I know someone else who thinks you are, too." Hayley pointed toward the clouds.

Olivia beamed. "Oh, I really hope she does."

"How could she not?" Hayley grinned and gave her a sideways hug. "You follow her Little Way."

TWENTY-SEVEN

"Jesus, help me to simplify my life by learning what you want me to be, and becoming that person."
—St. Thérèse

"Need help packing, girls?" Olivia's mom poked her head in the door. Olivia and Hayley were sitting on the bed talking and looking through magazines. They both could not believe it was time to go back home, that a month had passed at Keane Harbor.

"No, we're not ready to start packing, Mom," Olivia moaned.

Mrs. Thomas laughed. "I know. But all good things must come to an end. Aren't you ready to go back home and see your friends?"

Olivia nodded. "Before we left, I promised Chad I'd get him a Keane Harbor sticker, though. Can we go by a souvenir shop later?"

Mrs. Thomas laid a stack of freshly folded laundry on Olivia's bed. "We thought we'd go out to Captain Jim's for dinner in a bit. We can stop at one of the souvenir shops afterward."

Hayley and Olivia were pleased. They hadn't eaten out much on the trip, but no one had said anything about it because they knew the reason. It would be fun to go to the all-you-can-eat seafood buffet at Captain Jim's. Olivia loved shrimp cocktail and couldn't wait for dinner. Her stomach growled just thinking of all that seafood. They'd passed the popular restaurant many times and the parking lot was always crowded, so she knew it must be good.

"In that case, I'd better take a shower. I smell like the beach," Hayley announced, with a wrinkle of her nose. She hopped off the bed and grabbed some of her magazines. "See ya in a few," she chirped as she left the room.

Olivia sorted through the stack of clean laundry, setting Hayley's clothes aside.

"It's been a fun vacation, Mom. Thanks for letting me bring Hayley."

"You're welcome, Livvy. I hope she had a good time with us."

Olivia nodded emphatically. "She did. It was fun to have a friend along. Not that Lucy isn't good company, it's just…"

Her mom laughed. "I know. She's a lot younger than you. It's important to have time with friends your own age." She sat down on the edge of the bed and looked at Olivia with an odd expression.

"What?"

"I don't know," she said sadly. "You look so grown up to me now. I remember when you were little and you'd let me brush your hair while we sat on the bed. I miss those times."

Olivia did not know what to say. Sometimes she did feel grown up, but other times, she still felt like a child. It was so weird to be in between a child and a young woman. Every day she woke up and didn't quite know what she was or how she was supposed to act. Some days she wanted to have a temper tantrum and get mad when she didn't get her way; other times, she simply accepted it and moved on. It was strange.

"Mom," she began, trying to find the right words, "there's something I have to tell you, but I don't know how."

Her mom cocked her head. "What is it? You can tell me."

"Well, the trip's been fun, but some parts kinda weren't."

"Like what?"

Olivia took a deep breath. It would be best to just come out with it. She told her mom about following Hayley out to the beach, about Brandon and the turtles. Her mom nodded and listened without saying a word. Then Olivia plunged ahead.

"And I bought something I wasn't supposed to, and used up all my money in the process."

Her mom was silent for bit before speaking. "Your money for the project is all gone?"

"Mmhmm."

"That's a real shame, Olivia. You were saving for so long."

"I know." Olivia bit her lip. "But Mrs. Duggan paid me for yesterday. I'm starting to save up again."

"That's good to hear. What did you waste your money on?"

"Stupid stuff. Stuff to make me look popular and rich," she said sadly.

"I see. And this something you weren't supposed to buy, was it in there?" She pointed to the closet. "A pair of short-shorts?"

Olivia's jaw dropped. "Mom, how did you know?"

"I do your laundry, remember? And your hamper's in there."

"Oh." Olivia felt ashamed.

"I notice that they're gone. What happened to them?"

"I donated them to the rummage sale," Olivia said with a small smile, hoping her mom would not be too mad. She explained how Hayley had contributed her own clothes to the sale as well, and what had happened to them.

"Well, it looks like the clothes are right where they are supposed to be," her mom said brightly.

"You're not mad?"

"Livvy, no, I am not mad. Just disappointed that you'd buy them in the first place. But I am proud of you for doing the right thing and getting rid of them. What made you do that?"

"I don't know," Olivia admitted. "It just felt wrong."

"You know why it felt wrong?"

Olivia shook her head. "Not really."

"It's because you know, deep down, that God wants so much more for you than to be wearing clothes that take away the great dignity you have as a young lady."

Olivia stared down at her lap. "I want to be a lady. Sometimes I don't know what I am."

"Honey, you're only 12, I know that. But you don't have to dress in skimpy clothes in order to feel like you're growing up. I see so many ways every day that you are growing into a nice young lady. In fact, telling me about the shorts, and eventually doing the right thing by getting rid of them, speaks volumes about your character and maturity."

"Even though I bought them in the first place?"

"Even though."

"I only did it to fit in, Mom. Lots of girls my age wear stuff like that. The popular girls all do."

"I know they do. I've seen them, believe me. But I'm concerned with your eternity, not your wasting time trying to please everyone in the popular group. Maybe you're not 'popular,' as you say, because God's plan is to protect you for more meaningful things in life than just going with the flow."

"I just want to fit in and have friends," Olivia protested weakly.

"Of course you do. There's nothing wrong with being in a group of friends, but make sure you're doing what God wants you to do. Know what I mean?"

"I think I do."

"Every human person is God's own design, made with great dignity from the very first moment of their creation. Do your very best to honor that dignity by what you say and do and how you present yourself to the world, Livvy."

She continued, "Whether it's bad language, or immodest dress or behavior, just know that God has bigger, better plans for you than that. He, along with Our Lady, loves you and wants to keep you safe."

Olivia nodded. "I don't want people to think I only care about how I look on the outside. There's so much more to me than that."

Mrs. Thomas gave Olivia a hug. "Who does God want you to be? What does He want for you? Think about this the next time you are faced with a decision like that, when you are under pressure to do something you know isn't right."

"But...how do I know who God wants me to be?"

"Ask Him, Livvy!" Her mom then smoothed Olivia's hair and kissed the top of her head. "Ask Him, and He'll tell you."

TWENTY-EIGHT

*"How often have I thought that I may owe all the graces
I've received to the prayers of a person who begged them
from God for me, and whom I shall know only in heaven."*
—St. Thérèse

It was early, way too early to be up, she knew. Olivia had
tossed and turned the night before and finally awoke with the
sunrise while the household still slept.

Olivia stood by her parents' bedroom and listened. They were
still asleep. She peeked in on Lucy, who was sound asleep in
her bed. She tried Hayley's door, which was ajar. She could see
Hayley's long, brown hair spilled out all over the pillow. Hayley
was deep in dreamland.

She sighed, disappointed. She'd hoped to take a walk along
the beach with someone on their last full day in Keane Harbor,
but it was not to be. Even Grandma, an early riser, could be heard
softly snoring in her bedroom.

She went to the kitchen and rummaged through the drawers.
She found a pad of sticky notes, and jotted down a quick note for
her parents.

Went for a walk on the beach. Be back soon.

She stuck it on the refrigerator door where she knew it would be noticed.

Farther down on the beach, a few fishermen were seated in chairs on the sand, settled in for a morning of fishing. She saw their long poles stuck into the sand and jutting out into the water, awaiting a catch. The sun was glistening on the water brightly. As she looked out onto the horizon, Olivia was delighted to see a couple of dolphins jumping in and out of the water.

She wished she had thought to bring a towel, but it really didn't matter. She found a nice spot near the water's edge and sunk her feet in, not caring if she got too wet.

She really came out here to think, and talk with St. Thérèse. She felt like she hadn't spent much time with her lately. Digging her feet into the sand, she wiggled them until the sand fell off and she could see her pink toenails.

Olivia leaned back, her arms outstretched behind her onto the sand. It was peaceful here.

"St. Thérèse, I don't know where to start," Olivia whispered.

So she pulled out a little booklet of quotes from St. Thérèse that she had thought to put in the pocket of her cargo shorts before she left the house.

"'I'll never forget the impression that the sea made on me,'" Olivia read aloud from the book. "'I couldn't keep myself from looking at it without stopping. Its majesty, the roaring of its waves, everything spoke to my soul about the Greatness and the Power of God.'"

Olivia let the book fall into her lap. It was as if St. Thérèse were talking directly to her through the book.

"Oh St. Thérèse, you are right: God is very great," she said aloud.

Olivia was suddenly glad that she was alone on the beach; that neither Hayley nor Grandma nor her parents had come with her. She knew it was good that she was alone.

She wondered what people would think about a 12-year-old girl who came to the beach to be alone with God. Would they think she was strange, too old for her age? Then she remembered that it didn't matter what other people thought, and that she didn't really care. Like her mom had said, Olivia had to ask God who He wanted her to be, what He wanted of her. And she knew that God wanted this time with her, as much as she wanted this time with Him and His servant Thérèse.

The Greatness and the Power of God, Thérèse had written. Olivia squinted in the early-morning sun and looked out at the water. She suddenly felt close to Thérèse, because as she studied the majesty of the ocean, she felt the same way, like she couldn't tear her eyes away from it. For God was certainly great to create this masterpiece, to love her as He did, to forgive her sins through the sacrament of confession, to shower her with blessings. She had a loving family, wonderful friends, a nice school. She had a best friend in Saint Thérèse, who never gave up on her and was always praying for her. She knew it wasn't luck but blessings that were showered down on her from her heavenly Father.

Olivia reached for a tiny piece of driftwood nearby and wrote her name with it in the sand. She decided that she liked to be up early, before everyone else. It was a nice, quiet start to the day, a time when she could talk to God without being interrupted. The beach was mostly quiet except for the sound of the gentle waves and a few seagulls conversing with each other. Soon people would start coming down to the beach, loaded down with striped umbrellas, coolers, and beach chairs. Families would come with young children, eager to build sandcastles and lie lazily in the sun.

She tossed the piece of driftwood aside and admired her art-work. She dug in her feet and felt the coolness of the sand as they went deeper. She thought about what the priest had told her at confession—that she was to do something extra nice for some-one. What should she do? The Infant of Prague statue was a nice gesture, a gift for Mrs. Duggan. Yet she felt unsettled, like there was something more she had to do. She didn't know what it was, but it gently nagged at her that her penance wasn't quite com-plete with Mrs. Duggan's present. There was something more... but what was it?

In the distance, she spied the lighthouse and studied its shape, imagining it leading boats to safety on dark, stormy nights. A light in the darkness, a lamp, a path, allowing boats to sail in total security. *That lighthouse is like God*, Olivia decided. *We just have to let the lighthouse lead us and tell us where to go.*

She picked up her book again and stared at its cover. A pho-tograph of St. Thérèse smiled back at her, that tiny, gentle smile that had quickly made that particular photo Olivia's favorite of the great saint.

"St. Thérèse, whatever quote of yours I open this book up to will tell me what God wants me to do," she said softly.

She closed her eyes and everything went dark. She heard the sounds of the waves coming onto the shore and a seagull calling out. Still blind, she opened the book. Taking her forefinger and placing it on the page, she opened her eyes to read the following:

"I feel myself consumed with a thirst for souls and I wish at any price to snatch sinners from the eternal flames."

Sinners? A thirst for souls? Who could that be?

Then she knew: Brandon, Brooke, and the others on the beach who were destroying the turtle eggs.

She felt a sense of revulsion. Why should she pray for them? They deserved whatever they got. Then she read the next quote:

"I am sorry for people who lose their souls; it is so easy to miss your way when the paths of the world seem so attractive."

Was this it, what she was supposed to do for her penance? Did God really want her to pray for sinners? Could she, in some small way, help them not to lose their souls?

Then she remembered reading the story of young Thérèse, not that much older than Olivia, praying in secret for a terrible criminal in France. She had said she wanted to save his soul, believing anyone could turn back to God, even a horrible sinner. Thérèse so wanted everyone to know of God's love and grace, and she wanted to do her part to get everyone to Heaven.

Olivia had experienced God's love firsthand in the confessional. Maybe it was now time for her to share that foregiveness. She didn't totally understand it all, but the feeling in her was so strong that she knew she could not ignore it.

"God, You forgave me my sins and I am grateful. Now I would like to pray for Brandon, Brooke, and those kids. As bad as they are, they were created by You. Please help them to know You are there for them, no matter what."

It felt strange and exhilarating all at the same time, praying for people she despised—yet she found complete peace in doing so. It was a mystery to her, but she knew it was the right thing to do. The kids would never know she had done it, but she would know—and God would know.

She could not explain it, but at that moment she felt St. Thérèse smile down on her.

She stood up and brushed the sand off of her legs. Taking one last look out at the sea, she spied the lighthouse in the distance.

And she realized that she wasn't really alone on the shore after all.

TWENTY-NINE

"With the same little hand that caressed Mary
You upheld the world
And gave it life
And You thought of me."
—from a poem written by St. Thérèse

Olivia gently picked up the bag and walked outside. Winding around the path that led to Mrs. Duggan's house, her heart pounded with anticipation.

She peered around the fence at the Duggans' house. Their car was not in its usual spot in the driveway, and Olivia was relieved at her good fortune. She didn't want anyone to be home.

She crept next door, cradling the Infant of Prague statue close to her heart. After another quick look around, she gently placed the statue on the front porch. She looked down at it standing there by the door and smiled. Mrs. Duggan was going to be so surprised when she saw it waiting there for her. She giggled to herself, delighted at her idea, and suddenly felt a very close connection with her grandma's family in Ohio so many years ago. Then she hurried home before the Duggans came back.

A few hours later she returned, this time a little nervous about what she knew she had to do.

When Mrs. Duggan answered the door, she smiled and motioned for Olivia to come inside.

"Olivia! I'm so glad you had a chance to come over to say goodbye before you left today!" She led Olivia into the large living room and patted the sofa. "Come and have a seat. I'm afraid Danny is taking a nap right now."

Olivia frowned, disappointed that she wouldn't have a chance to say goodbye to Danny. "Oh, no."

"I could wake him up now. He's been asleep for a while..." Mrs. Duggan offered.

"No, no, that's okay, Mrs. Duggan. Then he might be crabby. I really just came to talk to you. I wanted to tell you something. That one day I told you I was sick and couldn't come over...I sort of made that up. I feel really bad about it, but some fun plans came up and...I'm really sorry, Mrs. Duggan."

Mrs. Duggan smiled warmly. "Oh, it's okay, Olivia. All work and no play is no fun. I understand. You've been such a big help with Danny, don't worry."

Olivia sighed. The relief was immense. She had been so afraid that Mrs. Duggan would be disappointed in her.

Mrs. Duggan got up to sit next to Olivia and hugged her for a long time. Then she pulled away and looked at Olivia, her face streaked with tears.

"Are you okay, Mrs. Duggan?"

Mrs. Duggan paused for a moment, trying to compose herself. "I'm sorry," she sniffed. "It's just that I've been saying a... novena. To the Infant of Prague. I'm just a little emotional about the timing of this."

"The timing?"

"Today is the last day of the novena, Olivia. I just..." she shook her head in awe. "I came home today to find the most wonderful, anonymous surprise on my front porch. It's so amazing that I can scarcely believe it."

Mrs. Duggan stared at Olivia for what seemed like a long time. "The Infant of Prague is very special to me," she said slowly. "I feel a certain connection to the Child Jesus, I guess because of Baby Gabriel..." her voice trailed off.

"I'm sorry," she said with a little laugh. "You didn't come over here to see me cry." She wiped her eyes with the back of her hand. "I'm okay. I'm just very touched. God is so good, isn't He?" Just then she cocked her head and smiled at Olivia, giving her a wink.

Olivia nodded, trying to hide a smile of her own, feeling that God was indeed very, very good.

"You know, Olivia, I've said it before, but if it weren't for you and your grandma..." her voice trailed off again, and Olivia knew Mrs. Duggan was thinking of the time when Olivia and Grandma had saved Danny from drowning. "This means so much to me. May God bless you for your kindness, Olivia."

Olivia's heart felt full and warmed with the love and happiness that can only be felt when a person has given the perfect present.

"You are the nicest young lady I know. I'll treasure it always."

THIRTY

"Just as the sun shines at the same time on trees and flowers, like each was the only one on earth, so does our Lord care for all souls in a special manner, as if they were each unique." —St. Thérèse

"Well, that's the last of it," Mr. Thomas said as he loaded some bags into the family's minivan. "I'll just go back inside and find Mom and Grandma."

Olivia stood on the driveway and craned her neck, looking around. She was hoping to say goodbye to Abby, but she was nowhere in sight. Yesterday evening on the beach, she said she'd come by in the morning to see them off.

"Potty!" cried Lucy as she scrambled to get out of the van. "Livvy take me!"

Olivia sighed. She really didn't feel like taking Lucy inside right now while she was waiting to see Abby.

"It's okay, I'll take her," Hayley said. "Come on, Lucy."

"Thanks, Hayley," Olivia said, grateful to be able to spend a few more moments outside.

Lucy took Hayley's hand and pulled her into the house.

Olivia stood alone on the driveway and took a last look around. Then she saw Abby walk through the bushes.

"Oh good, I'm not too late!" Abby cried, and ran over to give Olivia a hug.

Olivia grinned. "I was wondering where you were."

"I was on the phone with my mom," Abby said, beaming. "The doctor had some good news; he thinks my mom is improving!"

Olivia squeezed Abby tighter. "Oh Abby, I am so happy for you!"

"Thanks," Abby said, out of breath from her run and the excitement. "You guys all set to leave?"

"Yup. It was a fun vacation, and I sure am glad we met y'all."

"Me too. I'm sorry about all of the trouble."

Olivia waved her hand. "It's all over now. Don't worry about it." She wondered where Brooke and Brandon were; she had only seen them one other time on the beach, and they were far away. Abby had told her that they were trying to keep their distance.

They heard some noises in the bushes, and Brooke and Brandon appeared from behind the fence. Olivia shuddered a little. It was strange to see them again after what had happened.

"Hi," Brandon said. He didn't have that same smug look on his face that he'd had before. Neither did Brooke.

Olivia stared at them, thinking of the promise she'd made to God to pray for them, to pray for their souls. There was no way they knew about it, of course, but still she wondered if they did.

"We came to say goodbye," said Brooke.

"Oh. That was nice of you." Olivia did not know what else to say to them.

"So...maybe we can e-mail or something," Brooke suggested, and Brandon nodded in agreement.

"Maybe," said Olivia, knowing full well that they wouldn't, but she didn't want to seem rude. They really had nothing in common, and they all knew it. It was just something you said.

Hayley came out of the house holding Lucy's hand, and shock registered on her face to see Brandon and Brooke standing there.

"Hey," said Hayley.

"Hey," echoed Brandon. "We came to say bye."

"Hope you had a fun time in Keane Harbor," offered Brooke.

"Yeah. It was…interesting," said Hayley.

"Yeah."

In the distance, they heard someone calling Brooke and Brandon.

"Better go," said Brandon. "Mom and Dad keep a pretty tight leash on us these days."

They all shook hands and said goodbye. Brooke and Brandon walked away and were soon lost in the bushes. Abby followed them, turning one last time to wave goodbye. Then they were gone.

"That was nice that Brandon and Brooke came to say goodbye," Hayley said sadly.

"Yeah," replied Olivia. "It makes me feel sort of sad."

"Why?"

"I don't know. I guess it's because now they are finally, like, decent people and we have to leave!"

Hayley laughed and gave Olivia a playful shove. "Just get in the van, Olivia!"

Thirty-One

"I take refuge, then, in prayer, and turn to Mary, and our Lord always triumphs."—St. Thérèse

"Come on, Olivia, you missed a spot," teased Sabrina as she sprayed the hose onto the Thomas' minivan.

"I don't think she has a future career at Soapy Joe's Car Wash," Chad said as he tossed his sponge into the plastic bucket on the driveway.

"I never said I was any good at this," Olivia said, wiping her soapy hands on her legs with a smirk.

"Well, it's a hot day, what else was there to do?" Hayley was sitting on a beach towel on the grass, trying to dry off.

"I should be helping my mom clean the house for our Labor Day picnic tomorrow," Jenna said, frowning as she squeezed soapy water out of her sponge and into the bucket. "But this is way more fun."

"I can't believe school starts in two days," Olivia moaned. "Where did the summer go? It just flew by!"

"Yeah, I don't know about that," said Chad. "It was pretty long and boring around here last month when you guys were gone."

"Didn't you have fun?"

Chad shrugged his shoulders. "It was okay. But I had no one to pick on with you guys gone. Now I'm out of practice."

Olivia laughed sneakily and grabbed the hose, giving Chad a good soaking from head to toe.

Chad yelped in surprise. He stood on the driveway, dripping in water and trying not to laugh, while the rest of the friends howled in laughter.

Mrs. Thomas came out of the house carrying a tray with lemonade. She was startled when she got a good look at Chad.

"That was...cold," he deadpanned.

Mrs. Thomas frowned. "Chad! Did those mean old girls get you? Do you need a towel?"

"No, but Olivia will now," he sneered, and grabbed a soapy sponge, preparing to toss it at Olivia.

"NO!" she screamed and giggled at the same time.

Chad reconsidered and dropped the sponge. "Fine. I'll get my revenge out on you some other time...when you least expect it! Think snowballs at recess!"

Hayley, Sabrina, and Jenna fell into a chorus of laughter. They had all missed being together and acting silly.

Mrs. Thomas set the tray down on the grass. "Well, today's so warm that it probably feels good to get wet. But don't get any ideas about getting me wet, any of you!" Then she hurried to go back inside.

The kids each took a glass of lemonade and collapsed onto the cool grass under the shade of a big maple tree. "Oh man, I come over and your family puts me to work," Chad teased.

Olivia rolled her eyes good-naturedly.

"It's warm now, but soon we'll be freezing cold," said Sabrina, now that Chad had brought up the subject of snowballs.

"Yeah, I always think that summer is going to last forever," added Jenna, lying on her back and looking up at the late-summer sky. "Then one day you wake up and you're on the school bus."

"It wouldn't be so bad if I didn't have to take that smelly bus," Hayley complained.

"What would your majesty like to take, a limousine?" asked Chad.

Hayley giggled. "No, I think I've had enough of the rich life," she said, giving a knowing look to Olivia.

Olivia took a sip of her lemonade and said, "Really? No more Park Avenue apartment in New York City?"

Hayley shook her head. "Nah, I'm rethinking all of that."

"Yeah, me too," said Olivia, thinking about Brooke and Brandon and their rich lifestyle, which she now knew wasn't as great as it had first seemed. "Fortunately I don't have to worry about all of that, seeing as I'm broke anyway. Ha ha," she mocked.

"That's too bad about your project, Olivia," Jenna said sadly.

Sabrina agreed. "Yeah, sorry, Olivia."

"It's okay," said Olivia. "It'll just take me longer to do it, that's all."

Olivia got quiet just then. She felt remorseful that the poor child she was saving up to help in Guatemala would have to wait, whoever he or she was.

"Hi guys!" a voice from the sidewalk interrupted their conversation. They turned around from their spot on the grass and saw Tina from school riding up on her bike.

"Tina!" exclaimed Olivia. "I didn't know you lived around here."

"A couple of neighborhoods over," said Tina, who had stopped her bike on the sidewalk in the shade of a tree.

"Ready for school?" asked Hayley.

Olivia bit her lip. She had not told Hayley that Tina's family could not afford to send her to St. Michael's anymore. She felt it would be gossiping.

But Tina just smiled. "I started already."

"You did?" exclaimed Jenna. "What do you mean? We don't start for two days."

"I'm not going back to St. Michael's," she said. "I'm home-schooled now."

"You are?" asked Olivia, surprised.

"Yeah. My parents found a great homeschooling group at church and I love it. I met lots of new friends already over the summer and we have tons of fun stuff planned," she beamed.

Olivia smiled. Tina looked so happy and excited. She was pleased for her friend.

"We'll miss you at school," chimed in Sabrina.

"Glad you live close by. We can see each other still," said Chad.

"Wanna help us dry the car? It's going to get spotty if we don't hurry up," said Hayley.

"Next time. I've got to get home; my mom planned a lunch with some of the homeschool kids. See you guys!" Tina waved and pedaled away.

The group stood up.

"Yeah, I should get going too," said Jenna. "My mom will need my help."

They all grabbed towels and dried off the car, congratulating themselves on how shiny and clean it looked.

Later, when everyone had gone home and Olivia was up in her room going through her new school supplies, she heard the doorbell ring and her mother answer the door.

Olivia zipped up her backpack and sighed. She couldn't believe that in a few days, she'd be starting the seventh grade. It just didn't seem possible. She had to admit that she was a little nervous, but she tried to think about all of the things that she had to look forward to in seventh grade: the girls' basketball team, the talent show, the Halloween dance. She smiled as she thought of going to her very first school dance. She wondered if a boy would ask her to dance and how she would feel if he did. Hayley had already danced with a boy; she wouldn't be scared. Olivia shrugged her shoulders. She wouldn't worry about that now; there was plenty of time to think about that later.

"Livvy, package for you!" she heard her mom call from downstairs.

Olivia met her mom halfway down the stairs. "For me?"

"That's what it says," her mom said cheerfully. She handed her the package and hurried to grab Lucy, who had mischievously started to get into the pantry.

Olivia took the bulky package upstairs to her room. It looked so strange, wrapped in wrinkled brown paper. She turned it all around but it did not have a return address.

She sat down at her desk with it, intrigued. The handwriting on the package was large and childish. Using a pair of scissors, she slit it open and found an envelope and a smaller brown package tucked inside.

Olivia decided to open the letter first. She couldn't for the life of her imagine who it was from. Aunt Peggy and Uncle Jack? Abby? She unfolded the paper and read:

Dear Miss Olivia,

You do not know me, but I am girl who lives in Guatemala. I new to learn English so please excuse writing. I am ten years of age and happy to know you as my new friend. Thank you for sponsoring me. You are helping my family and we are grateful. With your money I can buy things I need for school. I have a new bag for books and new shoes.

I thank you from the bottom of my heart. You are a gift, Miss Olivia, and have made much difference in this girl's life.

So I have gift for you. It is made by friend of mine who makes things from wood and paints them. Please enjoy. Your friend Miss Hayley told me this would be perfect gift for you. I will write again soon.

God bless you,

Rosita

Olivia's jaw dropped. Rosita? Who was Rosita? And how did she know Hayley? She was utterly confused. Tucked inside the letter was a small picture of a girl wearing a yellow dress. She stood under a palm tree, holding a new, green backpack. She was posed leaning on the tree trunk sticking out her right leg, showing off her brand-new shoes. Her bright, crooked-tooth smile beamed with happiness.

The simplicity of the girl in the photo struck a chord with Olivia. A young girl so pleased to have the barest of necessities, thinking she was on top of the world with her new backpack and shoes. Olivia stole a glance at her old, scuffed-up sandals that she had kicked into the closet and felt a wave of shame at how she had thought them so irrelevant and used-up back in Keane Harbor.

She studied the picture of Rosita and shook her head in disbelief as the realization hit her: Hayley had done this. Hayley had sent in the money to the agency on her behalf. Sweet, funny, loyal Hayley. Hayley, who'd had faith in her and The Project from day one. She must have used up every last penny she had to give in secret.

She thought back to the faith of the blind priest with the Infant of Prague statue, and the candles from Mrs. Linden, who had faith in being a new mother to a child the world would not think was perfect. She thought of Grandma's faith as she went into the water after so many years to save Danny.

Rosita had faith that a nice family would help her. If a poor girl who had nothing could have faith, and a blind priest could have faith in what he could not see, then why not her, going into seventh grade and facing the unknown of a new school year, with all of its challenges?

Gently, she opened up the paper-wrapped box and reached inside. Nestled in pages of crumpled newspaper, a delicate animal made of wood peered up at her. Painted in blues and greens, the little face of a sea turtle looked up at her with a tiny smile.

Olivia cradled the little turtle in her hands and looked lovingly at the little creature that showed what just one person could do for another life.

Things still seemed uncertain; her dad was still laid off from his job. The other turtles on the beach were still destroyed. But Olivia suddenly knew what the saints know: that faith guides you, gives you hope in any situation. It's having faith in God and His Son, and forming a relationship with the saints, especially the Blessed Mother, who are there to help you and give a heavenly hand to hold in good times and bad.

Olivia kissed the tiny turtle, a gift from a poor girl in another country that she had never met. A girl named Rosita: a little rose.

"Thank You, God, for all life, big and small," she said as she touched her nose to the turtle's nose.

And she gave thanks for a loving God who would never, ever leave her alone on the shore.

THE END

GRANDMA'S LIME GELATIN SURPRISE
Feeds a crowd!

1 large OR 2 small packages lime-flavored gelatin

1 20-ounce can pineapple pieces not drained (You need 1 cup of liquid here. You may have to add water to make 1 cup of liquid.)

1 8-ounce package cream cheese, softened

1 cup ginger ale

2 cups boiling water

(Recipe needs a total of 4 cups liquid.)

Mix 2 cups boiling water with gelatin and dissolve completely.
Add softened cream cheese to ginger ale and mix well.
Add mixture to gelatin.
Add undrained pineapple and mix well.
Refrigerate until firm.

My Lord and my God, I have realized that whoever undertakes to do anything for the sake of earthly things or to earn the praise of others deceives himself. Today one thing pleases the world, tomorrow another. What is praised on one occasion is denounced on another. Blessed be You, my Lord and my God, for You are unchangeable for all eternity. Whoever serves You faithfully to the end will enjoy life without end in eternity. Amen.

—Prayer of St. Thérèse

Novena or prayer to the Infant of Prague

Jesus, You said, "Ask and you shall receive, seek and you shall find, knock and it shall be opened to you." Through the intercession of Mary, Your holy Mother, I knock, I seek. I ask that my prayer be granted (mention your request). Jesus, You said, "All that you ask of the Father in My name, He will grant to you." Through the intercession of Mary, Your holy Mother, I humbly and urgently ask Your Father in Your name that my prayer be granted (mention your request). Jesus, You said, "Heaven and earth shall pass away, but My word shall not pass." Through the intercession of Mary, Your holy Mother, I feel confident that my prayer will be granted (mention your request).

To be said for nine consecutive hours or for nine days

"Henceforth, dear Little Flower, I will fulfill your plea 'to be made known everywhere' and I will never cease to lead others to Jesus through you."
—Miraculous Invocation to St. Thérèse of Lisieux

Nancy Carabio Belanger is the author of the award-winning *Olivia and the Little Way*. The book received an award from the Catholic Press Association in 2009 as well as the Catholic Writers Guild Seal of Approval, which selects books for their faithfulness to the Magisterium. A wife and mother of two sons, she founded Harvey House Publishing in 2008 to create books for children and young adults that celebrate their Catholic faith, modesty, the gift of life, and a wholesome childhood. Nancy is a member of the Catholic Press Association, the Independent Book Publishers Association, and the Catholic Writers Guild. She has a great love for St. Thérèse, God's Little Flower. A proud Italian-American and Michigan State University graduate, Nancy lives with her family in Michigan where she is working on more novels for children.

Visit Nancy on the web at nancybelanger.blogspot.com.

Illustrator **Sandra Casali LewAllen** is an experienced artist in many types of media. A graduate of Wayne State University in art education, she studied studio art and art history in Perugia, Italy. She is working toward a master's degree in education at Michigan State University. Sandra and her husband Dave have two children, Nick and Sarah. She currently teaches art to high school students in Troy, Michigan. As time permits, she loves to draw, paint, sculpt, and create freelance art.

ACKNOWLEDGEMENTS

It is with sincere gratitude and appreciation that I thank the following:

Sandra Casali LewAllen, my incredible illustrator, who loves Olivia as much as I do;

Erin Sims Howarth of DDM Publications, who solved every problem and dotted every "i";

Roseann Nieman of Niemanartgraphics.com, the queen of fonts and logo design;

Michele Bondi Bottesi of Joseph Karl Publishing, for her warm friendship and support;

My great parents and brother, my friends and family, and a big hug to all of my readers, who begged me to continue Olivia's journey to holiness;

And to God, Who is everything.